Praise for

CAMERON HALEY

and the Underworld cycle

"Fast pacing, pungent wit, surprise twists, thoughtful discussions of morality and escalating, cinematic battles keep the pages turning."
—*Publishers Weekly* (starred review) on *Mob Rules*

"With so much urban fantasy currently on the market, it's hard for a reader to find anything that feels 'fresh.' *Mob Rules* feels fresh. I read it with the same sense of enjoyment and discovery that I felt when the first Tanya Huff and Laurell K. Hamilton fantasies came out years ago."
—*Fresh Fiction*

"*Mob Rules* is exciting and fresh, with a complex and conflicted heroine who grabs your attention and doesn't let go. This book will make you fall in love with urban fantasy all over again!"
—Diana Rowland, author of *Mark of the Demon*

"Gangsters and vampires, ghosts and sorcerers, and the mean streets of L.A. Add to the mix a woman who can definitely take care of herself, a plot full of twists and some clever magic, and you've got *Mob Rules*. And a whole lot of fun."
—John Levitt, author of the Dog Days series

"Domino is a new and interesting character for the urban fantasy world and I want to see…even more horrible, horrible things happen to her. Because she is the most interesting when horrible, horrible things are happening."
—*Dreams and Speculation* on "Retribution" in *Harvest Moon*

"Haley is definitely an author to watch!"
—*RT Book Reviews* on "Retribution" in *Harvest Moon*

**Also by
Cameron Haley**

Mob Rules

Harvest Moon
"Retribution"

...cycle

SKELETON CREW

CAMERON HALEY

LUNA™

www.LUNA-Books.com

LUNA™

SKELETON CREW

ISBN-13: 978-0-373-80326-2

Copyright © 2011 by Greg Benage

This edition published by arrangement with Harlequin Books S.A.

For questions and comments about the quality of this book please contact us at Customer_eCare@Harlequin.ca.

www.LUNA-Books.com

Printed in U.S.A.

For Mashenka

one

It was raining when Terrence Cole buried his soldiers. A late summer downpour was the rarest of miracles in Los Angeles, and I watched as the fresh mounds of earth beside the open graves slowly turned to mud.

Terrence stood in the center of the small, black-clad crowd, his head bowed and his hands clasped in front of him. He didn't have an umbrella, and the rain glistened on the coffee-colored skin of his shaved head. It trickled down his forehead and along his temples, and the wetness on his cheeks almost looked like tears.

The service drew to a close, the coffins were lowered into the damp earth and the mourners quickly dispersed. I wasn't sure if they were fleeing the elements or the sense of helplessness and despair that hung over the gathering. Probably both. I went to him when Terrence stood alone by the graves.

"Domino," he said, "I appreciate you being here." Stylish narrow sunglasses covered his eyes, but his head remained bowed and I didn't think he'd looked up as I approached.

"I'm sorry about your guys, Terrence. I just found out about it today."

He nodded, not at me but at the graves. "These two here were my nephews."

"Jesus, Terrence, if I'd known, maybe I could have—"

"Their moms was my favorite sister. Used to be. Now she just want to see *my* funeral."

"You're not responsible for this."

Terrence took off the glasses and lifted his head. There were dark circles under his eyes, and he had the look of a man on the run who knows he's all out of places to hide. "I brought them in. Thought it was the best way to keep them safe, thought I could protect them." He shook his head and the corner of his mouth twitched.

"What happened?"

"They didn't even have any juice. Mobley put a posse on them just to send me a message."

Francis Mobley ran the largest Jamaican outfit in the city. He'd been aligned with Terrence's former boss, but now he saw the outfit Terrence had inherited as a target, an opportunity to expand his territory. Mobley was brutal, but I knew the executions hadn't just been a message. The hits would have given Mobley a lot of juice and he'd be planning to use it for something even worse.

It was old-school gang warfare. With magic returning to the world in force, the stronger outfits had more juice than they knew what to do with. Back in the day it hadn't been like that. There hadn't been enough magic to go around, and the L.A. outfits fought for whatever piece of it they could get. They'd used tactics like this—one seemingly pointless act of violence feeding juice to the next—to move against their rivals. It was like a game of leapfrog played with murders.

My outfit was the strongest in the city and we didn't have to resort to those tactics to take care of business. But there was still something in it for a smaller, weaker outfit, as long as the guy calling the shots didn't let anything like conscience get in the way. I'd never heard Francis Mobley had much of a conscience.

"You're my ally, Terrence. Give the word and I'll crush that motherfucker like a bug."

"Then what, Domino? You gonna move on the Koreans? Word is they want a piece of me, too."

I hadn't known about the Koreans, but Terrence was right. As much as I liked the idea of hitting back at Mobley, he was a symptom and not the disease. Taking him out wouldn't make the problem go away. The problem was Terrence's outfit was too small and too weak to protect itself. It wouldn't survive for long—and never mind that it was weak mostly because of what I'd done to it a couple months ago. If it wasn't Mobley, someone else would move in to cull the herd. That's the way it worked, and if I put my personal feelings aside, I knew that's the way it should work. There was no room for weakness in the underworld.

"Are you ready to lay down, Terrence?"

He didn't say anything for a while. It surprised me, but maybe he was thinking about it. Getting your ass handed to you was no fun in any walk of life, but it really sucked in the underworld. I couldn't really blame him.

"No fucking way," Terrence said finally. "I ain't gonna lay down 'less someone puts me down."

"Okay, so what are you going to do about it?"

"Mobley ain't shit. He's not my problem—motherfucker's just exploiting my problem. I can hit him just like he's hitting me. I can drop bodies on his corners and put blood on his streets, but that just makes it worse. I need soldiers, Domino. It's simple as that."

"I know where you can get some."

Terrence narrowed his eyes. "Where's that, D? You can't send me muscle—that's no different than letting you hit the Jamaicans for me. I got to prove my outfit is strong enough to protect itself."

"I can't send you troops, but I could let them go if they got the idea on their own."

"Who you have in mind?"

"Simeon Wale's crew. The prick likes you a hell of a lot better than me, anyway. He'd cross if you offered him lieutenant. I'd let him."

"Simeon Wale is a bad nigger and he got juice, but I'm not sure I trust the motherfucker any more than you do. I'd be watching my back night and day if I brought him in."

"Why you think I'm letting him go? Nothing's free, Terrence. You know that. Question is, is watching your back better than lying down? I'm getting pressure. Everyone's worried. If you can't hold your ground, something else might move in that'd make the Jamaicans look friendly."

"The Turk is on you about this?"

"No, I don't even know where that son of a bitch is. He said he was going on sabbatical, left routine operational control of the outfit to the heir apparent."

Terrence laughed. "Adan's making trouble for you. My pops always said, be careful what you wish for—it might just get you."

"Your pops sounds like an asshole."

"He was, but he might have been right about that."

Adan Rashan was my boss's son. He'd been swapped out with a changeling as a baby and spent the first twenty-plus years of his life in Avalon, the fairy otherworld. A few months earlier, I'd killed the changeling and averted a war with the Seelie Court, but not before I'd fallen for the fucking guy. Now the real Adan was back and he was turning out to be a major pain in the ass. I couldn't just flip the switch and turn off the attraction, either. I didn't understand it, I didn't much like it, and I sure as hell wasn't going to make the same mistake twice.

"Adan's got no say in this. I'm still the wartime captain, you're my ally and supporting our alliances is part of my job description."

"He can still make trouble."

"No, all he can do is bitch and moan about it. He's been doing a lot of that. He can't move on you unless I give the word."

"You gonna give the word?"

"I wouldn't be here if I was ready to push you out." Even if Terrence hadn't been my ally, he'd betrayed his former boss to save my life. Maybe saving my ass hadn't been his only motive, but that kind of thing still counted for something. At least to me.

"So it got to be Wale's crew?"

I nodded. "Anyone else, it looks like I'm propping you up. This way it just looks like you're taking advantage of disloyalty in my ranks. No one will have a problem with that."

"Except Mobley. You think you can arrange a sit-down?"

I shook my head. "Not yet. Mobley thinks he has you by the short ones, Terrence. You're going to have to hurt him before you sit down."

"I can put Wale on him," he said, and laughed. "You got all this worked out, don't you? Remind me never to piss you off."

I shrugged. "It's time to play hardball. You turn Wale loose, Mobley will come to you. He'll be begging for a sit-down."

Terrence nodded and was about to respond when a sound

like a snapping tree limb split the air. The sound came from behind us.

From the graves.

Terrence and I turned together, toward the sound. Splintered wood from one of the coffins lay scattered around the gravesite. As we watched, one of Terrence's nephews climbed from his shattered coffin and stood up. He staggered and then braced himself with both hands on the sides of his grave. He looked down at himself, at the dark suit his mother had buried him in, and then he looked around. His gaze landed on us, and his eyes were a dull, filmy gray. They were a dead man's eyes.

"What the fuck, Uncle T?" he said. "Why you got to put a brother in the ground?"

The kid climbed out of his hole and stumbled toward us. He seemed a little stiff. After a few jerking steps, he wobbled to a stop and fell back on his ass, his legs splayed out in front of him.

Terrence and I just looked at him.

"I feel like shit, Uncle T," the kid said. He was holding his head in both hands and craning his neck to either side. It snapped and popped like dry kindling in a fire.

"You got shot seven times, Tony," Terrence said. His voice sounded dry and harsh, like he just woke up from a hard night of drinking and too many cigars.

"Damn, Uncle T, it's Antoine, I keep telling you that. No one calls me Tony anymore."

"You got shot seven times, Tony," Terrence repeated. "One of the bullets went in your brain. They didn't even bother to dig it out when they put you on the table."

I thought it was a little more detail than the kid probably needed, but Terrence sounded like he was saying it to remind himself more than for his nephew's benefit.

Tony raised a hand to his forehead and probed the gray, puckered entry wound with his fingertips. "Why ain't I dead, Uncle T?"

Terrence didn't say anything. I didn't either—I just relaxed my vision and looked at Tony with my witch sight. Terrence had said the kid didn't have any juice, but that wasn't exactly right. Every human has a little juice in them—an aura or whatever you want to call it. I could see what was left of Tony's juice soaking into the soggy earth with the rain. It was exactly what I'd expect to see on a human body that had been dead a couple days.

I dropped the sight and looked over at Terrence. He turned to me and I shook my head.

"Tell me what you remember, Tony," he said, looking back to the kid again. He stayed where he was, about ten feet from where Tony had dropped into the mud.

"I remember all of it. I remember getting shot. We were just hanging out at the store and the Rastas rolled up on us in a black Escalade. I didn't even have time to be scared, Uncle T. I saw them roll up and then I was down."

"What else, Tony? You remember anything after that?"

"I remember everything," he said. "I remember the uniforms showing up, and later the murder police. And after, when the doctors laid me out and started cutting on me. I was awake but I couldn't move. It didn't hurt, you know, but I could feel what they were doing." The kid started crying but there were no tears. His eyes were dry and gray. "I remember the funeral. But I was lying in that fucking box and I couldn't see anything. I was able to open my eyes but all I could do was lie there and look up at the ceiling."

"Any hoodoo on him, Domino?" Terrence asked. You could use magic to raise the dead, to make a zombie out of a corpse. I even knew the spell, though I'd never used it.

I shook my head. "Nothing."

"Maybe that fairy shit?"

"No, I'd see it." When I'd killed the changeling who'd replaced Adan, I'd also taken his magic. Now I could see fairy glamour as easily as human sorcery and there was no glamour on Tony. Raising zombies wasn't exactly the Seelie Court's style, anyway.

"What you think we should do?"

"No clue."

"We can't put him back in the ground."

"No, that doesn't seem right."

"Maybe if we wait awhile he'll die again."

"Fuck you, Uncle T. You think I can't hear you?" Tony had stopped crying and was scowling at us.

"Sorry, Tony, I didn't mean it like that. I'm just not sure what to do about this."

Tony staggered to his feet again. He was moving jerkily around the grave site when we heard a thumping sound coming from the other coffin. Terrence and I looked at each other and then at the grave. We walked over and looked down.

"I hurt, Uncle T," Tony called from behind us. "Before I couldn't feel nothing, now it hurts, real bad."

"Chill out, Tony. I got to help Keshawn." Terrence dropped to his knees in the mud, reached into the grave and unlatched the coffin. He opened the lid.

The body lying there didn't look quite as good as Tony's. Keshawn had taken one in the head, too, but the exit wound had torn away one side of his skull. The funeral home hadn't done much more than slap some industrial-strength Maybelline on it. I flowed a little juice to steady my nerves and calm my stomach.

"I think I'm hungry, Uncle T," Tony called.

"I said chill the fuck out, Tony. Give me a minute and I'll take you to Mickey D's."

Keshawn opened his eyes. They were gray, empty and lifeless, just like Tony's. His lips pulled back in a snarl and bared yellow teeth, and his hands flashed up and grabbed Terrence by the throat. Keshawn screamed and thrashed and pulled Terrence into the grave. Terror welled up from someplace deep in my mind and tried to paralyze me. I flowed more juice to take the edge off it and moved forward to help. Then I heard Tony step up behind me.

"I don't want Mickey D's, Uncle T," he said, and I felt his cold, cold hands on my neck.

Everyone has an irrational fear. For some people it's spiders, for others it's snakes, or maybe clowns. I have a big fucking problem with zombies. I can deal with ghosts— even the really creepy ones. Hell, I share my condo with a spook, an old woman named Mrs. Dawson. I can also deal with dead bodies—as long as they stay down. If they get up and try to eat me, that's just too fucking much.

So when Tony put his hands around my neck, I didn't spin a combat spell. I didn't trigger the defensive ring on my pinkie finger or do anything else that might have been vaguely constructive. Instead, my body seized up, my hands flew to my face and I screamed like a little girl. Actually, that's not quite right. I screamed just like a bimbo in a zombie movie.

I stayed like that, frozen in place and screaming at the top of my lungs, until Tony's teeth clamped down on my ear. In a zombie movie, flesh would have torn and blood would have sprayed, but fortunately, Tony's teeth weren't exactly designed for chewing ears. Blunt teeth or not, I can say one thing about having someone bite into your ear, and I think

Evander Holyfield would back me up on this: it hurts like a motherfucker.

It hurt enough that it probably saved my life, or at least my profile. When I felt Tony's teeth sink into my flesh, my scream turned into an outraged roar and I twisted, swinging an elbow into his face. I heard a sickening, crunchy, squelching sound as it slammed into his nose, and he staggered back from the blow. I turned to face him and put one hand to my ear. I looked at the hand and there was blood on my fingers. I looked up at Tony, who was staggering toward me again, his arms outstretched and his hands grasping like claws.

"You dirty, dead motherfucker," I said. "You bit my fucking ear." Tony made a terrible moaning, mewling sound. His lips curled away from his teeth, like that hideous thing chimpanzees do, and he kept coming.

"Vi Victa Vis," I said, and my force spell hit Tony in the chest like a wrecking ball taking a shot at a condemned building. His body hurtled through the air away from me and slammed into the side of a family mausoleum, the marble cratering from the impact.

"Terrence," I called over my shoulder, "your fucking nephew wants to eat me." I heard sounds of a struggle from the grave behind me and I remembered Terrence was having his own issues.

"Smoke him," he grunted. "He's family, but that shit only goes so far."

"A great flame follows a little spark," I said. A ball of fusion fire appeared in my hand. I flicked my arm and threw it at Tony, and it streaked toward him like a meteor burning through the atmosphere. The fireball exploded when it struck the zombie. I had to shield my eyes from the blast, and the shockwave lifted my hair from my shoulders. When

I looked again all that was left of Tony was a blast shadow on the mausoleum wall.

I turned and looked back toward the other grave just as Terrence leaped back. He flowed a rhyme from a gangster rap and liquid fire poured into the grave. Keshawn screamed as he burned, but the screaming stopped long before the fire did. I walked back to Terrence and stood beside him, and we watched the flames dancing in the grave.

"That was fucked up," he said.

"Yeah."

"It must have been Mobley. He must have put a spell on 'em, done a ritual or something."

"Maybe," I said. "But what if it wasn't Mobley?"

Terrence looked over at me. "What you mean, Domino?"

"I mean, what if your nephews aren't the only ones?" I looked around the cemetery, and shivered. "What if they're just the first?"

two

That night, I sat on my bed with my laptop in front of me and searched for Tony and Keshawn on FriendTrace.com. I typed their names in the search box and poured juice into the spell I use to contact the dead.

I got a white screen with the words *No Results Found* on it. I couldn't force Terrence's nephews to take my call, but that's not what my spell was telling me. It was telling me Tony and Keshawn weren't in the Beyond. Since they were dead—again—there was really only one other place they could be.

I shut down the laptop, threw on some clothes and went out to the living room. Honey, my piskie roommate, was on the coffee table with four of her sisters. They were playing Chinese checkers, but the game seemed more about pelting each other with marbles than the strategies I'd learned as a child. There was a fair amount of violence in it, since the marbles were almost as large to the piskies as a bowling ball would have been to me.

"Hi, Domino! Wanna play?"

"I need to cross over for a bit. Hold down the fort while I'm gone."

"I can come with you."

"Play your game. I should be in and out." I sank onto the couch, spun my spirit-walking spell and crossed over to the Between. I grabbed the Colt Peacemaker from the closet and belted the rig around my waist. The weapon had belonged to Wyatt Earp and they called it the Dead Man's Gun in these parts. They also said it was cursed, but it was still a comfort in a place where I couldn't use sorcery.

I left my condo and strolled down the blue-lit night-time street outside my building. I entered the pale mist that shrouded the streets of the shadow city, and the world seemed to spin around me like a vinyl record on a turntable. When I stepped out of the fog, I was standing at the gates of the cemetery.

This was my first time visiting a cemetery in the Between. I'd expected it to be a happening place, the ghostly equivalent of a busy hotel. Instead, it was deserted, quiet and still. In the real world, it had been designed from the sod up to ooze peacefulness and serenity. It was pleasant enough you could almost forget it had corpses buried in it.

In the Between, that calm and soothing ambiance was replaced by something else entirely. Not danger, exactly—I didn't feel threatened by it. The vibe I got from the place was more like loneliness, regret. The cemetery was the last station at the end of the line. "Everyone gets off here," it seemed to whisper. "There's no place else to go."

I went in through the gates and walked down the winding road toward the graves. The ambient blue light of the Between at night was dimmer here. There were no leaves on the trees that flanked the road, and they cast no shadows.

Tony's grave was still open, a stark, black shape like a doorway in the ground. I walked to the edge and knelt beside it. "Tony?" I whispered. No response. I tightened my jaw, lay down on my stomach and reached into the grave. It was empty—even the coffin was missing. I hastily stood up and brushed the grave dirt from my clothes. I looked around, and seeing nothing, I walked over to the mausoleum where I'd torched Tony with the fireball spell.

The blast shadow was still there. As I approached, it rippled and flowed away from the wall, and then floated toward me. I jumped back and drew Ned, pointing the pistol more or less at the center of the shifting shadow.

The apparition raised its hands. "Yo, Domino, it's me, Antoine."

"What the fuck, Tony, you scared the shit out of me."

The uppermost part of the shadow—presumably Tony's head—swirled around, like he was checking himself out. "Yeah, kinda creepy. Sorry 'bout that. You nuked me, guess this is the best I can do."

"You tried to eat me, Tony."

"Yeah, I got to apologize for that. Your ear okay?"

I nodded. Honey had dusted up a nice healing glamour for me and my ear was good as new. I'd have to get it pierced again, though. "So what was up with that? Why'd you bite me?"

"I don't know what got into me, Domino. I just needed it, you know? It's like when you're real thirsty and you see some water and you just got to have it."

"Like an instinct."

"Yeah, that's what I'm saying. I didn't decide to eat you, my body just needed it. I guess it's a zombie thing, like in the movies."

"That fucking bite better not turn me into a zombie, Tony, or I'll come back and kill you again. I'll come in with a plan and take my fucking time about it."

"I don't think it works that way, Domino. I didn't get bit by a zombie and I still turned into one."

"So what now, you're a ghost?"

"Yeah, I guess, but I'm stuck here." Tony floated toward me again and then stopped abruptly. "See? This is as far as I can go from where you lit me up. It's like I'm chained to the fucking muslim."

"Mausoleum."

"What?"

"It's a mausoleum, not a Muslim. So you're trapped in the place where your body was destroyed."

"Yeah," Tony said. "Keshawn still over there, too. We was talking earlier, before you showed up. He can't leave his hole."

I had a spell that bound ghosts and I thought I might be able to reverse it to free Tony. I even had a spell that could banish a ghost to the Beyond. Problem was, I couldn't cast either spell in this place. I could try to summon Tony into the mortal world but the odds didn't seem good with him tied down in the Between. "Have you tried to manifest in the physical world, Tony? If you can, I might be able to cut you loose."

"Nah, Domino, I can't go nowhere. Like I said, I'm stuck."

"I could shoot you. If I destroy your ghost form or whatever, maybe it would set you free."

Tony didn't say anything for a few moments and I got the feeling he was looking at Ned. "Maybe we could try something else."

"I can't really think of anything else, Tony."

"I can wait. Maybe something will come to you."

I nodded and was about to respond when a writhing mass of fleshy tentacles flashed down from above and coiled around the shadow. Tony screamed as the tentacles lifted him into the air. I looked up.

A severed head hovered in the air about ten feet above us. It looked male and mostly human, though the skin was a mottled gray and the features were twisted hideously. Long, black hair hung in greasy strands from the head, and the thin, glistening lips were drawn back to reveal a mouthful of pointed teeth. I realized the "tentacles" were actually flayed strands of muscle and tendon, impossibly long, extending from the severed neck. The tentacles were lifting Tony toward the toothy maw, and drool spattered down on the helpless shade.

All of this was enough to bump zombies down to Number Two on the list of things I just can't tolerate. I brought Ned up and aimed, but just before I squeezed the trigger I saw the thing's yellowed, bloodshot eyes snap to me. I fired, but the severed head dived with dizzying speed and the shot missed. Tony fell to the ground again and the tentacles released him. The creature turned its attention to me.

It zigged and zagged in the air as I tried to draw a bead with Ned. I fired and missed again, and then one of the tentacles flashed out and wrapped around my arm, immobilizing it. I struggled against it, but the tentacle was like a meaty vise and I couldn't bring Ned up to take another shot. More tentacles shot out and wrapped around my legs and my waist, and the creature laughed. It sounded wet and diseased. Blood and saliva sprayed from the thing's mouth and neck.

I reached for the fairy magic inside me, but I suddenly didn't have the strength. I could feel my magic being drawn from me, into those tentacles, and they throbbed like bulging veins as my juice pumped into them.

The creature extended yet another tentacle, slowly this time, and it coiled around my throat, almost gently, like a lover's caress. Tony finally picked himself up and flew at the monster, but its head snapped around, its mouth opened and Tony was swallowed up like smoke being sucked into an air cleaner. The creature made a vile gulping sound and licked its lips. Then it turned back to me. It drew close and its jaws stretched wide. Its hot breath smelled like rotten meat.

An arrow burst from the thing's throat, just above its Adam's apple, and blood and pus spattered my face. It was in my eyes and my mouth, and somewhere deep inside I started screaming.

I reached out with my free hand and grabbed a tentacle, pulling the creature to me. I took hold of the arrow and twisted it, grinding it against the raw edges of the angry wound, and then I head-butted the thing in the face. The creature shrieked and recoiled from me, and the tentacles withdrew.

"Big mistake, motherfucker." I brought Ned up and fanned the hammer with my left hand. The monster jerked around in the air like a kite in a gale, but it couldn't dodge all the ethereal lead the weapon threw its way. One shot pierced the wrinkled gray skin of its cheek and the other took it just above the eye. Black blood trickled down its face and sprayed from the exit wound in the back of its skull.

I heard a sharp snap and another arrow slammed into the side of the creature's head. The arrow penetrated the monster's temple and burst out the other side. It looked just like the arrow-through-the-head party gag, and I couldn't hold back the giggle that bubbled up from the part of me that had gone a little mad.

The creature remained in the air for a few moments, bobbing like a cork in a pool. Then its eyes rolled up in its head and it collapsed in a twitching mass of tentacles. I stepped up to it, stuck the Peacemaker's barrel in its ear and pulled the trigger a couple times. Maybe more than a couple.

I felt a hand on my wrist, pressing firmly but gently. "That's enough, miss. It's over."

I looked up and saw a ghost. He was wearing a long leather coat and a wide-brimmed hat. Brown hair shot with gray spilled down from the hat to his collar. He looked to be in his fifties, and his face had a seamed and weathered appearance that suited him. He was holding an antique wooden crossbow in one hand and a large leather pack was slung over his shoulder. I nodded and reluctantly holstered Ned.

"That was a disembodied head that eats ghosts," I said.

"The Karen tribesmen of Burma call it the kephn."

"Around here we call it Pac-Man."

The ghost shrugged and extended his hand. "I'm Abe," he said. "Abe Warren."

I shook his hand. "Thanks for your help, Abe. I'm Domino."

Abe nodded and then squinted at me. "You're alive."

"Yeah, barely. Like I said, thanks."

"What I meant was, you're not dead. You're not a spirit."

"Right on."

"So you're a witch."

"I prefer sorcerer. Or sorceress, if you have to be gender-specific about it."

"A witch spirit-walking in a boneyard at night…I probably don't want to know what you're doing here."

Abe didn't seem too fond of witches but at least he was polite about it. "Well, why are you here?"

"I'm a ghost-hunter."

"You're a ghost yourself, Abe."

"Well, yes, I was a ghost-hunter in life. I never saw the

point in changing vocations just because I died. Matter of fact, it's a lot easier to find the bastards this way."

"What do you have against ghosts?"

"Oh, nothing against most of them, just the troublesome ones. The haunts, revenants and vengeful spirits—those are my prey."

"Well, I don't think there's any ghosts like that here. Tony got eaten and Keshawn can't leave his grave."

"I'm glad to hear it. I'm on patrol, you see. It's my job to make sure there aren't any malevolent entities on the prowl." He drew a gold watch from his vest pocket and snapped it open. "Since there aren't, I should be on my way."

"Yeah, just the head. Thanks again for that."

"My pleasure. Well, there's plenty more graveyards to visit before the dawn." He smiled and tugged on the brim of his hat. "Good evening, miss."

He turned away and I watched as he walked across the cemetery toward the edge of the mist.

"Say, Abe," I called. He stopped and turned back to me.

"Yes, Miss Domino?"

"You got any idea why Tony and Keshawn were trapped here? It's like their ghosts were chained to the place where their bodies were destroyed."

Abe looked down at his feet and rubbed his chin. He looked back up at me and shook his head. "No, I'm afraid I don't know anything about that," he said. "But I reckon a powerful witch such as yourself will get to the bottom of it." Then he turned and disappeared into the fog.

I didn't want to chase him into the mist but I thought about going after him. Not because I needed the company, but because I was pretty sure the son of a bitch was lying.

★ ★ ★

"Why didn't you tell me the Koreans were making noise about Terrence's outfit?"

I was meeting with Adan in the second-floor office of his father's strip club, the Men's Room. It was early afternoon and there was a light lunchtime crowd in the club below. The girls danced onstage and gossiped in back of it. The men paid their money and pretended they weren't lonely for a while.

"It's a political matter, not directly related to the war effort. I figured you had more important things to worry about, and besides, Dad left this kind of thing to me. Anyway, I'm telling you now."

"Terrence is our ally, Adan. Supporting our alliances is critical to the war effort, and you damn well know it."

Adan's voice softened. "I'm not trying to undercut your authority, Domino. Really, I'm not. I just think you're being soft on Cole because you feel like you owe him something."

"Yeah, he saved my life."

"And we're all grateful for that. I'm grateful." Adan smiled and looked at me with his dark, soulful eyes. I'd gotten lost in those eyes once before. I didn't plan on doing it again.

"So you want to show your gratitude by stabbing him in the fucking back? Remind me never to do you a favor."

"No one has to get hurt, Domino. I'm not talking about taking him out. He'd get bumped down to lieutenant again, but in a stronger outfit. It's still a promotion for him, from where he was before. We annex his territory and he runs it for us."

"I'm pretty sure Terrence wouldn't see it as a promotion. I'm pretty sure I wouldn't blame him."

"Maybe. He's not stupid, though, and I think he'd come around. He'd listen to you, Domino."

"I'm not going to push him out without giving him a chance."

Adan sighed. "What do you suggest, then? The current situation isn't stable. If we don't push him out, someone's going to put him down."

"Simeon Wale's crew is going to cross. Terrence will give him lieutenant."

"No one mentioned this to me."

I shrugged. "I thought you had more important things to worry about. Anyway, I'm telling you now."

"You're weakening our outfit to support Terrence."

"Letting Wale cross doesn't make us weaker. I know *I'll* sleep better at night."

"The other outfits will know you're supporting Terrence. It will involve us in the conflict. It could escalate."

"I don't see how. The move is between Terrence and Wale. I'm just stepping aside."

Adan frowned and shook his head. "I don't like it, Domino. I should have been consulted about this. I don't like you dropping it on me after it's already done."

I smiled. "Yeah, it stings a little, doesn't it?"

"This is different, Domino. Okay, I didn't tell you about the Koreans. You made a move that impacts my responsibilities without discussing it with me."

"There wasn't anything to discuss. If we can help Terrence get right, we're going to do it. That's the way we treat our allies around here. Maybe it's different where you come from."

Adan flinched, and I had to admit it was a low blow. Adan may have been the crown prince and maybe he'd made his triumphant return, but he was still an outsider to most of the guys in the outfit. A few even suspected King Oberon of running a long con on us. They figured Adan would turn out to be some kind of Manchurian Candidate even more dangerous to our outfit than the changeling had been. Adan had inherited a certain amount of power— enough to make life difficult for me—but he was isolated. In the underworld, that's an uncomfortable place to be.

In my experience, men weren't usually very complicated, and Adan was no exception. In the last couple months, he'd made it pretty clear he wanted to be friends. Problem was, I needed an associate I could count on a hell of a lot more than I needed a friend, even if he was nice to look at.

"We're on the same side," Adan said, as if he knew what I was thinking. "I'm just trying to protect my father's interests, the same as you. We don't have to be rivals, Domino."

I wasn't sure how we could avoid being rivals if he challenged all my decisions. Maybe he thought we could avoid it if he were the one making all the decisions. If that's what he had in mind, he was going to be really disappointed.

"There's something else," I said. "Terrence had to bury two of his nephews yesterday. I was at the cemetery."

"That's rough, but from everything you've said about Mobley, that's the way the Jamaicans play the game."

"That's not what I'm getting at. After the service, the kids got back up and tried to eat us." I told Adan about the zombies and about my visit to the Between.

"And you're sure it wasn't something Mobley did?"

I shook my head. "There was no magic on the kids. I've been down that road before so I don't want to make too much of it. But it wasn't sorcery and it wasn't glamour."

"So what does that leave?"

"I was hoping you might have an idea." Avalon, where

Adan had grown up, was in the Beyond. He'd had more experience with this kind of thing than I had.

"It could be a plague, like in the movies."

"Jesus, Adan, I was hoping you'd have something a little more solid than fucking Hollywood. Anyway, I got bit by one of them and I haven't been feeling any cannibalistic urges or anything."

"Sorry, Domino, I really don't know. We didn't get much in the way of zombies. I guess it could be an Unseelie thing. They were hooked up a little more closely with the realms of the mortal dead than we were."

"The Unseelie?"

"Yeah. There are twin kingdoms in Faerie, one light and one dark. The dark one is called the Unseelie Court."

"So the Seelie are supposed to be the good fairies? They swapped you out for a changeling, killed a lot of my guys, tried to kill me and planned to take down your father."

Adan grinned. "Light and dark, not necessarily good and evil. The distinction is more about personality than morals. The Seelie fey are usually in a better mood."

I didn't know the Seelie king well, but I had to admit even when he was conspiring to kill me he'd been pretty cheerful about it. "So you think the Unseelie fey might be raising zombies?"

"I don't really know, Domino. I was raised by the fey but I was never one of them. Everyone knew who I was, what I was and why I was there. I wasn't trusted. If I had to guess, I'd say no. The Unseelie are still fey. If there were Unseelie glamour on the zombies you'd have seen it."

"Should we be expecting the Unseelie to move on us, just like the Seelie did?"

"Another thing I don't know. There wasn't much contact between the courts, except for the occasional war. I do know King Oberon has an army of spies whose only job is to keep tabs on them. You could ask him."

"Okay, thanks. I'll stay in touch." I stood up and left. Adan might have called after me but I was already out the office door and heading down the stairs to the club.

I'd like to say I was thinking about Terrence, about the Jamaicans, about zombies and the possible involvement of the Unseelie Court. But I wasn't. I was thinking about Adan. I was thinking about how badly I'd wanted him—or at least, the creature that had taken his place—just a few short months ago. At least I'd thought I wanted him. Looking back, it was hard to remember why. But then Adan would smile and those fucking dimples would soften his chiseled face, or he'd tilt his head to the side as he listened to what I was saying. Just like the changeling. I'd catch the scent of apples and cinnamon and I'd feel that familiar pull. It was just like waking from a pleasant dream and wishing for a moment you could go back to sleep.

This Adan wasn't a changeling. He wasn't a monster. But that didn't mean he wasn't dangerous.

I'd averted a war with the Seelie Court by giving them Hollywood. King Oberon had taken over a club on Sunset Boulevard that had belonged to one of the conspirators, a vampire I'd gotten to kill. It had been called the Cannibal Club under the vampire's management, but Oberon had since changed the name to the Carnival Club. He'd done some remodeling and redecorating, too. The Mardi Gras theme was a lot less played out than the Goth thing, and I had to admit the purple, gold and green decor was a lot more festive—gaudier, too, but what do you want from fairies? All in all, Oberon could have done worse. It wasn't like the world needed another Irish pub or anything.

I spun my parking spell and left my Lincoln out front, then went inside the club. I found Oberon behind the main bar polishing glasses with a white cloth. He was wearing a plain white T-shirt and faded jeans and looked more like the drummer in a garage band than a fairy king. The Carnival Club wouldn't open for hours but a few sidhe were hanging around, lounging at the tables and booths or drinking at the bar. The fairy queen, Titania, was there, and she didn't look old enough to be in the club.

"Domino, welcome," Oberon said. "Tequila? I'll join you."

"Too early for me, King. How about some of that apple cider you make?"

Oberon reached below the bar and brought out a carafe of the amber liquid. The cider wasn't too sweet, a little spicy, and I was pretty sure it had some narcotic qualities. I didn't care—it was one of the best things I'd ever tasted and it reminded me of better times.

"With ice," I said as he filled a glass.

"You're a barbarian, Domino," the king said, but he dropped a few cubes in my glass. He pushed it across the bar to me as I sat down. "What brings you in?"

"The Unseelie Court."

Oberon frowned. "What about it?"

"I maybe got a problem with zombies. Adan thought the Unseelie fey might be involved. He said they were more closely aligned with the realms of the dead, and all that."

"Queen Mab has, at times, made the mortal dead a part of her court. Mostly to torment them, from what I've seen."

"Queen Mab? Is she your sister or something?"

"They were lovers," said Titania.

Oberon glanced over at her. He looked worried. "That

was a long time ago, my dear. We've been enemies far longer than we were lovers."

"She doesn't do zombies, though," Titania continued. "Very few mortals can cross physically into Avalon, so you're not likely to find any animated corpses there."

"Many of the Unseelie sidhe can raise the dead, though," Oberon said. "When they cross into Arcadia."

"She hasn't crossed, husband. None of them have. I'd know."

"She will."

"But not yet. And Domino doesn't care about that. She's asking about zombies."

"Yeah," I said. "One thing at a time." Arcadia was the sidhe name for the mortal world. The idea that a grouchier sidhe nation would eventually cross over—that was a problem for another day.

"Tell me about your zombies," Oberon said. I gave him the whole story, and I have to say, neither he nor his queen seemed all that interested.

Oberon kept polishing his glasses. "I know of the kephn. Human souls are its food of choice, but it's been known to hunt the fey and other spirits in lean times. It feeds on juice and so it can be quite dangerous to the lesser fey. Graveyards, as you might guess, are its primary hunting ground."

"Well, I don't think it's my problem. It's dead, and anyway, it seemed to have a hankering for ghosts, not zombies."

"Yes, the kephn is incapable of manifesting in the mortal world. It would have no use for zombies so I doubt it was responsible for their creation."

"So what's creating them?"

"What makes you think there will be others? Perhaps it

was just something that happened to those two and you'll never know what caused it."

"Yeah, I'm not going to waste time hoping there won't be more. I'm not that lucky."

"Maybe it's a plague—a viral outbreak or something."

"Everyone watches way too many movies."

Oberon shrugged. "This is Hollywood."

"So you've got nothing for me?"

"I'm no expert on zombies, Domino."

I sighed. "All right, thanks anyway. How's everything else going? You settling in okay?"

Oberon grinned. "It's perfect. Hollywood may not be much to look at, but there's so much juice here. We're all quite content, I assure you."

"That's good."

"Are you coming to the Bacchanal Ball?"

"What's that?"

"I'm throwing a party. Here at the club. You should have received an invitation."

"Sometimes I forget to check my mail. When is it?"

"Tomorrow night. You must attend, Domino. It will be a celebration quite unlike anything you've ever experienced."

"What are we celebrating?"

"Him," said Titania. "What else?"

Oberon frowned at her. "Our return to Arcadia. The ceremony with which you celebrated our arrival was simple and elegant, but a little understated. That's not really how we roll."

"Yeah, okay, I'll be here. Thanks for the invite. Is it formal?"

"It's a masquerade, of course."

"So I need a costume?"

Oberon laughed. "You stole my shapeshifter's glamour, Domino. I'm certain you'll come up with something wonderful."

"All right, but I'm bringing Honey."

Oberon shrugged. "That's fine. I don't hold grudges." That was a lie—he held them better than just about anyone. "There's one more thing, Domino, a somewhat more serious matter."

"What's that?"

"It's Terrence Cole's outfit. We're concerned. We feel as though we've left the back door open while our family sleeps."

"I'm handling it, King."

"I've no doubt you'll do what you can, within the limitations of the political situation. I understand you've given him Simeon Wale's crew."

That didn't take long, but then Oberon's spies were better than most. "Wale crossed on his own. Wasn't my idea. I can live without the bastard, though—if it helps Terrence, that's just a happy coincidence."

Oberon nodded and smiled. "I don't know this man Wale as well as you do, of course, but I'm concerned that it won't be enough. I'm concerned that I was…too diplomatic… when I agreed to surrender Cole's territory."

I let the feeling drain from my face and looked at him. "Your diplomacy meant we didn't have to kill each other. That's still what it means."

Oberon held up his hands in mock surrender. "Easy, Domino. I'm not proposing a breach of our treaty. I'm merely pointing out that I could hold Cole's ground better than he can, with or without Simeon Wale."

"You couldn't hold it without the other outfits behind

you. And we're not. Remember that. Maybe there's something for you in Reseda if you're feeling cramped."

"What the fuck would I do with Reseda? Open a carwash?"

I shrugged.

"And it's not about feeling cramped, Domino. It's about security. You of all people should understand that."

"Yeah, I do. I remember when another outsider tried to move in and take my ground."

"Precisely. And the same thing can happen to Cole, only this time, the outsider may not be as understanding as I was."

"That's why we have a treaty, King. Something comes in, we're united against it. That's the way we do it. We protect each other. The strong don't feed on the weak."

"That's the way you'd *like* to do it. That's not the way it was done in the past. You can't even be sure your way is going to work. You still don't know if you can make an army out of a gang. The old way was less risky."

"Maybe now it is but not in the long run."

"In the long run we're all dead."

"That's an odd thing for an immortal fairy king to say."

"Okay, in the long run *you're* all dead."

I laughed and the king did, too. "That's better," I said. "The point is, you should appreciate that we can't be shortsighted about this. You're the master of the long-term plan. We're going to need Terrence. We're going to need all the outfits to be strong."

"Very well," Oberon said. "You're right, of course—I've been called many things, but never shortsighted. But as one who has a great deal of experience with long-term plans, let me offer a word of caution. The most dangerous thing about thinking ahead is that you wait too long when the time comes to act. The line between the short run and the long run is indistinct, Domino. Sometimes you can cross it without even realizing it."

"I understand, King. Terrence is on a deadline but we give him a chance to stand up. That's the way it's going to be."

"I concede, my dear, and once again you've proven that I'm no match for you in negotiations."

I smiled even though it was bullshit. Oberon's only reason for bringing this up was to put Terrence and me on the clock. We'd established the Seelie Court couldn't move on Terrence immediately. But if the clock ran down, I'd be all out of excuses and Terrence would have more than the Jamaicans and Koreans to worry about.

I promised Oberon I'd see him at the party and left the club. I wasn't real happy about how it had gone, but I wasn't exactly surprised, either. I'd learned Oberon was someone I could deal with, but the deals always left me feeling like I'd gotten the short end.

But again, what do you want from fairies?

three

I woke up to a phone call from Adan just after dawn the next morning.

"Simeon Wale hit the Jamaicans last night," he said when I picked up the phone.

"Yeah, good morning to you, too. What fucking time is it?"

"It's about five-thirty. Did you hear me?"

"Yeah, Wale hit Mobley. What did you think was going to happen?"

"He burned a couple apartment blocks in Imperial Courts, Domino. A lot of people are dead." Imperial Courts was the largest housing project in L.A., and it was the heart of Francis Mobley's territory between Watts and Compton.

I sat up and rubbed my eyes. "What the fuck did he do that for? How many people?"

"According to the news, no confirmed deaths but a lot of serious injuries."

"I thought you said people were dead."

"They are, but the news teams haven't figured it out yet. They're calling it 'The Miracle in the Projects.'"

"Oh, fuck me. Zombies?"

"Yeah. Maybe a hundred."

"Jesus Christ. What's happening there now?"

I heard Adan take a deep breath. "We're losing it, Domino. I think we maybe lost it already. They're taking them to the hospitals. There's not much we can do about it."

"What's Mobley doing?"

"Community service. He's got his posses out there helping with the relief effort. But you can forget about getting him to sit down with Terrence. There won't be any sit-down, not after this."

"Stupid fucking Wale," I said, and slammed the receiver against my skull a few times.

"What are we going to do, Domino?"

I really had no idea but I had to think of one, fast. "It sounds like containment isn't an option. We've got to start thinking about a cleanup. I'm not as worried about the projects, but we're going to have to put soldiers in the hospitals."

Adan laughed and there was an ugly edge to it. "That's it? You want to send death squads to the hospitals? Domino, it's on the news!"

"Okay, not our soldiers. We'll handle the projects—we won't attract much attention there. We can send the fey to the hospitals. They can deal with the zombies and glamour the civilians. They can keep a lid on it, if anyone can."

"That might work, if Oberon agrees to help. You'll be indebted to him, though."

I didn't answer. If I played my cards right I wouldn't need Oberon for this. "Why don't you go ahead and say it, Adan."

"What?"

"I told you so. You're thinking it, might as well be man enough to say it."

The line was silent for a few moments. "I wasn't thinking it, Domino. You didn't know Simeon Wale was going to do this. And the zombie problem definitely isn't your fault."

"It was my plan to send Wale over, and it went about as wrong as a plan can go."

"Look, I'm not going to pretend I agreed with your decision. I didn't, but not because I anticipated anything like this."

"No, you were just worried it would involve us in the conflict, that it would escalate and pull us in. You were right."

"Maybe," Adan said. "And maybe next time I'll be the one who fucks up. The truth is, I've been at this, what, ten weeks? Most of the time I'm just bluffing my way through and hoping no one notices. Neither one of us is my father, Domino. We need each other to do this thing."

"I'll try."

"As will I, starting now. I'll take care of Imperial Courts. You handle the hospitals."

"Done," I said. "Call me."

"I will. Good luck."

"You, too. And Adan?"

"Yeah?"

"Thanks," I said and hung up the phone.

"Honey," I called. I'd thrown on some clothes and I was in the kitchen nuking a frozen snack. Honey flew in from the second bedroom she and her family had converted into the Enchanted Forest.

"Morning, Domino. What's for breakfast?"

"Hot Pocket," I said, and looked at the box. "Ham and Cheddar."

"Ugh. I don't see how you can eat that stuff."

"I'm not in the mood for a burrito. Say, Honey, how do feel about killing zombies?"

Honey's face brightened and her wings scattered orange pixie dust. "Did you get an Xbox?"

"No, I mean real ones."

"Oh. I've never killed one. I bet it's not as fun as it is in the games."

"Probably not, but do you think you could handle some zombies?"

"Are they really slow, like in the movies?"

"I don't know. I've only seen two of them. I think it depends on how long they've been dead and the condition of the body."

"I think I can handle it. How many are there?"

"Maybe a hundred. Maybe more if we don't move fast. They're in the hospital."

"Oh. I'll probably need some help. I can bring my sisters."

"Yeah, bring your whole family. I'm going, too, but it could get nasty and we need to clean it up fast."

"Okay, sounds good. I don't think we've been spending enough time together."

"Thing is, it's not just the zombie killing. There will be a lot of civilians at the hospital. We need to dust them so they don't remember what happened."

"Sure, that's easy. We could do something even better. We don't have to just make them forget—we could make them think something else happened."

"Like what?"

"Maybe a weather balloon exploded and killed every-one."

"We could just make them forget."

"Gas pocket?"

"Nah."

"Whatever you say. Are you ready to go now?"

"Yeah, we need to hurry. You round everyone up and I'll finish my breakfast."

"Cool," Honey said, and she flew back into the bed-room.

Twenty-eight piskies, including Honey, piled into my Lincoln with room to spare. They huddled on the seats and dash, jostling for a favorable position. Honey perched on the steering wheel and pretended to help me drive. They were all invisible to human eyes so this was far less of a spectacle than it sounds.

All of the piskies were female. Along with Honey, there was a mother, grandmother, great-grandmother, a few aunts, a handful of sisters and several nieces and cousins. I'd asked Honey about it and she'd said piskie families were always female. The males, apparently, left the nest when they reached puberty and only returned to the females to mate. When the female was pregnant, they left again. Actually, it worked a lot like the barrio where I grew up.

Most of the "survivors" from the fire at Imperial Courts had been taken to Centinela Medical Center in Inglewood, so that was our first stop. I used my changeling mojo to assume the appearance of a blonde doctor with enough curves to make surgical blues look good. I spun my parking spell and we took a spot reserved for ambulances. I dropped a ward on the building so no one would be able to leave, and then we all went in through the emergency room doors.

The situation at Centinela had already gone to hell. When the automatic doors closed behind us, we saw a young nurse run screaming from a treatment room to our right. A black male who looked to be in his sixties was chasing her, dragging a metal stand behind him from the IV line still planted in his arm. He had third-degree burns over most of his body and the remains of his clothes were deep-fried into his skin.

"I got this," I said. "Spread out and clear the place, room by room. Make sure you only hit the dead ones. Some of the victims should still be alive."

My weapon of choice was my ghost-binding spell. "At first cock-crow," I chanted, "the ghosts must go, back to their quiet graves below." My working theory was that the zombie was just a ghost trapped in its mortal remains. Sure enough, the spell pulled the man's shade from its ravaged vessel and the barbecued corpse dropped limply to the tile.

The piskies used their glamour. I didn't really want to know what they did to kill the zombies. They just flew up to the victims and dusted them, and the walking corpses fell over and stopped moving.

We moved methodically through the first floor of the hospital and the heaviest work was in the emergency department and triage wards. By the time my kills reached double digits, I'd turned my brain off and stopped registering what I was doing. I saw enough before that happened to realize some of the zombies weren't victims of the fire. They were nurses, and doctors and candy stripers, and they'd died when their patients fed on them. Some of them were so badly ravaged they were barely recognizable as human. They were still moving, though, and they were still hungry. They dragged themselves along the white tile, leaving smeared blood trails behind them, and they reached for me eagerly before I tore their spirits free.

It took a little over three hours to reach the top floor of the hospital. When we were finished with the zombies, we started back down, floor by floor, glamouring the surviving employees and patients. None of them would remember what had happened and I felt like we were doing them a kindness.

It was a pretty thin cover-up and I knew there'd be an investigation. A lot of questions would be asked but none of them would have any real answers. There were going to be a lot of bodies but in the end it wouldn't lead anywhere. No witnesses, no leads, no case.

When we arrived at Broadway Hospital for the second phase of the cleanup, Agents Lowell and Granato were standing outside by their black sedan.

"Jesus Christ," I said. "As if I don't have enough to worry about without these fucking guys showing up. Honey, y'all hang back and let me handle this."

Agent Lowell spoke as I walked up to them. "Ms. Riley, please tell me you didn't have anything to do with this."

"I'm not in the business of raising zombies," I said. The fact they were here meant they already knew what was going on. No point in lying about it.

"And the project fire?" asked Granato. He always wanted to be the hard ass.

"Not guilty, but I know who did it. We'll take care of it."

"And do you know who's responsible for the zombies?" Lowell asked.

"I was hoping you might know what's going on. Before this, it was just a couple of gangsters." Tony and Keshawn hadn't really been gangsters, but it would have been too fine a distinction for Lowell and Granato.

"It's not just gangsters and it's not just the victims of the fire. We've gotten reports from all over L.A.—everyone who dies is getting back up."

"I figured it would go that way. And Stag doesn't have any intelligence on this thing?" Homeland Security's Special Threat Assessment Group had compiled a lot of research on the supernatural, even if Lowell and Granato were the only agents with any juice.

"We assume it's a PNC," Lowell said.

I'd gotten enough of asking him to explain his fucking acronyms the first time we met, when the sidhe came across in what Stag called an MIE—a Major Incursion Event. I glared at him and waited for the translation.

"Paranormal Contagion," he said finally. "You know, a zombie plague."

"Jesus Christ, not you guys, too."

"I can tell you this," said Granato, "if there's anything that concerns the government more than an MIE it's a PNC."

"This is extremely serious, Ms. Riley," Lowell said. "We can't isolate the pathogen or identify the vector, so we have no way of containing the outbreak. We could lose the city, just for starters. That pushes most of the contingency plans off the table and the decision-makers go right to the unconventional protocols."

It seemed like every time there was a little supernatural hiccup, someone in the government wanted to reach for the red button. "It's not a zombie plague, Lowell. I got bit by one of the damn things, and I feel fine—as fine as I can, considering I just had to clear a hundred-plus zombies out of Centinela Hospital."

"How do you explain what's happening, then?"

I exhaled slowly and shook my head. "Beats the hell out of me. From what you said, everyone that dies is turning into a zombie—everyone, no matter how they died, no matter where in the city they died. That sounds like a much bigger event than your horror-movie outbreak."

"A CMI," Lowell said, nodding thoughtfully. He looked up and noticed my irritation. "Critical Metaphysical Instability. A breakdown in the structure or natural processes of our reality."

"Yeah, that sounds more like it," I said.

"If you're right, this situation represents an extreme threat to the United States."

"No shit, Lowell."

"I mean, a CMI...this is End Times stuff, Ms. Riley."

"Well, I haven't seen Jesus or heard any trumpets sounding so I guess it's not all that bad. We just have to figure out what's causing it and put it right."

"How do you propose to do that?"

"Fuck if I know. Is it just L.A.? Have you gotten any reports from anywhere else?"

"Just L.A.," Granato said, "for now."

"That's good. Okay, I'll look into it. I'm not sure how, but I'll figure something out. I can ask Mr. Clean if he knows anything about it, though I consider it a last resort."

"Mr. Clean?"

"My familiar. We don't get along real well but he knows his shit." Problem was, every time I went to him he was playing another angle, trying to get me killed. It was a hate-hate relationship.

"How quickly can you move?" Granato asked. "We have to submit a report on this. We can try to buy you some time and we can...suppress...the media coverage of the story. But the government won't stand back and watch L.A. turn into a necropolis."

"A necropolis?"

"Yes," Lowell said. "Even in the best of times, more than two hundred people die in L.A. every day. We've done some, uh, testing in the last twenty-four hours. Everyone who dies seems to go mad and degenerate into cannibalism, eventually, and that just creates more zombies. It won't take long for this to become a city of the dead."

"How does the cannibalism tie into your CNE theory?"

"CMI," said Lowell. "Based on the experiments, feeding on human flesh seems to be the only way to slow the zombies' physical decomposition."

"So they eat people, they don't degenerate?"

Granato shook his head. "They don't rot as fast. Depending on how they died, some of these freaks don't even know they're dead. Either way, it drives them mad when they start in on the other white meat."

I nodded and rubbed my ear absently. "Okay, guys, I'll try to hurry. I have other things on my to-do list, you know."

"Like what?"

"Well, right now, I've got to clear some fucking zombies out of another hospital. Maybe you can help with that, it'll go a lot faster. Then, I've got a gang war that just went hot. I've got to make sure that doesn't blow up and put a lot more zombies on the street."

"Is that all?" Granato said, smirking.

"No, Granato, it's not—thanks for asking. I've also got a party to go to tonight, and I haven't even decided what to wear."

Attending the Bacchanal Ball with everything that was going on felt a little like fiddling while Rome burned, but I wasn't just in it for the free food and booze. I knew I probably wouldn't be able to roll back the zombie outbreak. CMIs aren't exactly my specialty. If it got out of control I'd need Oberon's help to defend my territory and my people, and I didn't want to irritate him by blowing off his little soiree.

I also knew most of the supernatural A-list would be at the ball and I hoped I might find someone who could tell me what was going on. I'd struck out with Mr. Clean. He said it was probably a zombie plague and noted that *Night of the Living Dead* was on his channel that night.

So I had good reasons not to cancel. Plus, there'd be free food and booze.

The problem was the costume. I thought it'd be cool if Honey and I picked a theme together. I suggested shape-shifting into a gorilla and she could go as a banana. Honey didn't care for that idea and told me to do something to myself with the banana.

"I know," said Honey, "you could go as a dominatrix and I could be your whip."

"Seems like it'd be a little boring to go as an inanimate object, even a whip."

"You wanted me to be a banana."

"Yeah, but you could be like the Fruit of the Loom guy, with arms, and legs, a face and stuff."

"Forget it, Domino. Anyway, I don't think the Fruit of the Loom guys have a banana."

"Okay, I could go as a pirate captain and you could be my parrot. You perch on my shoulder all the time anyway."

"Too unoriginal. There will probably be a lot of pirates there."

"Peter Pan and Tinkerbelle."

"Only if you're Tinkerbelle."

"Witch and black cat."

"We're going to a ball, not trick-or-treating."

"Jesus, Honey, we're never going to come up with anything."

"Oh, I know! You can be an angel and I'll be a little devil on your shoulder. Like the parrot, but sexier."

"Ironic. I like it. But I thought fairies didn't like Christian stuff."

"Christians didn't come up with angels and devils."

"Whatever, let's not get into it." I got enough blasphemy from Mr. Clean—I didn't need it from Honey, too.

What followed was a game of one-upmanship as we tried to outdo each other for the sexiest costume. Since I was shapeshifting and Honey was using her piskie glamour, it escalated quickly. We finally decided to call it a draw, but by that time we looked like we'd walked off the set of a porn video with a paranormal theme.

I was wearing a sheer white shift that might have reached midthigh if I pulled on the hem real hard. A halo of golden light encircled my head and elegant feathery wings fluttered at my back. I chose a pair of white stilettos that hurt like hell but did amazing things to my calves. I added some curves to fill out the shift, and most of them were plainly visible through the thin fabric. I thought I heard Mr. Clean's chuckling at one point, but the TV wasn't on.

I finished off the ensemble with a white garter, panties and stockings to maintain some sense of modesty, at least from the waist down.

Honey went with classic red leather. It started out as a bustier but was quickly reduced to a thong, thigh-high boots and something that might have been a bra or pasties, depending on where you draw the line. She completed the look with cute little horns, a tail and the requisite pitchfork.

When we were finished, we stood in the middle of my

bedroom and admired our handiwork in the full-length mirror hanging on the closet door.

"We're going to do some damage," I said.

"Yeah."

"Do you think I'm cheating with the shapeshifting?"

"No way, it's a masquerade. Besides, your boobs are spectacular."

"Yeah. I always hoped they'd look like this when I grew up."

"You should keep them."

"Nah, just for the party. One night is enough."

"Not for me it's not."

"You'll live. Buy a magazine or something."

"You're beautiful, Domino."

I smiled. "I have to be to keep up with you."

If the End Times were upon us, the Bacchanal Ball was the right kind of party to close things out. Oberon had glamoured the whole club. I could see the magic plainly enough, but even without the witch sight I'd have known it the instant Honey and I walked in the door. All my worries and inhibitions literally dropped away from me at the threshold. I'd had a little headache when we left the condo but it vanished when I entered the club. I didn't want to think. I only wanted to see, and hear, and smell and taste. I just wanted to *feel*.

Luckily, Oberon had provided plenty of amusements to indulge the partygoers' senses. Witch-light cast a soft, surreal glow across the club, and the space was filled with hundreds—maybe thousands—of exotic flowers. The main bar was gone and it had been replaced by a huge oak banquet table piled high with food and drink of every description. A chamber orchestra performed on the stage—all of the musicians sidhe—and the music they played made me ache with longing for something beautiful I'd lost and then forgotten.

The costumes were incredible—no surprise, given all the glamour and sorcery in the room. Oberon appeared as Pan, standing at least seven feet tall on a goat's legs, with curling ram's horns, golden hair and a roguish thatch of whiskers on his chin. Titania was a forest nymph, which meant she was more than half naked and had leaves in her long red curls. These images suited them somehow, and I found myself wondering if these were their true forms, or had been once.

"Welcome to Arcadia, m'ladies," the king said, bowing dramatically. "Welcome to the Dream."

And that's just what it was, that first true night in the fairy king's Arcadia. Later, the memories would dance away from my conscious thoughts like embers on the wind. I remember we ate and drank, and everything I tasted was the very *best* thing, each morsel and sip a unique delight.

Terrence was there, an ebon-skinned Egyptian god with the head of a jackal. I remember Adan, and he tasted like cinnamon and apples again. I remember Honey lying beside me and a handsome young piskie named Jack, and I remember the joy I felt when I saw them together.

I remember Anton was there but I don't remember what he was doing. I can only hope he wasn't doing much.

At some point during the endless revel, I heard a song I recognized. A single violin played a sad, sweet melody that was at once haunting and seductive. The instrumental went on for a long time, and then Titania stepped onto the stage and began to sing.

The song was "Hotel California." I remember looking around at the crowd. Some danced, slowly swaying as if in a trance, and others stood quietly watching the stage. All were weeping, and I realized I was, too. I can't describe what I heard, and anyway, the sound was only part of it. The queen poured an immortal lifetime of passion and sorrow into the song. I remember thinking if there were real angels, this was the song they would sing.

I don't remember the song ending, but Titania had left the stage when the dream turned into a nightmare.

I was reclining on a velvet couch with my dress bunched around my waist. Adan was draped over me and he was kissing my neck. Honey was curled around my forearm, naked and sleeping, and Jack was spooning her. He was also naked.

I heard screams and shouts, and I smelled sulfur and decay. Bodies were hurled away from the center of the room or crumpled where they stood. I heard the sound of tearing flesh and cracking bone. I saw blood splash like buckets of paint on the walls and the floor.

"Fomoiri!" Oberon yelled, and I saw him charge the dance floor with a silver greatsword in his hands.

I didn't recognize the king's name for it, but finally, I saw the demon.

It was massive, towering above the crowd, but darkness clung to it and its form was constantly shifting, twisting, so that my eyes didn't want to focus on it. It was vaguely humanoid and it was burning from the inside out, flame spilling from its eyes and mouth.

There were no batwings or horns. As I forced myself to look at it, I realized it was very like a human, except for the size, the special effects and the hideous deformities. Its back was hunched, its skull was misshapen and bone spurs pierced the mottled hide stretched over rippling bands of muscle.

The demon turned to Oberon as he charged, and it

roared. Fire exploded from its mouth and engulfed the king, but it didn't slow him down. He slammed into the thing and buried the sword in its side. The demon howled and swung one impossibly long arm. Its fist smashed into Oberon's head with a sickening crunch, and the king went down.

The fairy king went down.

This was enough, at last, to shock me from my stupor. I got up and advanced on the monster. I started spinning spontaneous combat spells as fast as I could pull the juice, and they flowed around the demon like water around a stone. I hit the thing with malevolent glamours and it didn't even notice.

By this time, the other survivors had recovered, too, and the air around the demon had become a storm of arcane energy. It just kept killing, and it finally dawned on me that there might have been a reason Oberon had attacked it with a sword.

"Physical attacks!" I shouted, and my words were followed shortly by the deafening sound of gunfire as all the gangsters who were still alive unloaded on the demon. I'd left my forty-five at home on account of my minimalist costume. I could have hidden it with glamour, but it would have ruined the experience. I snatched a semiautomatic from the waistband of a fallen soldier and emptied the magazine at the demon.

Bullets didn't seem to have much effect, either.

I turned and ran back the way I'd come, diving behind the couch I'd been lying on. "I have harnessed the shadows that stride from world to world to sow death and madness," I said, and I crossed into the Between.

In the spirit world, the demon was all special effects and no nasty body. It was a massive black shadow of shifting darkness marked only by the fire in its eyes and mouth. I got up and ran for the door. When I got outside, I kept running and plunged into the mist. I retrieved Ned from the front closet of my condo and made it back to the club in no more time than it would take the demon to kill a couple dozen revelers.

I eased inside and pressed my back against the wall, the Peacemaker gripped in both hands in front of me.

"I know you're cursed, Ned," I whispered. "I know this would be a really great time for the curse to show up, for you to earn your nickname. But the guy who sold you to me said you were an artifact, and I really, really need you right now."

I brought the gun to my lips and kissed the barrel.

"So please, Ned, I'm begging you, just this once. Get hostile with this ugly motherfucker." Then I extended my arms, aimed as steadily as I could, thumbed back the hammer and squeezed the trigger.

I squeezed it a lot, as fast as I could work the action. Ned danced gaily in my hands and burning sapphire holes opened in the demonic shadow. It threw back its head and screamed as the holes widened, the blue fire feeding eagerly on the darkness.

Then it turned and came for me. I closed my eyes and kept firing.

I'm not sure how long I kept at it after the demon was dead. When I finally opened my eyes, the thing was a smoking puddle of black tar on the floor, the ephemeral fire still flickering on the surface. Adan stood on the other side of the evil pool, the king's greatsword in his hands. Black tar oozed along the blade and spattered against the floor.

I sank to the floor and struggled for air with huge gasping breaths. "Domino, you silly bitch, you don't even really breathe here," I whispered, and then I started giggling.

"It's okay, Domino," Adan said. "You killed it."

"I did or you did?"

Adan grinned. "We did."

"How did you get here?"

"The same way I got to Arcadia—through that first gate you built for Oberon."

"You're really here. You're not spirit-walking, like me—you're physical."

"I don't know why I'm able to do it. Maybe it's a gift I was born with."

"Or maybe it's something Oberon did to you when he took you."

"Maybe," he said. "And still, you got here first."

I looked at the spreading, toxic sludge. I reached out and dabbed my fingers in the tar, and tasted them. The taste was foul, putrescence and fresh blood, with enough acidity to burn my tongue. There were a couple familiar notes, too. One of them I couldn't quite put my finger on; the other one pissed me off.

I stood up and holstered Ned. "See you on the other side," I said. I didn't want to leave the weapon in the club, so I had to make another round-trip to my condo. When I returned, I stepped back into the mortal world and into the slaughterhouse.

The dead were everywhere, but only the fey were staying down. The humans were nursing wounds they couldn't possibly have survived and some of them were already starting to look a little crazy.

Oberon was stretched out on the floor, his head cradled in Titania's lap. He'd returned to his youthful, sidhe form. He was bleeding but at least he was conscious. The queen wouldn't let anyone else get close, but she didn't object when Oberon waved me over.

"You slew the Fomoiri," the king said.

"We did," I said, nodding at Adan. I looked but there was no corpse in this world, not even a puddle of tar.

"I'm in your debt, Domino."

"Nah. Really it was just self-defense."

"This was my party. I'm the host." He paused and looked up at Titania, and smiled. "You defended my queen."

I shrugged. "You want to return the favor someday, I'm not going to argue much."

Oberon nodded and then his face hardened. "I'm sorry, but you're going to have to clean this up."

I looked around the room at the carnage. Most of the living dead were my soldiers. I saw Honey. She was sitting on the couch again with Jack, though I remembered hearing her battle cry during the fight.

I also saw Anton. He sagged against the wall with his legs stretched out in front of him. His torso had been torn open and he was trying to shovel his guts back into the cavity.

I shook my head. "No way, King. I'm not putting them down." Then I walked over to Anton. He looked up as I approached and I saw he was crying.

"I was dancing, Domino," he said. "Did you see me?"

"I missed it, Anton. I bet you danced real good."

"I was dancing with the pretty fairy." He looked toward the dance floor, and then tucked his chin into his chest and bawled. I turned and saw a bloody tangle of meat that might once have been a female sidhe.

I tightened my jaw, bit down on my lip and turned away. Honey and Jack flew over to me and Adan followed.

"What are you going to do, Domino?" Honey whispered.

I stared at her, blinked and ground my teeth. "I will *not* put that fat son of a bitch down."

"We don't have a choice, Domino," Adan said. "You know what will happen if we don't." He tried to put his arm around me but I jerked away.

"Honey, you and the other fey see what you can do. Save the ones that are still alive, then patch up the dead the best you can." I pointed to Anton. "Start with him."

I walked to the center of the dance floor and looked around. "Listen up," I said. "Those of you who died tonight, you're going to start getting hungry. You know the drill—you've all seen enough fucking zombie movies. You're going to want human flesh. You're going to need it."

I paused and looked at Anton. "You can have all you want," I said quietly, and then I looked out at the survivors again. "Eat up. It might keep your bodies intact, keep you more or less human. But there's only one place you can feed. If I find you anywhere else, I put you down."

"Where should we go, Domino?" Anton asked. "I'm hungry already."

"You go find Mobley and his boys, Anton."

Adan came up behind me and whispered in my ear. "Domino, no, you can't do this. You don't even know Mobley was responsible for that thing."

I turned and looked at him, and whatever he saw in my eyes made him step back. "I know," I said. "I tasted his fucking juice on it."

I turned back to Anton and nodded. "Go on," I said, and smiled. "Pig out."

four

The dream had become a nightmare, and now the party turned into a war council. Oberon had converted an unused storage space in the back of the club into a conference room. Terrence, Adan and I followed him in and joined the fairy king and his queen at the long, rectangular table.

"Who's Fomoiri?" I asked when we were seated. "It's a demon, isn't it?"

Oberon nodded. "Not who, *what*. A Fomorian. It is what some of your kind call the Firstborn."

I'd always thought demons were fallen angels, but Mr. Clean claimed they were actually Preadamites—the first race given souls and granted dominion over the earth. According to the jinn, they lacked empathy, conscience, the knowledge of good and evil, and so they had become corrupted and were cast out of the mortal world.

It seemed they were back.

"They are an ancient race," the king said. "An ancient enemy."

"Francis Mobley brought it here," I said. "A summoning of some kind."

Oberon looked at me and his face went hard. "No,

Domino. *You* brought it here. Your actions on behalf of this man," he said, gesturing at Terrence, "brought this thing into my house. Your efforts in defense of my queen do not absolve you of that crime."

"Ain't got nothing to do with Domino," Terrence said. "Mobley sent that thing after me." Terrence's Egyptian costume was gone, and he reached a hand inside his jacket. He pulled out a fancy parchment envelope and threw it on the table. "I guess I didn't invite myself here tonight."

Oberon stared at the invitation and then at Terrence. The muscles under the skin of his face shifted and rippled, like something hidden was trying to get out. "Nevertheless," the king said, "it was not prudent for Domino to throw in with you, Mr. Cole. Even the acting boss of her own outfit opposed her decision."

"I'm not Domino's boss, Sire," said Adan. "And I supported her decision. I still do. Terrence is our ally, just as you are. Mobley is our enemy. It isn't complicated." I looked at him and tried to keep the surprise from my face. He didn't return the look and his expression remained impassive. He was a good liar.

Oberon's cold stare locked on Adan for a few moments, and then his face relaxed. "Very well," he said, and looked at me. "It appears I misjudged the situation. Domino, I beg forgiveness for my ill-considered accusations. It has been a difficult night."

"Unnecessary but accepted, King. Adan has it right—Mobley is the bad guy. There's no profit in turning against each other. I figure that's why he sent the demon here and not to Terrence's bedroom some night."

Oberon inclined his head, deeply enough that it was almost a bow. "The question is, then, what do we do about it?"

"The bad news is the conflict between Terrence and

Mobley has escalated," I said. "The good news is, the political niceties just got flushed and the gloves are off. Mobley is an easy problem to solve."

"You sure, D?" Terrence asked. "Motherfucker summoned a demon. I don't know where he got the juice. Don't know where he got the chops. It ain't nothing *I* could do."

"And if he summoned one," Adan said, "we have to assume he can do it again."

"Okay," I said, "let's work that angle. How the fuck did he do it?"

"There are rituals, of course," said Oberon. "But I hadn't thought there was yet enough magic in the world to sustain the Fomoire—nor for a man like Mobley to call one."

"I got a taste of the juice. I can try to reconstruct the ritual." That still wouldn't explain where Mobley got the craft or the juice to pull it off, but it was a start.

"That sounds real good, D," said Terrence, "but Mobley ain't even our only problem. Zombie motherfuckers is getting out of control."

Oberon shrugged. "Our concern is the Fomoire, not the zombies."

"How do you figure?" I asked. "Looks to me like the zombies are everybody's problem."

"You may have noticed," the king said, "that my people are immune to this plague."

"I have a theory about that," Adan said. "The zombies are created when souls are unable to leave the body after death."

"So why are the sidhe immune?" I asked.

"We don't have souls," Titania said.

Awkward. I felt like I'd just told an off-color joke in mixed company.

Oberon chuckled. "There's no reason for discomfort,

Domino. It's not a matter of lack or misfortune. We are creatures of spirit wrapped in a thin veil of flesh. You are flesh that imprisons a small measure of spirit. Neither better nor worse, only different."

"Okay, so the Seelie Court won't go zombie," I said. "That's good. But it's still bad news for you if the rest of the city does."

Oberon didn't say anything and the expression on his face made it clear he didn't entirely agree. Was it possible he viewed a Los Angeles without humans—living ones, anyway—as an opportunity?

"She's right, husband," Titania said. "We need them." The "for now" at the end of the sentence was no less obvious for being unspoken.

"Yeah," I said, "you need us. Oh, and let's not forget the moral tragedy of the whole fucking human race being wiped out by fucking zombies. Maybe we should consider that, too."

Oberon and Titania looked at each other and then back to me. They smiled in unison. "Of course," they said.

"We are your friends, Domino," the king said. "We wish you no harm. But our first obligation is to our own people. We would expect no less of you."

"I'm overwhelmed, King. Thing is, I need your help with the zombies. Someone has to contain this thing and your people are obviously better suited to it than mine. I send my soldiers out to herd zombies, some of them are going to end up swelling their ranks. I don't like the math. Eventually, I'm out of soldiers and I've got more zombies than ever."

"And what of the Fomoire?"

"We can deal with Mobley. Anton and his crew should keep them busy for a while. Terrence, you help them out. Hit that motherfucker with everything you've got. There will have to be a reckoning with Simeon Wale at some point, but not now. We need him."

"Consider it done, Domino."

"In the meantime, I'll try to figure out how Mobley called the demon and what's causing the zombie plague. Adan, I'd like your help with that."

He nodded. "I think they may be related."

"How so?"

"The king is right—there shouldn't be enough magic to pull the Firstborn into this world and keep them here. Not yet. The dead rising, though…the normal rules are breaking down. Whatever's causing it, there are consequences to something like that. The walls are falling. It would make a summoning much easier."

"A Critical Metaphysical Instability," I said, and Adan cocked an eyebrow at me. "Never mind. But I'll bet you're right."

"I don't like the idea that your attention will be divided between the zombies and the Fomoire, Domino," Oberon said. "If Mobley is capable of summoning more of the Fomoire into this world, nothing is a higher priority. Not even a zombie plague."

"My attention won't be divided—not for long. I need to break down the spell because I tasted the juice. Once that's done, I'll give you and Terrence what I've got and you can deal with it."

The king smiled and bowed his head. "That is acceptable to us."

I'm so happy for you. "Okay, this sounds like a plan," I said. "Terrence and his outfit go stone-cold gangster on Mobley. The Seelie Court cowboys up on the zombies. Adan and I run down the summoning spell and then look for whatever's putting Death out of business."

There were nods all around the table and the council broke up. Adan and I sat together in silence after the others had left. He reclined in his chair, drinking wine from a crystal goblet, lost in thought. I knew what was coming—the Talk—and I really wasn't in the mood. The way I saw it, whatever happened between us at the party had happened, and that was all there was to it. Hell, I wasn't even sure what *had* happened—Oberon had slipped us all a magic roofie when we walked in the club.

But I just knew Adan felt the need to talk it over. I could see he was thinking about it, the way he sat there, staring at his goblet and turning it in circles on the table. The only question was what type he'd turn out to be. There was the annoyingly sensitive "we've got to share our feelings" type. Or he could be the irritatingly analytical "we've got to dissect this and figure out exactly what it means" type. If I was really unlucky, he could turn out to be the nice guy "I'll pretend I'm not needy and then stalk you" type. I *hated* that type.

Adan sighed and shook his head, and then looked up at me. Here it came. "I just have to know," he said, "did we have a foursome with those piskies?"

I laughed, choked and felt wine flood my nasal passages. Adan started laughing, too, and that made it worse. I hooted and howled, my eyes watering and my stomach clenching painfully. I finally managed to catch a little breath and gasped, "The guy, Jack, had to be a full nine inches." Adan doubled over and started slapping the table, and I lost it completely. All the pain, and fear, and horror of the demon attack and the zombie plague that threatened to tear the city apart from the inside out—all of it just got flushed away. It was the oldest and most powerful magic, the kind of magic humans had always used to banish the darkness.

After long, helpless minutes we finally managed to control ourselves. Adan took deep, shuddering breaths and wiped his eyes with the back of his hand. Finally, he looked at me and grinned. "Are we cool?"

"Like the other side of the pillow," I said.

As if on cue, Honey and Jack buzzed into the room. They stopped, hovering together in midair, and looked at us. "Oh, Domino, what's wrong?" Honey said. "Have you two been crying? Has something else happened?"

Adan and I looked at the piskies and then at each other. Adan made a sound that was half choke and half sneeze, like he'd taken a deep drag on a harsh joint. The laughter bubbled up again and brightened the world for a while.

I ran down a senior citizen on the way back to my condo from the Carnival Club. Adan, Honey and Jack were all with me in the car when it happened—Adan riding shotgun, the piskies in the back doing whatever. We were cruising down Silver Lake and I was using the traffic spell to make good time when an elderly gentleman stumbled into the street between two parked cars, arms windmilling, right in front of the Lincoln.

Adan shouted and braced one arm on the dash as I hit the brakes, but the old man never had a chance. There was a loud thump and the car shuddered as the grille slammed into his left hip. He flipped over the hood, twisting like a stuffed toy tossed into the air by a pit bull, and smashed against the windshield before somersaulting into the backseat of the open convertible. The piskies bailed just in time to avoid being crushed by the limp, broken body.

The Lincoln's tires squealed as I locked up the brakes and finally brought the car to a skidding stop. My hands gripped the steering wheel so tightly I thought my fingers might snap when I released it. I glanced in the rearview mirror. I couldn't see the old man, but the white upholstery of the backseat looked like it had been painted red by a really sloppy tagger. I looked through the starred glass of the windshield and saw blood there, too.

Adan and I just sat there for a moment, neither of us speaking. Then the screaming started. We looked to our right. An old woman with curlers in her hair stood on the sidewalk, one clutched hand wrinkling the front of her muumuu. And she shrieked.

"Tell me that didn't just happen," I said quietly.

"Where the hell did he come from?" said Adan.

"Domino…" Honey said. She was hovering at the edge of the street, between the car and the old woman.

"Pearl, stop that wailing!" the old man said, appearing in the rearview mirror as he sat up in the backseat. "You're like to wake the dead." He made a horrible hacking, wheezing sound and his shoulders shook. He was laughing. The left side of his skull was caved in and a wet flap of skin hung down over his cheek. His teeth were broken and bloody, and a couple of the lower ones were protruding from his bottom lip. He was wearing a nightgown, an old-school Ebenezer Scrooge number.

"Henry, you bastard!" yelled Pearl. "You bit me, you miserable old snake!" The woman shambled toward the car, raising her arm above her head. She was holding a butcher knife. Blood ran from a wound on her neck onto the green-and-orange muumuu. At least he hadn't gotten her ear. Adan and I jumped out of the car and backed away.

Henry twisted in the backseat and started crawling out onto the trunk. Most of his body didn't seem to be responding very well, and he dragged himself along on his belly, using his elbows for leverage. Point to Pearl—he did kind of look like a snake. He was also smearing blood all over my car.

I held up my hands. "Chill the fuck out, Pearl," I said. "Let's see if we can talk this through."

Pearl stopped and looked at me, still holding the knife in stabbing position. "Talk?" she shrieked. "You want me to talk? He tried to eat me!"

"I feel you," I said, rubbing my ear. "Believe me. But I'm not going to let you stick Henry, okay?"

"He died already!" Pearl yelled.

"Twice," said Henry. He'd rolled over on his back and lay splayed out on the trunk, chuckling wetly.

"Okay," I said. "How do you know he died, Pearl?"

"The machine! He's been hooked up to those damn machines for months, good for nothing except lying in bed shitting himself." She shook with fury. "I had to clean it up!"

"And he died?"

"Yes! He flatlined. When you get to be my age, honey, you'll know what it looks like. And he shit himself again!" Now that she mentioned it, Henry did smell a bit fragrant.

"Code Blue!" Henry said, cackling.

"Okay, okay. Then what happened, Pearl?"

Pearl calmed a bit and the knife dropped to her side. "I was feeling poorly myself, so I turned off the machines and went to lie down a bit. I must have dozed off, so then I got up and came back and unhooked him. And I was going to clean him up again, for the last time, praise Jesus, and he… he…he fucking bit me!" Pearl dropped the f-bomb like she hadn't dropped one in a few decades. Maybe never.

I looked at Henry. It hadn't taken him long to go cannibal. I had the idea he may have been homicidal even before he turned, at least where Pearl was concerned.

Henry returned my stare and bobbed his head, like he knew what I was thinking. "I ate the old bag's terrible cooking for fifty-seven years," he said. "Figured it was time I got a decent meal out of her!" He convulsed with laughter, blood and bile burbling over his lips.

"Charming," Adan said.

"Let me dust this asshole," said Honey.

"Wait!" Henry said. "That's not even the funny part."

A crowd had gathered. Cars and pedestrians had stopped and people stood at a safe distance, not understanding what they were seeing, unwilling or unable to either approach or run screaming.

"We're on crowd-control," Honey said. She and Jack buzzed over the onlookers' heads, crop-dusting them with some discombobulating piskie glamour. The civilians began to mill about in confusion, some standing slack-jawed and others wandering in circles or just walking away. It wasn't really *control*, if you asked me, but at least it would keep the rubberneckers from getting up in our business.

"The funny part is," Henry continued, his torn mouth slurring the words, "when I bit her, she was already cold! Can you believe that? I finally get a chance at a nice dinner and the bitch serves it up cold!"

I peered at Pearl with my witch sight. What little juice she'd had when she was alive was settling in her tissues like lividity and just beginning to ooze from her skin. She stared back at me, her eyes wide and glassy. Pearl was dead as disco but she obviously hadn't noticed it yet.

"Let's just do what we have to do and get out of here, Domino," Adan said. "No point in having a conversation about it."

"Henry and Pearl are zombies, Adan," I said.

"Well, I never!" Pearl protested. "I'm Presbyterian, young lady."

"Yeah, so we have to put them down," Adan said.

"We're talking to a couple of zombies."

"What's your point?"

"Braaaiiins," Henry said, giggling. He slid his broken body off the trunk and staggered to his feet.

"Let's say your home computer wasn't working, and you needed to figure out what was wrong with it. What would you do?"

"I don't have a computer," Adan said.

"Damn, you're country."

"I grew up in Faerie."

"If you had a computer and it wasn't working, you could run a diagnostic program...okay, skip the analogy. The point is, we need to figure out what's causing the zombie outbreak. Here we happen to have a couple zombies. We could ask them."

"That's the worst analogy I've ever heard."

"It's not my strong point," I allowed.

"You already talked to Terrence's nephews. One of them, anyway. You said he really didn't know anything. Pearl here doesn't even know she's dead."

"I am *not* dead!" Pearl said.

"See?" Adan said.

"I never finished talking to Tony, because Pac-Man ate him. Plus, no disrespect to the mostly dead, but Tony wasn't that bright. Pearl might have better answers."

"What about Henry?"

"What about him?"

"He's stepping up on you." Adan nodded his head, looking over my shoulder.

I jumped, turning, and sure enough Henry was creeping

up on me from behind, his arms outstretched and his hands grasping spasmodically. His eyes shone with madness and wickedness, though I had the feeling the wickedness, at least, had probably been there even before he died.

"Vi Victa Vis!" I yelled, and the force spell hurled him back and slammed him into the Lincoln's rear suicide door. His already abused skull made a pulpy sound when it struck steel, and he slumped to the ground, moaning.

I pulled juice from the streets—I was on my home turf now and it came easily. "At first cock-crow the ghosts must go back to their quiet graves below," I said. The magic burned through Henry's ravaged body and wrenched his spirit free of the flesh. The corpse toppled over and lay still on the sidewalk.

Pearl screamed and rushed to Henry's body. She dropped to her knees on the concrete hard enough to tear skin, but it didn't seem to bother her. She cradled him in her arms and sobbed, and then she jerked her head around to look at me. There were no tears but there was genuine hate in her eyes. "What did you do," she snarled.

Jesus Christ. "He was dead, Pearl," I said. "I just ended his suffering."

"You killed him!" she wailed.

"No, Pearl. He was already dead, remember? You told me that. You also told me he tried to eat you. I had the idea you hated his guts."

"He was my *husband*. For fifty-seven years. Of course I hated him! But he was the love of my life. He gave me three beautiful children. Oh, God, how I loved him when we were young. He was so handsome and strong…all of my friends were jealous and I was so proud. He was a good man. What am I supposed to do now?" Pearl buried her face in Henry's chest and sobbed uncontrollably.

You're supposed to get hungry and start eating people, I thought. "I have to ask you some questions about what happened, Pearl," I said. "This is going down all over the city and it's *wrong.* You see that, don't you?"

Pearl lifted her head and nodded. She sniffled and dabbed at her eyes with wrinkled hands. "How can you stop it? Are you a pastor or something? I don't hold with women pastors."

"Not a pastor, Pearl, but something like it. Will you answer my questions?"

"What do you want to know?"

"Tell me what happened after Henry died."

"I already told you—I didn't feel well, so I went to lie down for a while. It was just *too much,* finally, do you understand? I just couldn't deal with it all right then."

"I understand, Pearl. But tell me more about what you felt. Did you notice anything unusual?"

"It was my heart," she said. "It's always my heart. I had chest pains, dizziness. Maybe it was a little worse than usual. I took one of my pills but it didn't seem to help. I felt worse, so I went to lie down on the bed for a while. And like I said, I must have dozed off because the next thing I remember is waking up."

"How did you feel when you woke up?"

"Strange, I suppose. Nothing I could put my finger on that felt wrong...just, nothing felt quite right. You get used to the way your body feels—you even get used to your pain, when you're my age. It just felt *off,* like it wasn't the body I was used to. Was Henry right? Am I dead, too?"

"Yes," I said. I couldn't think of a good lie, or any reason to use one on her if I could.

"Why hasn't the Lord called me home? I'm ready to go."

"That's what I'm trying to figure out. Tell me anything else you remember."

"I felt alone," Pearl whispered. "I thought it was just because of Henry dying, but now I don't think so. It felt like… waiting."

"Do you know what you were waiting for, Pearl?"

"No, it's not like that." Pearl shook her head and thought for a moment. "I was born during the Great Depression," she said finally. "We came out here from Oklahoma when I was a little girl, and my father worked in the orchards and the fields. He'd be gone for weeks at a time, and sometimes we didn't know when he'd come back. When I was a little older, he enlisted and went away to the war. That was even worse—we didn't know if he'd come back at all. I know what it feels like to wait for someone, honey. This feeling wasn't the same. With Daddy, the feeling was always about him. I was waiting *for him*. This time…it was just an absence and a sense of expectation that hung there in the room, thick enough to breathe. I was just waiting."

I glanced at Adan and he shrugged. I turned back to Pearl. "Is there anything else you can tell me? How are you feeling now?"

"I hurt. Everything feels…tight. Inside. Like cramps, but sharp and hot." She started crying again and covered her curler-studded hair with her arms. "I'm *hungry*. Oh, God, I'm so hungry, and I know what I want. I know what I want and I can't *bear* it!" She began rocking herself and clawing at her head, pulling out fistfuls of fine, white hair and blue curlers.

"Domino…" Adan warned.

"You won't have to wait much longer, Pearl. I promise. It'll just be a little while and then you can go home." I knelt down and touched her wrinkled face, tilting it up to me. I smiled at her, putting as much warmth in it as I could find, and then I spun the spell and pulled her spirit free. I laid her body down beside Henry's as gently as I could.

"We need to get out of here," Adan said.

I stood there looking down at Pearl's body. "I know, but we can't just leave them here like this."

"Let's get moving," he said. "I'll call 911. I do have a cell phone," he added, smiling.

I nodded and whistled to the piskies, who were still flying air patrol over the crowd. We all piled into the Lincoln. I reached for the ignition and then slumped back in my seat. "It's never like this in the movies."

"What's that?" Adan asked.

"This shit is cruel, man. Dying's got to be bad enough, but this is just brutal. It's just *wrong*. I don't care if it's God Himself fucking with us—I'm going to find out who's responsible, and I'm going to break off a foot in his ass."

five

When we got back to my condo, Honey took Jack in to meet her family. They seemed to be moving pretty fast, but I wasn't exactly qualified to offer relationship advice. The last time I'd gotten involved the man of my dreams turned out to be a shapeshifter who wanted to skin me and steal my magic. Honey couldn't do much worse than I had with Adan's changeling. And Jack seemed okay—the strong, silent type, as piskies went.

"What?" Adan said.

"What, what?"

"You were staring at me."

Damn. "I was just thinking about, uh, where to start." I gestured vaguely at the living room. "Have a seat." I went into my bedroom and came back with my laptop. I pushed the Chinese checkers board out of the way and put the computer on the coffee table.

"Domino, I told you, I'm not really into gadgets."

"Gadgets? It's a computer, Adan. And I use it for divination magic."

"Why? You could just use—"

"Skip it, Adan. Okay, we do the summoning ritual first,

just so we can get it off our plate and deal with the zombie problem."

"You want to identify the ritual," Adan said, and I nodded. "Okay, what can I do to help?"

"Let's see what I get. Then you can help me think it through." I brought up Wikipedia on the browser and tapped the ley line running under my condo. As the magic poured into me, I fed in the juice I'd tasted from the demon's manifestation in the Between. The screen flickered and displayed the results.

The entry was titled Interdimensional Gate and I already knew most of what it said. "What the hell? It's just a gate. It's not that different from the one Honey showed me. It's built to draw a lot more juice and it's more complex…"

"Your gate was only designed to open a way to the Between," Adan said, scanning the words and diagrams on the screen. "This spell is meant to tunnel all the way into the Deep Beyond."

"Like to Avalon or something?"

"No, a lot deeper than that. Wherever the Fomoire were banished, I guess. The Celtic legends say the ancient fey drove them into the sea."

"The sea? That doesn't make any sense."

Adan shrugged. "Eire is an island. To the Celts, the sea was the edge of the world. They tried to make sense of it the best they could and I guess they were close enough. What do the Christian legends say? They were cast into the Pit or something?"

I frowned. "No clue. Either way, it doesn't help us much. And the point is, the spell's just a gate. This isn't a real summoning, Adan. There's nothing here to bind and command an entity. Mobley just threw open a door."

"Yeah, but look here." He pointed at a diagram that

looked like something Leonardo might have drawn after a particularly bad nightmare. "Mobley *is* the gate. He allowed the demon to possess him. That's how it crossed into this world."

"That thing we fought definitely wasn't Mobley."

"No, once it came through, it could go anywhere it wanted, in the Between or in the mortal world. Actually, it makes a little more sense this way. This gate would be a lot easier to handle than a demon summoning, especially with the zombie outbreak softening things up."

"Yeah, easy—you just have to let a demon possess you. Okay, let's say Mobley has the juice to do this. Where did he learn the ritual? And how did he talk the demon into doing his dirty work without any magic to compel it?"

"Well, look, Mobley wasn't pulling all that juice. He was giving some of his own magic up to the demon. It fed off him. Otherwise, yeah, you're exactly right," Adan said. "Mobley ran the same game Papa Danwe did with Oberon. He cut a deal."

"How exactly did he make a deal with something that couldn't manifest in this plane of existence?"

"The demon couldn't get here without the gate, but that doesn't mean it couldn't communicate with Mobley."

"Maybe," I said. "But maybe not." I went to the kitchen and came back with a couple beers. I handed one to Adan, popped the cap off the other and took a long pull. "The last time, with Papa Danwe, I made a lot of assumptions. I was wrong about most of them and right about just enough to be dangerous. I don't want to do it the same way this time."

"Fair enough. All we really know is Mobley created a gate using his own body and soul, and a demon came through and attacked Oberon's party."

"Yeah, and we know he didn't command or compel the demon with magic."

Adan shook his head. "We don't really know that. We just know you didn't get anything from the juice the demon left behind."

I felt like arguing, but he was right. Actually, Adan seemed to be in the habit of being right and I didn't like it much. It was like having a neat-freak for a roommate—occasionally useful but mostly just irritating. This was probably one of the useful times so I decided to let it go.

"Okay, but I think there's one more thing we do know. Look at the spell. Never mind how Mobley learned it—it doesn't take *that* much juice. I know better than most, it's not that hard to tear holes in the world. This one's deep, yeah, but it's doable, especially since he can feed the demons with his own magic. Mobley will be using the war with Terrence, and if he puts everything he has behind it, he's got this kind of juice."

"So he can do it again," Adan said.

"Yeah, but only if he's got more demons lined up he can cut deals with. Otherwise, he's just letting them in with no way to guarantee they'll do what he wants. They could come after him. And he can't play host for long—from what Mr. Clean told me about demons, letting them possess you has to be bad for your health."

"The demons probably don't want to put Mobley at risk. They want all the players back in the game."

"We're speculating again," I said. "Truth is, we don't really know enough to hand this off to Terrence and Oberon. We saw what one of those things could do. If Mobley can bring more in, it's fucking stupid to give him an excuse."

"Mobley isn't giving Terrence much of a choice. He's either got to soldier up or lay down."

"You're picking up the lingo pretty good, even if you are country. Terrence has to fight, no doubt. Hell, Mobley will get suspicious if he does anything else at this point. But we can't go at him directly. We can't back him into a corner as long as he might have some demons in his back pocket."

Adan nodded. "The only way we can stop him from gating in more demons is to deny him the juice he needs to work the ritual."

"Right on, so it's just another gang war. Terrence needs to take his streets, muscle him off his corners. No juice, no demons. Once we dry his ass out real good, then we can move in and take him down."

"It's a good strategy," Adan said.

"Thanks."

"But I don't think it's going to work."

I frowned and did my best to keep the annoyance out of my voice. "Why's that?"

"Look at it from Mobley's perspective. He put a demon in King Oberon's house. Maybe you're right and he was just trying to sow dissension in the ranks, but even so it's a damned aggressive move. He didn't have to bring the fey into it. He didn't even have to bring us into it. Yeah, he knew what it meant when Simeon Wale went over to Terrence's outfit, but he could have let it go. That gave him an excuse to escalate but he didn't have to seize the opportunity if he didn't want to. He's fully committed, Domino. He's got to know he doesn't see the other side of this thing unless he takes us all out—you, me, Terrence, Oberon. Everyone's got to die. Which means…"

"…if he's got more demons, he'll use them," I finished. "And we can't just put a crew together and take him down.

Even if we bring in the other outfits, it's not clear we'd win an all-out war."

"We need time," Adan said, "but Mobley obviously isn't going to give us any."

"So we don't give him any choice in it. All we really need to do is avoid committing our forces to a fight we can't win. We can do that as long as Mobley has something to keep him busy."

"Terrence. You're willing to sacrifice him?"

"Call it what you want, Adan, Terrence is on the frontlines. If I'm going to be the wartime captain, some hard decisions are going to come with that. It's the right move. If this is a fight we can't win, our objective has to be not losing. The only way we do that is by not fully engaging the enemy. We need cannon fodder."

"I agree, it's the best play we've got. I'm just surprised. I know it can't be an easy decision." I met his gaze and saw something in his eyes. It was something I'd become used to seeing but had never really earned. It was respect. I didn't feel like I'd earned it now, either. What's so respectable about giving up a friend?

"Damn it!" I said, and slammed the laptop closed. I rubbed my eyes and temples and let out a long breath. "I was going to make an army out of this outfit, Adan, but I haven't done shit. We should have been doing…army stuff. Training, organizing, gathering intelligence. Our guys are gangsters. They don't know anything about being real soldiers. I don't know anything about it, either. Now something happens, it's exactly the kind of thing we were supposed to prepare for, and we're sitting here with our thumbs in our asses. And the only move I've got is to sacrifice a friend just to buy a little time."

"I'm not sure how much training or organizing you can

do with this bunch. Even if you can turn the outfits into that kind of army, it's not going to happen overnight. You've got them looking at the big picture. They're willing to fight with you, and for something more than their own corners and rackets. That's a small miracle in itself."

"Intelligence is the big problem," I said. "I may not be much of a soldier, but even a gangster knows you can't win a war if you're always reacting. You have to know who the enemy is, what he's planning, and you have to go on the offensive. We can't do that because we don't know what's coming or when. That's why we don't have any options with Mobley. We're on defense and it's getting our people killed."

"We can talk to the other outfits," Adan said. "Maybe some of them have more capabilities in that area than we do. I'll put Chavez on it. I need to check in anyway, make sure nothing else is on fire."

"Yeah, that's good. Make sure he talks to Sonny Kim— the Koreans pride themselves on having better informa- tion than anybody else. And if they do have something, it'd be just like them to keep it to themselves unless we come asking."

"What's your next move?"

I sighed. "I have to tell Terrence to charge the fucking machine-gun nest. I have to figure out what to do about the zombies, and there's another angle on the intelligence problem I want to try."

"What's that?"

"I'm going to the Feds. Those motherfuckers have to be good for something."

All the bosses in L.A. have front businesses. Sometimes these businesses are juice boxes, like Rashan's strip clubs and massage parlors. Other times, though, they're just mundane enterprises meant to grease the wheels of the illegal commerce that keeps the juice flowing in the boss's neighborhoods. Sometimes they're even legitimate.

Terrence owned about a dozen Laundromats in South Central, and I met him at the store on Normandie the next morning. The business shared a battered, peach-colored concrete building with a tiny storefront Baptist church and a check-cashing joint. There were tags on the walls but they were defensive wards—Terrence wasn't getting any juice from it when people fed quarters into his machines. Of the three businesses, the Laundromat seemed to be doing a more robust trade, but that may have been because it was a Tuesday.

Once the muscle out front passed me through, I found Terrence in the back working on a seventies-era dryer. The venerable machine was partially disassembled, and Terrence knelt on a drop cloth on the stained, concrete floor, pounding on something with a crescent wrench.

"Seems like you could find someone else to beat on your washing machines for you," I noted.

Terrence jumped and banged his head on the edge of the access panel. He swore impressively and wiggled back a ways on his knees so he could turn around. He wasn't exactly the right size to get inside most home appliances.

"It's a fucking dryer, Domino. And I do it because it relaxes me. All of a sudden, I ain't too relaxed, though." He rubbed the back of his head and winced.

"What I need to say isn't going to make you feel any better," I said. I found a folding chair and turned it around, straddling it and crossing my arms on the backrest.

Terrence got up and smeared the grease into his hands

with an old rag. He nodded and leaned against the dryer. "I guess I wasn't expecting good news," he said.

"Mobley gated the demon in. It wasn't a summoning spell. We don't know how he controlled it, or even if he controlled it, but he can probably do it again."

Terrence didn't say anything for a while and I could tell he was turning it over in his mind. Finally, he lifted his eyebrows and nodded his head once. "You got to throw me under the bus."

"God, I'd like to shoot whoever came up with that saying. Seems like everyone's getting thrown under a fucking bus every time they're a little inconvenienced or get their feelings hurt."

"I ain't complaining, Domino. Seems like that's the only thing you can do. You got to look at the big picture, and that means you can't go after Mobley until you're ready."

"I'm not happy about it, Terrence."

"I know that. This is a war, Domino. You made it pretty clear it wasn't going to be much fun." He shrugged. "We'll do our part."

I didn't deserve the respect Adan had shown me for giving Terrence this raw deal. But Terrence deserved a hell of a lot for manning up and accepting it with grace. I hoped he could see it in my eyes, the way I'd seen it in Adan's.

I nodded. "We don't need you to be a hero, Terrence. You go to the mattresses. You have to let Mobley come after you, but you don't have to stick your neck out. Stay alive and when we get in front of this thing, we'll put that motherfucker down together."

"Wasn't planning to stick my neck out. I was planning to let Simeon Wale stick his out. Plus, we got Anton's crew. He already growing that motherfucker, Domino. Got Zeds hooking up with him that ain't even in our game."

"Zeds?"

"It's what they call the zombies. Anyway, maybe it's just that Anton knows more about eating than anything else but he makes a pretty fucking good zombie. They turning Mobley's hoods into a slaughterhouse and Anton's keeping the peace with the civilians. I figure Mobley will need a couple demons just to keep Anton's hands off his fucking brains."

I chuckled. "Maybe he's found his calling."

"Yeah. The rest of it, we'll lock this shit down and see how it goes. I got some of my guys working on wards, maybe give us a couple safe houses the demons can't get to." He looked at me and cocked his head to the side. "Maybe you got some assets could help with that."

"I'll send you some warders and I'll get some taggers working so you can draw juice from our blocks. You should be able to keep at least some of the demons out of some of your juice boxes. Truth is, Oberon could have kept the demon out of his club if he'd been thinking ahead. It's kinda nice to know you can catch the motherfucker off guard, I just wish we hadn't been there at the time."

"Yeah, Mobley can still bring them in somewhere else and put them on us, but it be nice to know a demon won't show up in my bathroom while I'm taking care of my business."

I stood up and swallowed against the tightness in my throat. "Just stay alive, Terrence. I'm going to make this right."

"I know you will, D." Terrence walked over to me and we clasped hands. Then I pulled him in and hugged him. Just a couple slaps on the back, but I had to do it. I wasn't sure I'd ever have a chance to do it again.

★ ★ ★

The Department of Homeland Security's Special Threat Assessment Group had purchased an ashram just east of San Bernardino when the resident guru had been convicted on multiple counts of tax evasion, fraud and sexual assault. The compound was nestled at the base of the mountains, a hidden oasis of landscaped lawns and gardens and brightly painted cottages and bungalows built in the forties and fifties. At one time, before the lawsuits and criminal charges, the ashram had been a favorite destination for spiritualists and New Agers from all walks of life—as long as they could pay the price of admission. Now it had been turned into Area 51, Southern California style.

When I'd called Agent Lowell and told him what I was after, he'd seemed pleased. Maybe it gave him some sense of affirmation in his career choices, or maybe he figured I'd be easier to control if I actually needed him for something. Either way, he was probably kidding himself. But the fact that the Ashram—the Feds were nothing if not creative— was a black operation with no official oversight or budget meant Lowell could extend an invitation to a gangster on nothing more than his personal authorization.

I checked in at the front gate and a soldier in black fatigues with no insignia or identification handed me an access badge. The badge was just a white plastic card with a barcode on it—no name, no photo. It did have some juice, though, and I could smell Lowell on it. I drove the Lincoln along a winding road and parked in a gravel parking lot.

Lowell and Granato had set up offices in a yellow building with white shutters and trim, and flower gardens flanking the wide porch. The whole compound had a Dharma Initiative vibe I approved of, but maybe with a little more style. I slapped the access badge against the card reader by the front door and walked in. Lowell saw me through the open door of his office and waved, and he and Granato both came out to greet me.

"Couldn't you have found something a little closer to civilization for your secret hideout?" I always felt an irresistible compulsion to annoy Granato, and his scowl didn't let me down. "Malibu Canyon is nice. You could probably pick up something on the cheap, with the foreclosure crisis and all."

"We had specific requirements for the work we do here," said Lowell. "And the isolation is convenient."

The truth was, it had taken me less than an hour with my traffic spell. There was no getting around the fact it was San Bernardino, though. "You can skip the nickel tour," I said. "I hope you've got something for me now that I drove all the way out here. You mentioned something about zombie experiments."

"Let's go," Lowell said, and he and Granato escorted me back outside and along a narrow path that wound its way deeper into the compound. We walked in silence and arrived at a cluster of cottages arranged in a semicircle around a small duck pond. "This is where we're doing the CMI research...uh, that's Critical Metaphysical Instability."

"I remember," I said.

"Okay, let's go to Building Thirty-four," Lowell said, and led the way to one of the cottages. He swiped his badge and then hesitated. "What you're going to see isn't pleasant, Ms. Riley. It's not pretty but it's necessary. We're doing what we have to do to protect the city."

"I guess I wouldn't be here if I thought otherwise," I said. "And most of the shit I see from day to day isn't all that pretty, either."

Lowell nodded and pushed open the door, and we went

inside. The interior of the cottage had been remodeled in sanatorium chic. The front door opened into a small viewing area where a young woman in a white lab coat sat at a metal desk and occasionally tapped on the touch screen of a tablet computer. She looked bored.

Most of the far wall was dominated by a rectangular window through which I could see a large, padded cell. A little girl in a straitjacket huddled in the corner with her knees drawn up and her head down. I drew in a sharp breath, and even to my own ears it sounded like a hiss.

"Runaway," Granato said, glancing at me. "Multiple stab wounds. Homicide. We picked her up before LAPD found her."

"I guess it doesn't bother you they won't find her killer," I said, my voice tight.

Granato shrugged. "Not my job, Riley. What is my job is figuring out why she can't rest, and making sure it doesn't happen to anyone else."

"How's that going?" I asked. The words had a little more bite to them than I'd intended.

"Cindy," Lowell said, speaking to the woman in the lab coat, "this is Ms. Riley. Tell her what we've got."

"This is Subject Number Eighteen," Cindy said. "She's a Stage One—"

"What's her fucking name?" I said.

Cindy's mouth opened and froze. She looked at Lowell and Granato. "We, uh, find it easier not to think of them as people."

"Easier for you, right? I guess it's not easier for them."

Cindy swallowed hard. "Gretchen," she said. "Her name is Gretchen. She's eleven or twelve years old."

I nodded. "Go on."

"She's a Stage One. She died between one-thirty and three this morning."

"What are you doing with her?"

"We're observing the transition. Ideally, we'd monitor and record vital signs, but..."

"...Gretchen doesn't have any vital signs," I said.

"That's right. Physiologically, she's dead. No pulse. No brain activity. So there's not much we can do except observe and record changes in her appearance, behavior. When she reaches Stage Two, we'll do some tests, measure her response to various stimuli."

"Sounds fascinating," I said. I didn't want to know what kinds of "stimuli" she had in mind. "Have you actually learned anything?"

"Her animation is completely nonphysical," Cindy said. "Um, it's paranormal. I mean, there are absolutely no physical processes animating her body—no chemical activity, no electrical activity."

"She's running on juice."

"We believe so, but it appears to be a finite source."

"She's burning it, Ms. Riley," Lowell said.

"Right," said Cindy. "They burn it very quickly. We believe this condition is responsible for the cannibalistic compulsions. As they burn up their own, uh, juice, they must feed to survive. It's not a biological process but there are obvious parallels."

"What happens when they don't feed?" I asked.

"We could show you," Granato said. "We can show you Stage Three, Four and Five. You probably won't enjoy it."

"Their condition begins to deteriorate," Cindy said, "physically and mentally. Their bodies begin to decompose and they begin to present symptoms of acute psychosis. This acts as a kind of survival mechanism because the psychosis enhances their ability to find food."

"Problem is," said Granato, "the hunting and feeding drives most of them bat-shit crazy, too. Either way, they wind up insane."

"Most, but not all," said Cindy. "The transition's timeline is different for each subject. Some animate immediately, while for others it takes hours. The original personality is intact at the time of death. Some are more successful than others at coping with their undead state."

"And the cause of all this is that their souls can't leave their bodies?"

"Their souls *are not* leaving their bodies," Lowell said, "and that's causing the undead state. We don't know why it's happening. We don't know if the souls can't leave or won't leave."

"Maybe hell is full," Granato said, snickering.

"Fuck you, Granato." I felt like saying more but he pissed me off so much I couldn't think of anything.

"We do know a little more," Lowell said, "based largely on your reports and our own efforts to control the outbreak."

I nodded. "We can free the souls from the bodies. But they still can't move on—the ghost remains trapped with the remains."

"That's the part we haven't figured out yet," said Lowell. "We haven't identified the cause. We're not even sure how to go about looking for it."

"Not for lack of trying," said Granato.

I glanced at him and narrowed my eyes. "What do you mean?"

Lowell drew in a deep breath and let it out slowly. "We felt the only way to identify the cause was to observe subjects at the moment of death..."

"You didn't."

"We have, yes. Hospice patients. Their estates receive sizable settlements and they're all volunteers. By the time we make contact, many of them have already pursued illegal end-of-life options."

"Do you at least warn them they'll turn into fucking zombies?"

"Not exactly," Lowell said. "But we're hopeful we can resolve this crisis and give them the rest they deserve."

"They were going Zed, anyway," Granato said. "At least this way we might learn something from it."

"And did you?"

"Not yet," said Lowell. "The fact is, it's hard to observe a negative. At the moment of death, we observe all the physical changes we'd expect—cessation of life functions, basically. But neither Granato nor I can identify anything supernatural happening. Clearly, something is *supposed* to happen and it's not."

"So how is your little shop of horrors supposed to help me solve the zombie problem, Lowell?" I couldn't see I'd learned much, and what I had learned didn't seem all that useful.

"We're sharing the information we have, Ms. Riley," Lowell said.

"We've also modeled the contagion mathematically," Cindy said. "We looked at multiple scenarios—unconstrained outbreak, quarantine, eradication. The scenarios are complicated by the fact that we don't know why the phenomenon is localized—limited to the Greater Los Angeles area—or whether it will remain so. However, none of the scenarios produced markedly different results." She tapped the screen on the tablet and brought up a graph. A green line showed human population and a red line represented zombies. The green line sloped downward, sharply, from left to right; the red line sloped upward, just as sharply. "As you can see," Cindy said, flipping through multiple screens, "all scenarios end the same way."

"Zero human population," I said.

Cindy nodded and tapped the screen again, displaying rows of mathematical equations that meant absolutely nothing to me. "Since all the eigenvalues are nonpositive, the apocalyptic equilibrium is asymptotically stable. At least within the affected environment."

"What the hell does that mean?"

"We're fucked," Cindy said, and shrugged. "The biggest problem will be population clusters."

"It will spread fastest in the most densely populated parts of the city," I said.

"That's right," Cindy said. "The models depend on assumptions, and one of those assumptions is the reproductive efficiency of the zombies."

"How quickly they turn humans into zombies."

Cindy nodded. "This isn't a normal outbreak scenario. A human cannot be infected. Only fatalities will produce more zombies, so we have to estimate the number of fatalities each zombie will cause each day. The bad news is that any fatality produces a zombie, even humans not directly killed by them. It includes death by natural causes and those indirectly caused by the zombies. The bottom line is that reproductive efficiency could be quite high. It will begin in the population centers, as you said, but even in the suburbs there are population clusters."

"Like what?"

"Stay away from the shopping mall and multiplex," Granato said.

"This scenario is actually good news," Lowell said. "Even eradication doesn't work—it just creates more zombies."

"That depends on the protocol," Granato argued. "Eradication works if there aren't any bodies left."

"You're talking about fucking nukes again," I said.

"Probably," Lowell said. "Chemical and biological agents don't work. It's possible you could get the desired effect with conventional weapons—fuel-air explosives, for instance— but we're still talking about total annihilation. You just don't have the radiation to deal with in the aftermath."

"I can't believe you're even considering this," I said.

"It's *almost* unthinkable," Lowell said. "And that's the point. The lack of less radical protocols buys us a little time. Our containment efforts—your efforts—buy us a little more. We *can* neutralize the zombies with magic."

"Even with outside help," I said, thinking of the fairies, "I've got Adan Rashan rallying the troops, but I don't have enough manpower to stay ahead of this thing. I'm outnumbered and the zombies create more zombies faster than my people can put them down."

Lowell nodded. "Like I said, it just buys us a little time. It's not a solution."

"You guys are the spooks," I said. "You're supposed to find out what's going on. It would be really great if you could figure it out before it's too fucking late, but maybe that's too much to ask. I'd settle for something—anything— that would help me clean up the mess."

Lowell and Granato shared a glance. "We have one more thing to show you, Ms. Riley."

Building Three was a large Quonset hut that might have once been used as a motor pool. It was tucked away at the back of the compound and security was tight. There were armed patrols—more soldiers in black, unmarked fatigues— and there were security cameras and magical wards all over the grounds. Lowell and Granato claimed they were the only sorcerers in their outfit, so I assumed they'd been out there laying down the protections and defensive spells.

We went in through the front door and I found myself in a control room. I was starting to wonder if Stag had gotten all their control rooms off a studio lot in Hollywood. This one was larger and more sophisticated than the observation room in the cottage. There was a long row of computer workstations, with technicians tapping frenetically at keyboards or studying LCD displays. There was another long, rectangular window but the view through this one was blocked by a closed panel.

When we walked in, a short, round man in the mandatory lab coat looked up from one of the computer terminals and grinned. He stood and approached us with his hand extended. He seemed excited. He was almost skipping. "You must be Domino Riley," he said, nodding his head rapidly. The grin widened. "I've heard all about how you contained the MIE, killing the changeling and foiling the fairy king's diabolical scheme!"

I squeezed his hand and twitched one side of my face at him. I didn't really feel like smiling. "Well, I gave him Hollywood."

"I know! Brilliant!" He nodded and grinned some more. "I'm Dr. Tyler Niles."

"Okay," I said, and looked at Lowell. "Why am I here?"

Lowell nodded to the scientist and was about to say something but Dr. Niles started talking first. "Okay," said the scientist, "you're a sorcerer, so you already know ectoplasm flows through the earth's crust. Arcane energy, magic, juice—call it whatever you want. There's certainly no scientific name for it. We call it ectoplasm. It's funny." He bobbed his head and grinned.

"Hilarious," I agreed.

"Right, so the ectoplasmic flow is concentrated in ley lines. This building is constructed on the site of a major convergence of two ley lines—the trunk lines that follow the Santa Ana River and the San Andreas Fault." He crossed his forearms and giggled. "*X* marks the spot."

"There's a ley line on the San Andreas Fault?"

Dr. Niles nodded. "The largest in North America."

"That doesn't concern you, though, because…"

"Why should it? There's no evidence the ley line interacts with the tectonics of the region, if that's what you're getting at."

"So it's a coincidence that this huge flow of…ectoplasm… in the earth's crust follows the same course as this huge seam in the earth's crust?"

Dr. Niles shrugged. "Okay, like you, we've been thinking about ways to empirically measure—and monitor—the ectoplasmic flow."

"I haven't really been thinking about that," I said.

"Early warning," said Lowell. "Magic is returning to the world. If we can measure and localize it, we might be able to predict the instabilities and other events it produces."

"Right," said Dr. Niles. "There's just one problem." I waited. He bobbed his head and grinned some more. "Ectoplasm doesn't interact at all with machines. Our technology can't detect it, can't measure it, can't do anything with it. As far as the machines are concerned, ectoplasm doesn't exist."

I frowned. "That's not right. I have spells that affect machines."

Dr. Niles thrust an index finger in the air. "Precisely!

Spells can affect machines, but raw ectoplasm cannot. Magic can only interact with a machine through a *medium*."

"A sorcerer," I said.

"A human, or at least a sentient mind. As we discovered, the medium doesn't have to be a sorcerer." The scientist leaned down and tapped on the keyboard in front of him. The panel in front of the viewing window retracted into the ceiling with an electric hum.

The control room looked out onto an open space that must have occupied most of the building. A massive green wheel pattern was etched into the concrete floor, and three glass and steel cylinders were positioned at the center of the wheel. The cylinders were filled with liquid and a woman hung suspended in each of them. The women wore respirators but were otherwise naked. Tubes snaked from their arms, and electrodes spotted their bodies.

"Jesus fucking Christ," I said. "Who are they?"

Dr. Niles glanced at Lowell. The agent frowned and cleared his throat. "They're indefinite detainees. Another agency sent them to us from Pakistan. They're sisters. They're all widows and they were being trained as suicide bombers."

"This is disgusting."

"I agree," said Dr. Niles. "It's fucking fascist. If it makes you feel any better, the Sisters volunteered." I could hear the capitalization in his almost reverent tone.

"Why?"

"Because we promised to keep them together," Lowell said. "Their other life options were blowing themselves up or detention in separate cells at Bagram."

"What's the green shit in the floor?"

"Algae growing in nutrient solution," said Dr. Niles. "Organic matter is the most efficient conductor of ectoplasm.

The ectoplasmic flow is concentrated in the ley lines but it diffuses through the crust. Agents Lowell and Granato created the pattern you see to channel the flow."

"And the women are your mediums?"

"Yes. All three are sensitives—the strongest we've ever documented. And...do you hear it?"

Now that he mentioned it, I did hear something. Whispering, multiple voices—I went out on a limb and guessed three, to be exact. There was nothing ordinary about the sound. It wasn't really sound at all. The whispering was inside my head.

I nodded. "How are they doing it?"

Dr. Niles shrugged. "Telepathy? We can all hear it. It's pretty damned distracting at times but you learn to tune it out. It's not a spell, though. It's a projection."

I shook my head. "I'm not following you."

"Okay, so you know ectoplasmic energy flows through the earth," he said. "But did you know there's an intelligence in the flow?"

"A what?"

"A sentience. A mind." He nodded at the women suspended in the cylinders. "Can you understand what they're saying?"

"It's Greek to me."

"Exactly. A proto-Greek language, to be precise. Pre-Thracian, a dead-end branch of the Indo-European tree."

"So what are they saying?"

Dr. Niles frowned and shook his head. "We brought in a team of linguists from UCLA," he said, nodding to one of the researchers sitting at a computer workstation. "They work in shifts around the clock. We can translate the language but we can't interpret it. It's poetry."

"Maybe you can't interpret it because it's gibberish," I suggested.

"No, it's poetry. It has pattern and structure. It is metaphorical language and we need observable phenomena to match it to. We need referents."

"And you think this...intelligence...in the flow is projecting this telepathic poetry through your prisoners?"

"We're sure of it."

"Okay, so what is it?"

"We don't really *know* what it is," the scientist said. "We call her Hecate."

"The goddess?"

Dr. Niles nodded. "Of magic and the crossroads. Other names are Chthonia, of the earth or underworld. Enodia, on the way, and Propulaia, before the gate. Triodia, she who visits the crossroads, and Trimorphe, three-formed."

"Wikipedia?"

"Yeah."

"How did you...find her?"

"By accident!" he said, and snorted charmingly. "Our working hypothesis was that we couldn't measure ectoplasmic energy directly but we *could* measure its effect on the mediums. So we basically immersed them in the convergence and began monitoring their physical responses to the stimuli. We discovered Hecate even before the projections started. Think of her as a signal. She's fragmented and lost in the background noise but every once in a while we're able to pull a little bit of the signal out of the ectoplasmic soup."

"She's fragmented?"

"Yeah, but we're putting her back together, bits and pieces of the signal at a time. Or she's doing it herself. We're not really sure what's causing it."

"You're experimenting on something you call a god in a laboratory built on top of the San Andreas Fault and not one but two massive ley lines…and you're not really sure what's going on. Is that about right?"

"This is science, damn it, not a knitting circle."

"I like your style."

"Thanks."

"So what do you hope to get out of this nightmarish excursion into mad-scientist territory?"

"We're flying blind," Dr. Niles said, nodding to Lowell and Granato. "We speculate about the events that are coming but we don't really know. We can't predict them. We can't even really identify them after the fact with any precision or rigor, except by studying the shit on the fan."

"And you think Hecate can tell you."

"We think she already is, but we can't understand what she's saying." He tapped a few more keys and the screen displayed the text the linguist was transcribing in real-time. I read some of it as it scrolled across the LCD.

smoke at the green circumference
the invisible man jumps and swallows nothing
ripe coffins like swans on the floor
a sluggish place for some to fill

ants on the tongue
meager hopes in glass, screaming
away beneath life and leaf
sallow jewels and opulent flesh

bells bleed in the watchtower
animal skin at canyon fields

blossoms of hunger
and blue falls under the tree of swords

silence calling loose light
in palaces of white mountains
phosphorous machinery touch the gradient
naked night in tiger dreams

I looked from the screen to Dr. Niles. "You've definitely ruled out gibberish?"

"You're reading a fragment out of context," he said, frowning. "It almost starts to make sense when you look at it long enough."

"I'm sure. So can you tell me what's causing the zombie problem?"

"Not exactly."

I glanced at Lowell. "Remind me why I'm here again?"

"We don't know what's causing the Zed problem," Dr. Niles said. "But Hecate *has* been talking about it."

"How do you know? I didn't get that from 'phosphorous machinery touch the gradient.' It's not even good grammar."

"She spiked just before we started getting reports of Zed on the loose."

"She spiked?"

"Yeah, both the intensity of the signal and the strength of the projections. We're pretty sure she knew what was happening before it actually happened."

"How do you figure?"

Dr. Niles went to the keyboard again and pulled up another fragment of text.

claimant and messenger, lost
stone circle, grasping the harmonic motion

fire-lit shell on darkened shore
madness sings the red song

"We have no idea what the first two lines mean, so don't ask. But we think the last two are about Zed."

I squinted at the words on the screen. "'Darkened shore' sounds like death, if you're in a high-school poetry class. 'Fire-lit shell' means the zombies?"

"Right, a corpse is a shell on the shores of death."

"But 'fire-lit?' The shell's on fire?"

The scientist shook his head. "What's unusual about these particular shells, Ms. Riley?"

"They're walking around trying to eat people." I saw it as soon as the words were out of my mouth. "Wait, they're lit from *within*. They're dead, but they still have their souls... their divine spark. Fire-lit shells on the shores of death."

"A-plus!" said Dr. Niles, grinning. "Now, this kind of interpretation isn't exactly scientific, of course. But given the timing and the instability in the ectoplasmic flow...well, we think we may have found the first of our referents."

"And 'madness sings the red song'?"

"That's the walking-around-trying-to-eat-people part. We think the 'red song' is a metaphor for hunting."

"So these shells go mad and then they go hunting."

"Yeah. We figure the first two lines might indicate a cause but we can't decode them."

I shook my head and chuckled. "It's fucking obvious. The claimant and messenger is lost. When people die, they don't just catch the next bus to the afterlife. They need psycho-pomps to guide them."

Dr. Niles frowned. "What are psychopomps?"

"Reapers."

"Oh. What about the second line?"

"I have no idea. What the hell is harmonic motion?"

"It's a mathematical term. Simple harmonic motion is like the movement of a pendulum. Complex harmonic motion is what you get when you combine simple harmonic motions, such as in musical chords. It could describe planetary motion or the music of the spheres. Or it could just be a metaphor that has nothing to do with modern mathematics."

"Okay, skip it. The point is, the psychopomps have stopped doing their jobs." I felt more than a little stupid for not considering it sooner. At the club, I'd even made a comment about something putting Death out of business. Then again, I'd never actually seen a psychopomp. It's not like there were skeletons in black robes wandering around L.A. whacking people with scythes on a typical day. Despite the world I lived in, I had a tendency to assume folklore was bullshit until proven otherwise.

"And they're for real? Reapers, I mean?" Dr. Niles had gone a little pale.

"Apparently."

"You don't know anything about them?"

"Not really," I said. "But I know someone who does."

six

My mother was a psychic. She never had quite enough juice to be a real sorcerer, but she knew her game well enough to do fortune-telling, palm reading and the occasional séance. I figured if anyone could tell me about psychopomps, she could. She met me at the front door of her little bungalow in East L.A., as she always did, and we shared a hug before going inside. I waited patiently at the kitchen table while she made coffee and set out fresh-baked empanadas.

"You're here about *los zombis*," she said as she took her seat across from me at the table. Like I said, Mom's a psychic—you get used to it. It didn't surprise me she knew why I'd come, or that she knew about the zombie problem. She wouldn't have been much good at her job if she didn't.

"I need to know what's causing it. I got a tip it might have something to do with psychopomps."

Mom nodded. "The Xolos are missing," she said.

"Mexican Hairless Dogs?" I mumbled around a mouthful of empanada. It was delicious—light and fluffy with a golden-brown crust, filled with fresh strawberries and some kind of cream.

"*Xoloitzcuintli*. Not all of them are hairless. Just the psychopomps. Usually one in every litter is coated, and they're just normal dogs."

"Psychopomps are *dogs?*" I wondered who'd come up with the bit about skeletons in black robes wielding scythes.

Mom shrugged and sipped her coffee. "Here, and in Mexico, God has given the Xolos this duty. It has always been so. I don't know how it is in other places."

"Tell me about them, Mom." I'd learned long ago to let my mother get to the point by her own path. Besides, I loved her stories.

"The Xolos are a gift from God," she said. "They were created from a shard of Adam's rib. God gave them to us and commanded us to love and protect them, and in turn, they would guide us to Heaven when we die."

"That sounds like a Christian story. I thought the Xolos predated the Conquest."

"Adam also predates the Conquest, child." My skepticism toward dogmatic Catholicism was no secret, but Mom never missed an opportunity to chide me for it when it slipped out. "The Mexica had their own stories, of course, but I believe it is the same story with different names. They believed the god Xolotl created the Xolos from the Bone of Life that they might safely lead the dead into Mictlan, the underworld."

"I see what you mean about it being the same story. Okay, so the Xolos are psychopomps. They've gone missing and the souls of the dead are trapped in their bodies. That's what's causing the zombie problem. How do the Xolos get the souls out of the dead bodies?"

"With their teeth, I suppose." She said it like it was common sense.

"Any idea why they'd be missing? And isn't it kind of

strange they're missing and no one has noticed? I mean, they're not the most common breed but they're not exactly rare, either. Not in this part of the country."

"I don't know why they're missing or where they've gone, Dominica. But there aren't as many of them as you think. Not all Xolos are psychopomps."

"Yeah, you mentioned the coated ones are just dogs."

"Not all of the hairless dogs are psychopomps, either. Only the purebred ones, and there aren't very many of them left. At one time, they were almost extinct. Now they're bred for shows, and as pets."

"You think they might have died out? And even if they did, wouldn't other psychopomps move in to pick up the slack?"

Mom pressed her lips together and shook her head. "We were charged with protecting the Xolos, Dominica. If we failed in that, it is not God's responsibility to spare us the consequences."

God lets humankind lie in the bed it made. News at eleven.

I watched my mother as she refilled our cups. Her hands seemed a little unsteady as she poured. I saw her often enough that the little physical changes sometimes escaped my notice. Mortality was a patient beast. It stalked its prey slowly and you never saw it coming until it was too late. I tried to look at her with fresh eyes and I didn't like what I saw. Mom was only in her fifties but she looked older. She looked tired.

I knew very soon I'd have to make a hard decision. I used youth spells to slow my own aging. I tried not to overdo it but I used them. Fuck getting old if you don't have to. I could probably stop aging altogether if I chose—my boss had been kicking around for six millennia and he didn't look much older than forty. But in a year or two, maybe five at the outside, I'd have to decide whether to use that magic on my mother or to let her go. I'd never talked to Mom about it and I never would—she'd *hate* me if she ever learned I'd used magic on her. The chances were pretty good I was going to lose her either way.

"People die," my mother said. "Like the Xolos, this is God's gift to us. Perhaps He sent *los zombis* to remind us of that."

"Speaking on behalf of humans everywhere who still prefer the taste of chicken, message received. How do I make it right?"

"The commandment hasn't changed. Find the Xolos and protect them."

"But what if they're gone? What if there aren't any more purebred Xolos to protect?"

Mom crossed herself. "Then perhaps it is a different message God is sending."

"Game over."

"'But the day of the Lord will come like a thief. The heavens will disappear with a roar; the elements will be destroyed by fire, and the earth and everything in it will be laid bare.'"

"Yeah, and the eigen variables are asymptomatically stable," I said.

"I don't know what that means, Dominica."

"It means we're…uh…in trouble," I said. "I have to find out what happened to the Xolos. The psychopomp ones, I mean—they can't all be missing. If every Xolo in L.A. had suddenly died or vanished, we'd have heard about it. There must…" I stopped in midsentence and slapped my forehead.

"What is it, dear?"

"If anyone knows where the psychopomps have gone, it'll be the Xolos who were left behind. The normal dogs."

"It's possible, I suppose."

"You have to get out of town, Mom. Today. I don't know how bad this will get, but it could get *really* bad. Go visit Aunt Teresa—you should be fine in Calexico, at least for now."

"*Los zombis* will not frighten me from my home. I have nothing to fear from the dead. The Lord will protect me."

"The Lord is sitting this one out, Mom. You said it yourself." I reached across the table and grasped both of her thin hands in mine. I looked into her eyes and held her gaze. "I'm not asking, Mom. If you don't leave on your own, I'm going to make you leave. You won't even know what I've done. I don't want to do it—I hate the idea of it. But I will if it's the only way to get you out of here. Don't make me. Please."

My mother looked at me for a while without speaking. "I will do as you say, Dominica. May God have mercy on you, *mi hija.*"

I stood up and gave my mother a hug and a kiss on the forehead. "Thanks for the coffee and the empanadas, Mom—they're wonderful. I've got to have a sit-down with a dog."

When I got bumped up to wartime captain, I'd made Rafael Chavez my lieutenant. I'd known him since I was a kid. We came from the same neighborhood and grew up on the same streets. He was probably the only gangster in Rashan's outfit I really trusted.

Chavez had a nice little Spanish Colonial on Amalia, not far from Atlantic Park. With its clean white stucco walls and red clay roof tiles, the house would have looked like nothing much in some L.A. neighborhoods, but it was a palace in this one. A low stone retaining wall and white wrought-iron fence fronted the small yard, and a vibrant palm tree gave the house a little shade. The grass was so green it almost glowed, and the ferns and flowering plants that hugged the walls of the house gave it the feel of an oasis in the barrio.

I rang the doorbell and winced at the bedlam that erupted inside. One of Chavez's five kids opened the door, a dark-haired, dark-eyed boy maybe seven or eight years old. His face split in a jack-o'-lantern grin when he saw me, complete with missing front teeth.

"Carlos, right?" I said, and returned the smile.

"I'm Miguel," the boy said. "Carlos is with his *girlfriend*." He said it like he didn't think much of his older brother's judgment. Jesus, how long had it been since I'd stopped by? Miguel was the little one. The last time I'd seen him, he'd been a toddler. Or maybe that was Jorge.

"No way," I said. "Miguel is a little kid. You're obviously a young man. Where are you hiding the real Miguel?" I poked my head in and pretended to look around.

"*I'm* Miguel!" Miguel said, giggling. He grabbed me by the hand and pulled me into the house. "Come on, Aunt Domino, I'll take you to Papa."

Miguel led me through the kitchen where Chavez's wife was making sandwiches and struggling to control the damage inflicted by her youngest daughter's assistance. She smiled when she saw me and stopped wiping mustard from the countertop long enough to give me a hug.

"Domino, you don't visit us anymore," she said. "It's been too long."

"I know, I'm sorry, Cecilia. Things have been a little crazy at work."

"Yes, but you still have to take time for yourself. Like the king back there." She nodded in the direction of the backyard and laughed.

"Can I have a few minutes with him? I promise, I won't be long."

"You're always welcome here, Domino. Elsa will make you a sandwich." The little girl nodded and smiled, reaching for the mustard bottle.

I went through the back door and out onto the patio. Chavez's backyard wasn't much larger than the front, but it was big enough for a grill, a picnic table, a few patio chairs and an above-ground pool. A small wooden trestle canopy provided shade for the patio. Chavez lounged in a wicker chair, drinking a Tecate and watching a couple more kids splashing in the pool. He was wearing plaid shorts, flip-flops and a faded red tank top with enough holes to let his belly breathe.

"Looking good, Chavez."

"Hey, *chola*," he said, pulling another of the wicker chairs closer to him. "Come and sit with me." He opened a plastic cooler next to his chair and grabbed another beer. He popped the top and handed it to me. I noticed there were three cell phones sitting on the glass-topped wicker table next to the cooler. Chavez never completely stopped working.

I sat down and took a pull on the bottle. It was cold, and crisp, and little flecks of ice clung to the bottle and slowly slid down the glass.

Chavez leaned back in his chair and took a long swig. He sighed. "Life is fucking good, *chola*," he said. Then he looked sharply from side to side to see if any of the kids were in earshot. "Cilia works me over when I cuss around *los niños*," he said.

I laughed. "The domestic bliss is almost more than I can take, Chavez."

He shook his head. "This shit here's what it's all about, *chola*. It doesn't get any better. You should try it."

For some reason, I felt a little lump in my throat and took another drink to wash it down. "Hey, Chavez, you have a Xolo, right?" I'm not sure whether it was the sense of urgency I felt or I just wanted to change the subject.

"Yeah, he's around here somewhere. Why? You thinking about getting a dog? It's a start, I guess."

"I was wondering if I could talk to him."

Chavez stopped with his beer halfway to his lips and looked at me. "You want to talk to my dog, *chola?*" I filled him in on my theory about the zombie problem and the missing psychopomps. When I finished, he just shrugged and whistled.

"Caesar!" he called.

"Your dog's name is Caesar?"

"Yeah."

"Caesar Chavez."

"Yeah," he said, grinning. "Like Cesar Chavez, only Caesar instead of Cesar."

"Yeah, I get it," I said.

Caesar turned out to be somewhat smaller than you might expect from his name. He might have come up to my knee. He was long and lean, with an angular snout and a tapered tail that whipped back and forth. And he was hairless. His color was something between a dark gray and blue. Honestly, he looked a bit like he had a full-body bruise. He came loping around the side of the swimming pool and sat down in front of Chavez with his tongue lolling out.

Chavez scratched his head and nodded to me. "Go ahead. I can't guarantee he'll have much to say."

"I won't freak out your family?"

Chavez shook his head. "They know the game. They see what you're doing, they'll probably want you to translate so they can talk to him, too."

I'd learned the Doolittle spell when I was a teenager. It hadn't taken long to figure out most animals weren't much for engaging conversation. It had probably been close to twenty years since I'd last used the spell.

"Our expression and our words never coincide," I said, incanting the words of the spell, "which is why the animals don't understand us." The pattern formed in my mind and I let the juice wash over Caesar. He yelped and jumped to his feet, then turned in circles a few times before sitting down and looking at me.

"Tickles," he said.

I nodded and smiled at him. "Hello, Caesar. I'm Domino."

"I remember. You were here before, when I was new to this pack. Smell is the same." He had a slight Chicano accent, though it must have been coming from my subconscious, through the magic.

"That's right," I said. "I remember you, too, Caesar. I have some questions for you. Will you answer them?"

The dog's tongue flopped out of his mouth again and he lay down. "I will answer. Maybe the male will give me food. The female is making sandwiches."

"Yeah, with lots of mustard."

"I like mustard," Caesar said.

"Okay, answer my questions and I'll bet Chavez...uh, the male...will give you food." I'm not above bribery to get what I want, and anyway, it was Chavez's sandwich.

"You want to know about the ghost walkers?" Caesar asked. "The Xolos who walk with the dead?"

I was so surprised, my jaw dropped open. Most of what

humans would call intelligence was coming from the magic, but even so, Caesar was one insightful dog. "You know about them, Caesar? About what they do?"

"Yes, the truebloods, they set humans free when they die. Xolos don't need any help with dying, but humans are too stupid to find the way on their own." He dropped his head to his paws, and added, "No offense."

I laughed. "None taken. How do they do that, Caesar? How do they set the humans free?"

"With their teeth," Caesar said. He said it in exactly the same tone my mother had. Okay, so maybe it was a stupid question.

"They bite the, uh, bodies? How is it no one notices this?"

Caesar sighed. "Not the bodies. They cross to the other side and bite the spirits, to tear them loose from the bodies."

"How do they cross to the other side?" I asked, and then had an idea. "Is it when they're dreaming?"

"No, when we dream, we mostly just chase rabbits. Sometimes birds. Or cats—but cats can be scary." Caesar laid his ears back.

"So how do they cross?"

"They just do. They can cross over whenever they want—only when they're awake, though. Usually they wait until no humans are looking."

I'd never heard of anything that could cross physically from our world to the Between without a gate. Maybe ghouls. I'd run into a ghoul once and it wasn't my fondest memory. "But you can't do this, Caesar? Cross over and free humans, I mean?"

Caesar whined. "No, I'm not a trueblood. I think I've got

some Chihuahua in me." I thought I detected a disgusted note in his voice.

"You're a wonderful dog, Caesar. Your pack loves you." I wasn't sure he needed any encouragement from me but I didn't want my spell to leave him with an inferiority complex.

"I love my pack. They give me food, and I have my own house at the back of the yard, and I have my own bed in the kitchen where all the best smells are, and I don't even mind when the little ones pull my tail or twist my ears."

"That's great, Caesar, it sounds like you have a nice life here. Can you tell me about the ghost walkers? Do you know what happened to them?"

"The Hunter has been taking them. Everyone's talking about it."

Oh, *hell* yeah. "Who is the Hunter, Caesar? A human?"

"A dead one. He takes the ghost walkers when they cross over."

"The Hunter is a dead human? A ghost? He takes the Xolos when they cross over to the Between?"

"Yes, he's been doing it for a while. The Xolos try to stay away from him but the Hunter is very sneaky."

Something was bubbling up from the back of my mind, something I knew, something obvious I couldn't quite get my mental fingers around. "A ghost called the Hunter is taking the Xolos," I muttered. "A ghost. Hunter. A ghost-hunter! Son of a *bitch!*"

"Yes?" asked Caesar.

"Not you, Caesar. I just figured out who the Hunter is. His name's Abe Warren and I've actually met the bastard. In a graveyard. He said he was looking for ghosts."

"He was probably looking for Xolos," Caesar said.

"Probably. You have any idea why he's taking them?"

"No. Not unless he likes the zombies. I don't like the zombies. They're smelly."

"Truth, Caesar. Really smelly."

"If you want to find the Xolos, you should ask the Hunter. You'll have to find him first. It won't be easy—like I said, he's sneaky."

"Yeah," I said. "I'm going to need some bait."

seven

"I beg your pardon?" said Mrs. Dawson.

"I need a ghost to draw out the ghost-hunter," I said. "And you're the only one I know. It'll be perfectly safe. Trust me." Mrs. Robert Dawson—Maggie to her friends, Margaret to God-knows-who, and Mrs. Dawson to me—had once lived in my building. Now she unlived in my condo. I hadn't even known she was there until I learned to cross over to the Between. Then she tried to strangle me. We'd since settled into an uneasy peace—I tried to keep my socks and underwear off the floor and she tried to ignore me.

"I don't really think it's any of my concern what you need, Miss Riley." She was standing by the French doors in my living room—the blue-lit, nighttime Between version of it, anyway—with her stick-figure arms crossed and an expression of stern disapproval on her wrinkled and powdered face. "Ghost-hunters and cemeteries and the like, I've never heard of such a thing!"

It was too bad she'd never heard of a cemetery—if she'd been properly introduced to one, maybe she wouldn't be haunting my condo. "It's really important, Mrs. Dawson. I wouldn't ask if it wasn't. This ghost-hunter has been bagging our Xolos—Mexican Hairless Dogs—and that's causing the dead to rise when they, well, die, on account of the Xolos are psychopomps."

Mrs. Dawson just stared at me as if I were a raving madwoman. Maybe I hadn't explained it as clearly as I might, but really, you'd think a ghost would be a little more open-minded where supernatural shit was concerned.

"Okay, look. I know this is a big favor to ask. I'd owe you one." Somehow I knew if I wanted Mrs. Dawson's help, I'd end up haggling for it. It always seemed to go down like that in the underworld. Humans may be greedy motherfuckers on the whole, but we've got nothing on the not-quite and no-longer human.

Mrs. Dawson eyed me suspiciously. "I'm quite certain there's nothing you could 'owe me' that would convince me to act as your...your...your bait!"

She didn't *look* certain. Gotcha, Maggie, you cranky old bitch. "Oh," I said, turning away. "Well, if you're sure there's nothing I could possibly do that would be worth a short—and perfectly safe—stroll through a cemetery or two..."

"Move out," Mrs. Dawson said.

"Dea—" I cut the word off midsyllable and jerked my head back around to peer at her. "What the fuck did you just say?"

"Cursing shows your true color," she said. Color—not colors. Mrs. Dawson was a bigot from the old school. It was kind of refreshing. "I said, move out. I was here before you. This place belongs to me—what's left of it. Move out, tonight, and I'll go with you to the cemetery."

I laughed. "You want me to move out of my own house?" I let the anger and frustration drain out of my face, and I looked at her like I might look at a guy I'm going to clip. "I'll move *you* out first, Maggie. I'll bind your lily-white ass to a public toilet in Crenshaw. I've done it before." Technically, the toilet hadn't been public and it hadn't been in Crenshaw, but I was improvising.

"Go ahead and try it, Riley! I'll claw your eyes out and grind them into the floorboards if you try to force me from my home." Mrs. Dawson's eyes grew large and black, and the spectral flesh began melting away from her face like blood in the rain. Her jaw seemed to protrude from her skull and her bared teeth lengthened as her lips dissolved. She was going full spook on me.

So much for the fucking peace. I held up my hands and backed away. "Chill the fuck out, Mrs. Dawson. I was bluffing. I'm not going to do anything to you." My calves brushed the edge of the sofa and I sat down on the edge of the seat. And just like that, the harmless little old lady was back. She smoothed the front of her elegant dress with trembling hands, and then crossed her arms again.

Jesus Christ. "Okay, I tell you what, I'll move out of my bedroom—"

"Done!" said Mrs. Dawson.

"I wasn't finished!" I protested. "I was saying, I'll move out of my bedroom for a month."

"No."

"What do you mean, no? I'm offering to give you the bedroom for a whole month!"

"No."

"Two months?"

"No."

"Come on, Mrs. Dawson. Please? The piskies have the second bedroom. I'll have to sleep on the couch."

"I'm well aware of that. There's barely anyplace left

in this house for me to have some quiet time to myself. And n—"

"No...yeah, I got it." I sighed and buried my face in my hands. "Fine," I mumbled. "You win. I'll move out of the bedroom."

"What?" Mrs. Dawson said, cocking an ear my way. "My hearing's not what it was when I was—"

"When you were alive? Yeah, I guess it wouldn't be."

Mrs. Dawson sniffed. "I was going to say, when I was younger."

"Which century would that have been, exactly?" I dropped the volume and made sure to mumble directly into my palms.

"Insulting me won't get you what you want, young lady."

I lifted my head and squinted at her. "How the hell did you hear that, if you're so deaf?"

Mrs. Dawson sniffed, again. "I didn't, but I'm not an idiot. I'm no stranger to bad manners and worse breeding, Miss Riley. It was hard to find good help, even in my day."

I suddenly wondered if the tormented souls of pool boys, groundskeepers and maids were haunting the halls of my building. "Okay, drop it," I said, shaking my hands in the air as if I could fling the frustration from my fingertips. "Let's, just, the deal is done...let me get my crew together and we'll meet you back here."

"And when will you remove your things from my room?" I was pretty sure I could see a grin tugging at the corner of her withered mouth.

"When we get back," I said. "I'll move my shit when we get back." I pressed my hands against the cushions and bounced up and down a couple times, trying to gauge the comfort level. Never mind that concepts like firmness were of dubious value in the Between. I'd slept on the couch before but only when I was hammered. Doing it sober would take some getting used to, but that went for most things.

Even after we'd reached an agreement in principle, it took us two hours to get Mrs. Dawson out of the house. First she had to do her hair. She was inexplicably unable to locate the brushes and combs she remembered from the early sixties, so this mostly involved a half-hour or so of preening in the mirror and brushing the white tangles with her fingertips. When she was finished, her hair still looked like she'd rolled Phyllis Diller, Albert Einstein and a troll doll for it.

Then she had to select the proper outfit. She accomplished this by disappearing through the living room wall for more than an hour into what must once have been her boudoir. She emerged wearing a combed cotton seersucker suit, white heels, white gloves and a white pillbox hat. I pointed out it was nighttime, we were going to a cemetery and I needed her to look spooky, and she pointed out I knew absolutely nothing about fashion. In ordinary circumstances, the hat at least would have been an improvement but her hair had been the spookiest thing about her.

"You look quite elegant, Mrs. Dawson," Adan said. He'd crossed into the Between with Honey and Jack through the gate in my condo. I wanted to strangle him.

"Thank you, my dear," said Mrs. Dawson. "Men are in and out of here all the time, but you're the first real gentleman to set foot in this house since my Robert passed." She glanced at me and sniffed. I wanted to strangle her more.

"Jack's a gentleman," Honey said.

I glared at her. "You're not helping." I'd still never heard

Jack say anything. I was beginning to wonder if he was a mute. At some point the Silent Bob act starts to get creepy.

"I beg your pardon, young man," Mrs. Dawson said. "I'm sure you people can learn proper manners as well as anyone else."

"Nice," I said. "You're even bigoted toward fairies."

"I am not!" huffed Mrs. Dawson. "I don't have a bigoted bone in my body."

"You don't have any bones in your body," I said. "You don't even have a body."

Mrs. Dawson burst into tears—well, she no more had tears than she had bones, but she gave it her best shot. "You are so cruel," she whimpered. "Do you think I like what's become of me? Do you think I like being trapped here, separated for eternity from everyone who ever cared about me?"

"Gods, Domino," Adan said. "Ease up a little."

I tightened my lips and looked at the floor. "She could leave whenever she wants," I muttered. "She's just too damn stubborn!"

"So how are we going to do this? What's our plan?" Adan asked.

"We get to the cemetery, Mrs. Dawson does the vengeful spirit bit. The rest of us use our glamour to remain hidden. When the ghost-hunter shows up, we grab him."

"We grab him?" Adan said.

"That's our plan?" said Jack.

"You're not a mute!" I said. Jack shrugged. "Yeah, that's our plan. I like to keep it simple."

"What if he hurts me?" Mrs. Dawson said, her bottom lip trembling pitifully.

"He's not going to hurt you. He has a crossbow, but we can grab him before he shoots you with it."

"But what if something goes wrong?"

"Nothing's going to go wrong. That's the virtue of a simple plan."

Something went wrong. It started with Mrs. Dawson herself. I hadn't expected her to have any real acting chops, but it wasn't unreasonable to expect a ghost to be scary. In fact, I'd seen it. The skeletal hag thing she'd pulled when she lost her temper with me had been a little scary. Problem was, she couldn't fake it. At all.

Our first stop was the cemetery where I'd originally encountered Abe Warren, the one Antoine had formerly haunted and where his brother Keshawn still lurked. Keshawn might have provided an understudy in the event Mrs. Dawson bombed, but it seemed his ghost was deteriorating, fading. When I went to his graveside I could barely make out his shade in the darkness and his voice was a barely audible whisper. He didn't have anything coherent to say, either. He couldn't actually go anywhere without a Xolo to guide him, but that apparently didn't stop him from decomposing. The ghost was dying and there was fuck-all I could do about it.

So it was all on Mrs. Dawson. I didn't have a script— all she had to do was meet some basic standards of scariness. She just needed to haunt the graveyard and raise a little hell. We all got into position, the piskies hovering overhead, Adan and me skulking invisibly behind tombstones.

"We're ready," I said. "Show us the spooky stuff, Mrs. Dawson."

She stood there clutching her purse and looking lost. "Well, I'm sure I don't…" She cleared her throat. "Boo," she said.

I looked toward Adan. I couldn't see him, even with my

fairy sight, but I knew where he was. "Did she just say *boo?* Tell me she didn't fucking say *boo.*" The only answer was a choking sound that was frankly scarier than anything Mrs. Dawson had thus far produced.

"Mrs. Dawson," I said, struggling to keep my voice even, "boo isn't scary. I'm not sure it was ever scary, but it definitely isn't scary anymore. Come on, give me some ghost. Express yourself. Let out that tortured soul."

She just looked at me with a dazed expression on her face and shook her head.

"You're fierce," I offered. She wasn't. Eventually, it got bad enough I was afraid the ghost-hunter would sniff out the trap even if he did happen to wander by. We hit the mist and relocated. Mrs. Dawson repeated her performance at Inglewood Park, Angeles Abbey down in Compton, Roosevelt in Gardena and Park Lawn.

By the time we got to Evergreen Cemetery in Boyle Heights, the night was wearing thin on multiple fucking levels. Honey assured me it was almost dawn, though I hadn't noticed any change in the television glow of the Between. I'd never spent this much time in the shadow-world and I was beginning to imagine all the ways my body would protest the treatment when I finally got back into it. Most of all, I had a splitting headache that had started pinching my temples in Inglewood and got a little worse each time I used the invisibility glamour.

I crouched by a headstone, pressing the heels of my hands against the sides of my head. I tore one away long enough to wave it at Adan. I had to concentrate on keeping my ethereal brains inside my ethereal skull and steel myself to pull off the glamour one more time. Adan could coach Mrs. Dawson if he was up to it.

"Let's do it," Adan said, smiling at her. "Get angry.

Think about Domino." I growled at him, but he continued. "Think about her living in your house and…doing whatever she does. Come on now, let it all out."

Mrs. Dawson's face darkened. Her eyes narrowed and her lips tightened into a thin line. She began to puff up like she was going to blow. Adan looked over at me and nodded. "This is it," he said. I ground my teeth, swallowed drily and tried to bring up that ice-cold juice from the Beyond I'd taken when I squeezed the changeling. Pain lanced through my head and hammered me to my knees. I gasped and looked desperately toward Mrs. Dawson. After all this, I was going to blow it because I couldn't handle the glamour.

"Ooooo," she said. "Wooooooo!"

Rage flared inside me and purged the pain in my head, leaving an empty and cold space in its wake. I stood up, drew Ned from the holster on my hip and stalked toward the ghost. I raised the gun, fully extending my arm in front of me, and placed the barrel against the center of her forehead.

"That's it," I said, my voice low and calm. "I'm done with you, lady. I'd gun you down right here, but shooting's too good for you." I moved the barrel down and pressed it against the bottom of her chin, tilting her head up to the starless cobalt sky. I leaned in until our noses were almost touching. "I'm going to banish you from your precious house, Maggie," I whispered. "I'll bind you across the street, where you can see it, but you won't—"

"Nooooooo!" she screamed. Her face disintegrated like a sandcastle in the wind and her voice became a distorted, low-pitched moan. Her fleshless mouth stretched wide in a tormented snarl, revealing a blackness as thick as the bottom of a grave. Her head jerked spasmodically atop her gnarled spine and she reached for me with skeletal hands.

"Now *that's* some scary shit," I said. Then I turned and ran.

I didn't even try to summon the glamour. I'd temporarily psychoed the pain away, but I was pretty sure it'd be back with a fucking party hat on if I tried the fairy mojo again. If it came back, I knew I'd go down. And if I went down, I'd have Maggie's freaky ass all up on me. So I just ran, and screamed. Mrs. Dawson put me solidly in touch with my terrified inner child, so I didn't even have to fake it.

Abe Warren appeared out of the mist directly in front of us with his crossbow in one hand and a small wooden music box in the other. The music box was open and it was playing "Frère Jacques." The tempo was too slow, like the box was winding down, and the music was just slightly off-key. It was eerie, like the sound was being pulled from the bottom of a well, or pulled into one. The melody bent and turned in my mind and I could almost hear another song, a different song, in the spaces between the notes. If I could focus, if I could just *listen,* I was sure…

The sound froze Mrs. Dawson in place, her head cocked to the side, listening. Her form wavered and she was the little old lady in a seersucker suit again. Her wondering smile and bright eyes almost made her beautiful.

I watched in dreamlike fascination as Abe set the music box on the ground and lifted his crossbow. It was a plainly wrought weapon, a brutal tool without artifice, dark, un-adorned wood bound in dull iron fittings. The bow was lashed to the stock with what looked like hemp cords. The bolt was short and heavy with a wicked steel tip and rested lightly in the shallow groove that ran along the top of the stock.

"Boneyards are no place for the living," the ghost-hunter said. "Even witches." He braced the weapon and aimed carefully. "Rest now, spirit," he said, and he squeezed the trigger.

Adan hit him just as he loosed the bolt. It flew wide and never reached Mrs. Dawson. It stopped when it buried itself in my stomach. The impact knocked me onto my back and I felt a cold numbness spreading through my gut. I heard Mrs. Dawson scream and it sounded pretty good—too bad she couldn't have managed it earlier. I heard Honey's wind-chime voice, and maybe even Jack's only slightly deeper one. I lay there on the ground and looked up into the darkness that hung like a velvet curtain overhead. The mist seemed to roll toward me, a slowly tightening circle, the shadow-world collapsing in on me as my vision dimmed.

From somewhere far away, words hammered at my re-treating consciousness. I knew the voice—I'd just been thinking about it, hadn't I? Maybe not. Maybe the voice was one I'd known long ago, a voice that pulled at the thinning threads of memory. It didn't matter. I was sinking, falling into that endless black ocean—hadn't I been looking *up* at it?—where words and voices had no meaning.

"Domino, you stupid cow!" Honey yelled, right in my face. "Magic and mind! That's all you are. Remember!"

I opened my eyes and sat up, forcing Honey to spring away from my chest and hover in the air. I looked down at the crossbow bolt protruding from my belly. Azure juice poured from the wound and pooled on the ground around me. I pulled it out and tossed it away.

"Feel weak," I said.

"Of course you feel weak! You've lost a lot of juice. But you've got plenty left. You're not going to die unless you lie there and let yourself bleed out."

"Oh," I said. "That's cool." Adan and the ghost-hunter were rolling around on the cemetery lawn, occasionally landing a punch but mostly just wrestling. When he noticed I was up, Adan glared at me through a headlock. "Grab him," he croaked through clenched teeth. "Hell of a plan."

Jack was flying circles around the scuffle. He had a silver sword, just like Honey's. I looked at him and spread my arms. "Dust the son of a bitch, Jack."

He shook his head and kept circling. "Protected," he said.

Damn. I probably should have seen that coming. Just because he was dead didn't mean Abe was stupid. I didn't know what else he did to pass the time, but he hunted ghosts and abducted psychopomps in the Between. He'd probably *have* to be juiced up some kind of way. I looked at him with my witch sight and immediately saw the talismans. A medicine bag hung from a leather thong around his neck. An eagle feather dangled on a braided cord from his hat. He even had a brass Civil War belt buckle that was juiced with fairy magic, or something like it.

I walked over to where I'd dropped Ned when I got plugged by the crossbow and picked it up. I felt something cold and wet on my mouth, and brushed the back of my hand across it. It came away slick with glowing blue juice. I had a fucking nosebleed. I was pretty sure it wasn't on account of being shot, either—it was the glamour.

I walked slowly toward the wrestling match, holding the gun at my side. When I got close enough that I could probably shoot Abe instead of Adan, the ghost-hunter somersaulted out of the fracas and rolled deftly to his feet. He flicked out his hand and a net blossomed in front of me, its silver, silken threads as fine as a spiderweb. It expanded to an impossible size and settled gently over me. And Adan. And Honey. We all went down in a tangle.

Jack was the only one who'd avoided the snare—besides

Mrs. Dawson, I mean, but I wasn't exactly counting on her to save the day. She'd removed a white handkerchief from her white purse. She was sobbing quietly and dabbing at her eyes. Jack wheeled around in a wide arc and flew at the ghost-hunter, his sword at the ready in a two-handed grip. Abe leveled the crossbow—he'd somehow managed to reload it—and backed away.

"Don't make me do it, son," he said. "You're fast, but I don't miss."

Jack pulled up and looked over at me. I thought about pointing out he'd missed Mrs. Dawson, but I shook my head. We all watched as Abe tipped his hat and backed into the mist.

The piskie cut us free with his sword as soon as it became clear we'd never get out of the net without his help. The strands were so thin and delicate-looking they were almost invisible, but they were also incredibly strong. We couldn't tear them apart and every effort to do so only entangled us further. It took Jack a good ten minutes to saw a big enough hole in the net that we could pull ourselves free.

"It's important at a time like this not to point fingers," I said.

Adan tilted his head from side to side and rubbed his neck. "It's okay by me if no one ever finds out about this."

"What are we going to do now, Domino?" Honey asked. "The ghost-hunter will be on the lookout for us. He'll never fall for the trap again."

"I'm not sure it counts as a trap if the trappers all get their asses kicked," I said.

"Not a good trap, at least," said Jack.

I scowled at him. "Yeah, so I'm going after him."

"How are you going after him?" Adan asked. "He could be anywhere."

"I can track him. I was just really hoping I wouldn't have to do it."

No one said anything but they all had rather skeptical expressions on their faces. I gave them a mean-spirited smile and turned into a barghest.

Once upon a time, King Oberon had sicced a pack of the ghost dogs on me. I'd also seen the dogs with his armies. I'd asked the fairy king about them later, and he'd told me the hounds were useful because they could track quarry through the mist in the Between. The sidhe used them for hunting and also for war.

I couldn't really check myself out but I knew from previous encounters it was an impressive beast. The barghest was a massive black mastiff, far larger and more powerful than any mortal hound. The blocky, muscular body was nearly four feet tall at the shoulder and had to be pushing five hundred pounds. Thick, curved talons sharp as knives curled from its paws, and its mouth bristled with long, yellowed fangs. Its eyes blazed red like hellfire.

Unfortunately, using the changeling's glamour damn near killed me. The bone-chilling cold of the Beyond flared inside me, and icy blades of mindless agony scraped across every nerve ending in my new body. The breath went out of me and I collapsed in a furry heap on the ground, whimpering and mewling.

"Domino, stop it!" Honey yelled, swooping down to me and alighting by my head. I watched her with one burning eye as she looked up at Adan. "I told her this magic was not for her. I told her it would kill her."

Adan knelt beside me and placed his hand on my shoulder. His touch caused the pain to flare up again and I flinched, but I lacked the strength to move. I growled at him and my gums hurt when I bared my fangs. I lay there, my breath coming in short, fast spasms, and the play of my hide across my ribs sent white-hot needles lancing deep into my core.

"Most humans can't survive this magic, Domino," Adan said, gently. "Not even sorcerers. I'm different—I told you, I don't know why—but even I can't shapeshift. This magic isn't for us."

I wasn't sure what the lectures were supposed to accomplish since I was already a dog. They were probably just getting warmed up for later—I knew I'd hear about it again. And again. For now, I just tried to curl my oversized, vaguely canine body into the smallest possible ball and wait for the torture to pass.

Eventually, it did. I struggled awkwardly to my feet and shook myself, the convulsions beginning at the ruff of my neck and working their way along my body, more than eight feet to the tip of my tail. I was fucking huge.

I trotted over to where Abe Warren had disappeared into the pale mist. I sniffed at the air. I wasn't completely sure I'd be able to track the ghost-hunter. I knew the changeling's magic covered a lot more than shape or form—when I'd used it to shift into a copy of Anton, I'd been able to speak Russian. I had no idea how it was possible, but I knew it worked, at least to that extent. But I really didn't know if it could mimic the abilities of a supernatural creature. I figured it must have some limits—the changeling had not, in fact, assumed a godlike form and pounded me into sand—but I had no idea what they were.

As it turned out, the shapeshifting glamour was able to reproduce the barghest's magical nose well enough. I immediately caught the scent of the ghost-hunter on the wind and followed it into the mist. I heard distant shouts behind me but they were quickly swallowed by the fog.

Abe hadn't gone far. I found him walking along Whittier Boulevard west toward downtown. I came out of the mist about a hundred feet behind him, and immediately skulked into the deeper gloom that hugged the buildings lining the street. I trailed him silently, slowly narrowing the distance between us. I was maybe thirty feet behind him when he ducked through a gap in a chain-link fence and walked across a basketball court toward a small, Catholic elementary school. He skirted the school grounds and headed for the back of the modest, redbrick structure of Santa Isabel church that fronted Soto Street.

I loped across Whittier and darted through the fence. A plastic banner reading Our Future Is Bright, Drug Free hung by one corner next to the hole in the wire. The ghost of a junkie did the dope-fiend shamble at midcourt. He looked more like a proper zombie than the actual zombies I'd seen. "Nice doggy," he mumbled when he saw me. I ignored him and quickened my pace as I stalked the ghost-hunter through the night.

Abe was headed for the back door of the church. Once this became clear, I had a decision to make. I knew I couldn't let him enter the sanctuary. I was already probably on consecrated ground. It felt uncomfortable, unwelcoming, like God had posted a No Hellhounds Allowed sign at the property line. I was pretty sure I couldn't pull off another glamour anyway, but I knew I wouldn't be able to do it inside the church. The ghost-hunter might have allies in there, too. The question was whether to make a play in doggie form or risk shifting back.

Abe made the decision for me. He froze about twenty feet from the door. He turned and looked behind him. His gaze panned over the cramped schoolyard, and then...I couldn't be sure, but since my coat was black and I was skulking in the deep shadows of the nighttime Between, I guessed he might have spotted my baleful, burning red eyes in the darkness. Really, it was a pretty crippling design flaw. Good for scaring the breakfast out of unwitting civilians, maybe, but worse than useless if you needed to do some serious stalking.

I snarled and crouched, feeling the muscles coil along the length of my powerful body. I launched myself into the air and saw the ghost-hunter's eyes grow wide. He started to turn, thinking to make a dash for the church door, but he might as well have been trudging through half-dry cement. He had just about enough time to gulp, and then my massive body crashed into him. Damn it feels good to be a monster.

The impact didn't send Abe flying through the air; there wasn't even any sprawling or tumbling. He went down where he stood and stayed there, like a piano had been dropped on him. He tried to turn under me, to get his arms up to protect his head, but I dug my claws into his chest and clamped my jaws onto his neck. Actually, I got a piece of one shoulder and part of his head, too—my mouth wasn't exactly a precision instrument. It did the trick, though, and I felt his body go limp. I'd been as gentle as I could and I assumed he was surrendering rather than dying.

I lifted him effortlessly and trotted back across the playground to Whittier. I wasn't sure I could get through the gap in the fence without snagging Abe on it, so I leaped over it and into the street. I landed easily, my claws digging into the asphalt, but the ghost-hunter got knocked around a little. I heard him whimper and shook him a couple times—it was barghest for "hush." Then I turned and loped into the mist.

Adan, Mrs. Dawson and the piskies were still at the

cemetery. Adan reclined against a tree with his eyes closed and the piskies were huddled nearby, making out. Mrs. Dawson stood clutching her purse and looking timid, as usual. It looked like they hadn't missed me much. I trotted over to them and tossed Abe at Adan's feet—this time the ghost-hunter went sprawling. Adan knelt beside him and lashed his hands behind his back with a short length of cord. The piskies hovered to either side of him, their swords drawn.

When I was sure Abe was well and truly captured, I shifted back. I was prepared for the soul-rending agony, but there wasn't any. In fact, the feeling of relief that flooded through me was almost as incapacitating as the pain. It felt like I'd finally dug out a splinter that had worked its way deep into my flesh. It felt so good I wanted a cigarette.

I stood over Abe and grinned at him, and then I kicked him in the ribs. "That's for shooting me," I said. I kicked him again. "That's for making me chase you."

Abe winced and shifted his position, trying to get comfortable. "I feel compelled to point out," he said, "I wouldn't have shot you if I hadn't been assaulted by your companion."

"Yeah, but you tried to shoot my friend," I said, nodding to Mrs. Dawson. She sniffed.

"Right, well, it was an honest mistake given that she was chasing you and you were screaming like a lost child."

"Yeah, that was our trap."

"An effective one, in the end, witch. The question, I expect, is why you felt the need to trap me in the first place."

"I really do prefer sorcerer, buddy," I said. "You keep calling me a witch, you might hurt my feelings."

"Very well, sorcerer, looks like I'm at your mercy. What would you have of me?"

I crouched down so I could look him in the eye and rested Ned on my knee. "I wouldn't have much of you, Abe," I said. "Just need to know what you did with the dogs."

The ghost-hunter nodded and smiled. "This is where I'm supposed to tell you I don't know what you're talking about."

"Except you do and you're smart enough not to waste my time."

"Yes," he said, chuckling, "I am at least that smart. I was hired to take the dogs. You may not believe me, but I didn't anticipate the effect it would have on the mortal world."

"Once you figured it out, maybe you could have stopped."

"I couldn't stop," Abe said. "And, as a point of fact, there weren't that many of them. By the time I realized what was happening...what I'd done...it was too late. You must believe me, Miss Riley."

"Well, I don't think I must, but it doesn't really matter. Who are you working for?"

"Now I say, 'If I tell you, she'll kill me.'"

"And I say, 'If you don't, *I'll* kill you.'"

"Right," he said. "I do believe you would." He looked down at Ned, nodded and lifted his eyes to meet my gaze again. "She is called La Calavera."

"La Calavera Catrina?" I said. "Like the etching?" The famous image of a skeletal woman wearing a fancy hat had been created by a Mexican craftsman in the early twentieth century. It had become an icon of *El Día de los Muertos,* the Day of the Dead. I'd had a mask of La Calavera, and a wooden doll, when I was a little girl.

"Not just any etching," Abe said, "a portrait. It was the image of a spirit that visited the engraver, Señor Posada, and commissioned the work."

"What would a spirit want with an engraved portrait?"

"She wanted to extend her influence in the mortal world, and thereby increase her power in this one. It was remarkably successful."

"So why'd she want you to steal the dogs?"

"There is an underworld in this place, just as there is in your world. A criminal underworld, if you will, though there is no law. Indeed, in the absence of law, the gangs rule this world. The bosses are its kings."

"Yeah, I met one. The Burning Man. He deals hardware out of a warehouse in Van Nuys."

Abe nodded. "The Burning Man is small potatoes compared to La Calavera, but they are of the same breed. The Burning Man runs guns—La Calavera runs Hollywood."

I snorted. "Maybe she runs the monochrome version. The fairy king runs Tinseltown on my side of the tracks."

"Yes," Abe said. "La Calavera was none too pleased with that development. Her turf has become a kind of highway and staging area for the fairies passing through to the mortal world from Avalon."

"Okay, she's got a beef with Oberon. What's this got to do with the Xolos?"

"Nothing, so far as I know. The point is, La Calavera is a boss and she has her bony little fingers in lots of different pies. One of those rackets is a dogfighting ring."

I let the words sink in. I felt like spitting or hissing or something melodramatic like that to express my revulsion and disgust. Blood sport hadn't exactly been unknown in my neighborhood when I was coming up. The cultural roots of animal fighting went deep and poverty tended to harden even good-hearted, life-loving people. I'd always hated it, though. It seemed like the worst kind of perversion to domesticate animals, to tame them and then to turn them into murderous killing machines for the amusement of humans. It turned out there was an even worse perversion—doing that to a sacred animal like the Xolo. I wasn't even sure what the sacred was to me, what it meant to me. But whatever it was, the Xolos qualified.

"Why would you do it, Abe?" I said, my voice low and harsh. "What could she possibly offer you to do something like that?"

Abe swallowed and nodded once. "She has something I want. The only thing I want."

"What's that? You don't need money. Near as I can tell, you don't need anything. You're supposed to be past needing."

"You never get past needing, Miss Riley. You see, I'm not on some mad, eternal quest to fulfill my life's mission. It's my wife. She's out here somewhere, lost amidst the thousands, millions of ghosts that wander this city. Every night, I look for her. I will keep looking for her until I find her or until the last shred of my will falls to dust as my body did more than a century ago. La Calavera claims to know where she is, Miss Riley. She says she will take me to my wife."

"She hasn't, though, has she? You took the Xolos and handed them over to her, but she hasn't kept her part of the bargain."

Abe laughed bitterly. "Honestly, Miss Riley, I'm not at all sure she even knows. She says I haven't yet completed my service. I think she just wants to keep me on the string. But I haven't lost hope. Not yet."

"I understand you must have loved your wife, Abe, but

why do you have to find her? How do you even know she's out here? She could be waiting for you on the other side."

"I know because I killed her, Miss Riley. I put her here. She can't rest until she has her revenge and I mean to give it to her."

"Why did you kill her?"

"'Suffer not a witch to live,' Miss Riley."

"She was a witch?"

"Not a powerful one, and in the end, it was that lack of power that corrupted her. She started with small things, little charms and spells meant to ease people's lives. But she was so frustrated with her limitations, so angry that she couldn't do more. In those times, things were different and even a little power was hard to come by. She pursued that power into ever more esoteric arts and her magic became blacker and blacker." Abe blinked and cleared his throat. "Well, the darkness was stronger than she was, Miss Riley."

"Where is La Calavera holding the dogfights?"

"I don't know. The Mocambo club is the center of her empire."

"Wait, I've heard of that place—it was famous back in the day. But it closed a long time ago. It used to be over where Sunset Plaza is now."

"Yes, I believe the site is a parking lot," Abe said. "The club was torn down in the mortal world, Miss Riley, but it wasn't torn down here."

"Okay, how often does she have the dogfights?"

"There is no set schedule. I've heard she holds them a couple times a week. They aren't widely advertised. Only the Mocambo crowd hears about them, and I'm told invitations are exclusive."

"Does she keep the dogs at the club?"

"I don't know that, either."

"How can you not know where the dogs are kept or where she holds the fights? You're stealing the Xolos for her."

"I do not run with that crowd, Miss Riley. I deliver the dogs to a secluded overlook in the hills. I hand them over to her thugs. Then I leave. I do not know where they are taken after that."

"Okay, that's a soft spot in her racket, then. Here's the plan. You set up a meet. When the mooks show up, we ambush them and get the Xolos' location out of them."

"There will be no more meets, Miss Riley. I have already explained to La Calavera that there are no more Xolos for me to bring her. You understand, only the psychopomps are able to enter the Between."

"Yeah, I get that," I said, thinking of Caesar. "Still, you could tell her you missed one. The thugs wouldn't know we were hustling them until it was too late. It could work."

"It would not. It would be…irregular. In addition to being a very old spirit, La Calavera is a gang boss. She does not like irregularities. She sees them as potential threats, because they almost always are. She would sniff out your trap before you even had a chance to spring it."

I wasn't exactly on a roll as far as traps were concerned, so I was willing to take Abe's word for it. "How do we find the Xolos, then?"

"Perhaps you could track them the way you tracked me," Abe suggested.

"You can't keep using the changeling's glamour, Domino," Adan said. "Especially for shapeshifting. It *will* kill you—it's only a question of when."

I nodded at Abe. "Yeah, I could probably track a Xolo if I

could get a good whiff of one. But it doesn't help me much if I have to find them before I can find them."

"If the shapeshifting magic is a danger to you, perhaps it will not be necessary," Abe said. He glanced at Adan and then back at me. "You must secure an invitation to the dog-fights. If you were to infiltrate La Calavera's inner circle, you will learn where the fights are held and you may be able to discover where the Xolos are kept. If not, you will have an opportunity to catch their scent so you can track them as a last resort."

"That's not bad, Abe. Not bad at all." I looked at Adan and cocked an eyebrow. He nodded. "So how do I infiltrate La Calavera's inner circle?"

"You're going to need an introduction," the ghost-hunter said, "someone with enough juice to get you by security at the Mocambo."

I knew just the person. The only question was how much it would cost me.

eight

The piskies escorted Mrs. Dawson back to the condo. Adan and I went to call on the Burning Man at his warehouse in Van Nuys. The shapeshifting and other shenanigans had taken their toll and I desperately wanted sleep. But I wasn't sure how long it would take the Burning Man to get me in at the Mocambo club, and in the meantime, my city was being overrun by zombies. Like the man said, I'll sleep when I'm dead.

We let Abe go. Even if I'd had a mind to punish him, I couldn't think of anything I could do to him that he hadn't already done to himself.

Adan's relationship with the Seelie Court meant he had contacts in the Between, but none of them were likely on good terms with La Calavera. So it was the Burning Man or bust. We walked into the mist in the cemetery. When we came out in Van Nuys, it was full daylight—granted that "full daylight" in the Between amounted to a dim yellow illumination that suffused the air like pollution. The warehouse looked exactly as it had the last time I visited, when I'd purchased Ned from the Burning Man. The Asian gangbanger who'd been standing guard out front had been replaced by a Latino gangbanger. The AK slung over his shoulder looked about the same. There was no challenge this time—the kid opened the office door as we approached. "Go on up," he said in Spanish.

A small group of thugs lounged on battered vintage office furniture watching the Stooges on an old black-and-white TV. They didn't acknowledge our presence and I didn't see any reason to interrupt their show. We crossed the small room and climbed the metal staircase set into the far wall.

When we reached the upstairs office, the Burning Man was fully combusted, a human torch standing behind an ornate wooden desk. Greasy smoke twined from the curled strips of burnt flesh that still clung to his bones. He smiled as we entered, and a little tongue of flame escaped between his blackened teeth. We shook hands and the fire caused me no more discomfort than it did the Burning Man.

"You're looking fit as ever," I said, as we took our seats in front of the desk. The Burning Man grinned wider and a thin clump of burning hair and skin fell from his scalp and drifted slowly down to rest on the desk. He brushed it aside.

"Domino Riley," he said, "it's a pleasure as always. And Adan Rashan—it's an honor to finally make your acquaintance. Tell me, Miss Riley. I've learned of your promotion, of course. How goes the war?"

I shrugged. "Same as it ever was."

"Yes, well, that's not what my sources tell me. The dead walking the earth, demons on the rampage—it all sounds positively delightful. In wartime, of course, one must assure that one's army is well armed. What is an army without arms, after all?" The spirit laughed, belching smoke. "I see you still carry Mr. Earp's Peacemaker... I trust you haven't forgotten our arrangement?"

"No, you're still my supplier for weapons in the Between," I said. "I just haven't had occasion to call upon your assistance yet."

"Until now," said the Burning Man.

"Right, except I'm not in need of hardware at the moment. I came to see you about another matter."

The Burning Man was whole again. He smoothed the lapels of his dark gray suit and shot the cuffs. He unbuttoned the coat, sat down and clasped his hands on the desktop. "Very well," he said. "Tell me how I may be of service."

"I...uh, we," I said, glancing at Adan, "need to get into the Mocambo club. I thought you might be able to introduce us."

The Burning Man arched his eyebrows. "To La Calavera?"

"Yeah, I understand she runs the club."

"Oh, she does. She does indeed." The spirit tapped two fingers against his lips, considering. "I am, of course, acquainted with La Calavera, and as it happens, I am a member at the club. I'm confident I could arrange an introduction."

"That's great," I said, reaching across the desk and offering my hand. "How long you think it will take to set that up?"

The Burning Man smiled and started burning again. He held one finger up and a thin line of smoke coiled from his cuff. "First, there is the question of price."

I'd yet to run into a spirit—with the possible exception of Honey—who didn't want their pound of flesh for every little favor you asked of them. They were worse than gangsters. "The price, of course," I said. "Yeah, okay, what can I do for you? You've already got my gun business, when I need it."

"Well, you and I are alike, Miss Riley. The business

we can do need not be limited to conventional trade in merchandise."

"Spit it out," I said.

"I need you to make a problem go away."

I laughed. "You want me to kill somebody."

The Burning Man burned and smiled. "With occasional rare exceptions such as Mr. Rashan and yourself, Miss Riley, those of us who inhabit this world are not, strictly speaking, alive, and therefore I would hesitate to describe what I'm asking as a killing. Think of it as…an exorcism, if you like."

"Yeah. So who do you need clipped?"

"A competitor, of sorts," said the Burning Man. "Not a true threat to my operation, you understand, more of a… nuisance."

"A nuisance you apparently can't get rid of yourself. Who is he?"

"He is called Dedushka," said the Burning Man. "You would not believe how many tired, old spirits there are in the Between called Grandfather, in a thousand tongues and local variations. It's as if they lack even the rudiments of creativity or imagination."

I didn't think "the Burning Man" was a real dazzler in terms of creativity, all things considered. "Sounds Russian," I said, thinking of Anton. I wondered how he was doing. Was he still alive…or undead, or whatever the fuck he was? Had he gone mad?

"Yes," said the Burning Man. "Dedushka is a vodyanoy. He is supposed to be a river spirit, as I understand it, but the Los Angeles River apparently holds no appeal for him. Perhaps this is because the river is so often dry, or perhaps he simply lacks an aesthetic appreciation for concrete.

In any event, he has a home in Malibu." He gave us the address—an exclusive little enclave on Carbon Beach.

The Burning Man was having trouble with a river spirit. Fire and water. It was the kind of thing that might count for something in the Between. "Well, what's he done, exactly? I guess I'm not eager to gun down some old grandpa."

The Burning Man laughed. "This old grandpa drew his power from drowning mortals and taking them as slaves. That was a long time ago, but still you'll discover that many of his enforcers have a certain sogginess about them."

I looked over at Adan. "Sounds like a bad guy…" I remembered a time not too long ago when I'd promised myself I was going to change the game. I wasn't going to murder people anymore just because they were bad guys. I was going to be a real soldier. Somehow I'd imagined looking at my enemies across a battlefield and killing them fair and square. I was still waiting on some sign this was going to be that kind of war. So far, it was pretty much business as usual for the underworld.

"I know the vodyanoy," Adan said. "We'll be doing the world a favor."

I nodded. It was so easy to agree. This guy was a monster. He was in the war and he was my enemy. I wouldn't be breaking any promises if I put him down. "We can take this guy at his house in Malibu?"

"I wouldn't advise it," said the Burning Man. "A certain history, you see, has brought us to this point, and his security is tight. He does have a vulnerability, though, one of which I cannot easily take advantage. It should, however, present you with a perfect opportunity."

"What's the vulnerability?"

"He goes for a swim every evening. He strolls along the beach in front of his house for a spell, surrounded by bodyguards. But they wait for him while he swims. None of them, you understand, have any real enthusiasm for entering the water with him."

I didn't have any real enthusiasm for it, either, but at least he'd be out in the open. "Okay," I said, "I'll kill this Dedushka for you. But it's a heavy lift just for an introduction."

"You think perhaps I should sweeten the pot?" the Burning Man asked.

"Yeah, I want you to set up my compadre here with a firearm. Something good, like Ned, only a long gun."

"Ah, yes, I noticed that he is somewhat lightly dressed. If he is to aid you in your mission, I suspect a rifle might come in very handy, indeed. Of course, I have just the thing." The Burning Man opened the cage and retrieved an old rifle from a rack bolted onto the wall. He placed it carefully on the desk and nodded to Adan.

It was a simple bolt-action rifle with a wooden stock and black hardware. The weapon looked somewhat crudely made. The grain of the wood was rough and I could even see tool marks and shoddy finishing in several places.

"This is the Mosin-Nagant used by Vassili Zaitsev at Stalingrad," said the Burning Man.

"Am I supposed to know who that is?" I asked.

"Jude Law," Adan said. "*Enemy at the Gates*." He hefted the rifle and worked the action. He seemed pleased. I wondered how he kept up-to-date on movies growing up in fairyland.

"That's right," said the Burning Man. "Zaitsev killed two hundred and twenty-five enemy soldiers with this weapon at Stalingrad."

That was more than Wyatt Earp ever killed with Ned. I shrugged. "There was a war on."

"That was his confirmed count during a single five-week

period in the winter of 1942, Miss Riley. And, if I do say so myself, there would be a certain delicious irony in it if you were to use this legendary Russian rifle against the vodyanoy."

"It'll work," said Adan. He set the butt on the floor and leaned the rifle against his thigh. Boys.

"It's like Ned, then?" I asked. "He doesn't have to worry about ammo or anything?"

"It is just the same," the Burning Man agreed, "with, perhaps, a bit more 'muscle,' as you say."

"I doubt that," I said, scowling.

"The terms of the weapon's possession must be the same, too, of course. Should Mr. Rashan die—"

"No. When he's done in the Between," I said, "Adan gives up the gun. That was our agreement." I hadn't fallen for the Burning Man's little trap-clause the first time. I wasn't sure why he thought it'd be any different now.

"Done," said the Burning Man, and we shook hands again. "I will make the necessary arrangements with La Calavera. Once your business for me is concluded, I will be most pleased to introduce you."

"Okay," I said, "we'll be in touch. Let's go, Adan." We rose and went to the door.

"Just one more thing," the Burning Man called from behind us. We turned to see him sitting behind the desk again, blazing merrily. "I know I didn't specify in the course of our negotiations, but if it wouldn't be too much trouble…"

"Get on with it already," I said. "What do you want?"

"Once you've killed Dedushka, bring me the mother-fucker's head."

The clock radio by the sofa—the one that had previously been on my bedside table—said it was just after nine in the morning when we got back to the condo. There was no sign of Mrs. Dawson or the piskies. I assumed Honey and Jack were taking a little private time in the Enchanted Forest, and the ghost was wherever. Adan wanted to plan the Dedushka assassination, but I wasn't up for anything except lying down. I needed sleep. If I didn't get it, there was no way I'd be able to clip a spirit, rescue some dogs, save the world from a zombie apocalypse or even speak coherently.

Adan gave up the argument shortly after my ass hit the couch and it became obvious I wasn't listening to him. I felt his weight settle on the other end of the sofa and I opened one eye. He tucked his hands behind his head and stretched out. One of his feet was touching mine. I wondered what would have happened if I hadn't given up my bedroom to Mrs. Dawson. Would he have jumped in bed with me? Or would he be out here on the couch while I was in the bedroom? Did it matter? There was nothing you could do on a bed that you couldn't do on a sofa. Whatever had happened at Oberon's party had happened on a couch.

That had been pretty good, probably. Whatever it was. Adan was kind of a pain in the ass, but he really wasn't so bad. He was real nice to look at—the changeling had copied him well—but he had a brain on him, too. He had juice, though I hadn't decided if that made him more appealing or just a bigger pain. He had a good sense of humor when he wanted to…which wasn't often enough, but he probably had a lot on his mind. He had a great smile. What was it about dimples, anyway? Why did just thinking about what amounted to dents in his face make me as frisky as a schoolgirl? And why was I asking myself all these stupid fucking questions?

Adan was a distraction. I was thirty-five years old. I was wise to his evil ways and immune to his charms. No way

I'd let him work me over again, even if it hadn't really been him the first time. I had better things to think about than some guy—like zombies, and ghosts and Russian spirits that lived in Malibu.

His foot was still touching mine. He shifted on the couch and it rubbed against my ankle. I hoped my feet didn't smell.

Adan had me pinned to the teacher's desk in my fifth grade homeroom when the alarm woke me. "Come on," he said, "it's almost three o'clock." He was sitting on the edge of the sofa, tying his shoe. I sat up and shook the lascivious dream images out of my head.

"Three? I set the alarm for two."

"You kept snoozing. You must have hit the button at least five times. I don't think you even woke up. It was kind of freaky."

"Yeah, I do that." I hoped I hadn't been talking in my sleep. Or making any noises. "You want a burrito? I'm cooking." I got up and walked into the kitchen.

"Sure," he said. "We can lay down a plan while we eat. You need some help?"

"No, I got this," I said, taking two burritos out of the freezer and popping them in the microwave. Two minutes and forty-five seconds later, I set the paper plates and a couple beers on the coffee table. I sat back down on the couch and crossed my legs under me.

Adan looked at the burrito and then looked at me. "What?" I said around a mouthful of beans and cheese. "Eat it. It's good for you."

He took a tentative bite and made a face, then put the burrito back on his plate. "I don't mean to be critical or anything," he said, "but it's cold inside."

"Yeah, but other parts are hot as hell, so be careful." I reached over and placed my index finger on his burrito. "Dance, Monkey, Dance," I said, and flowed some juice. Refried beans began bubbling from the end.

"Dance, Monkey, Dance?"

"For the molecules," I said, and shimmied my shoulders in a little dance move. "Try it."

He bit into the burrito again and chewed hesitantly. Then he titled his head and nodded. "Not bad."

We ate our burritos and drank our beers in a comfortable silence. I didn't get to have breakfast very often with guys who slept over. Usually they beat a hasty retreat at the first opportunity, or else I chased them out. Adan crashing with me on the couch hadn't been the usual kind of sleepover, but it was still nice. It made me feel almost human.

"So the vodyanoy's house on Carbon Beach," Adan said. "Do you know anything about it?"

So much for almost human. "Not really. They call it 'Billionaire's Beach' on account of all the celebrities and rich folks that have houses there. In the real world, anyway. In the Between, who knows what it's like."

"It's probably pretty close but we won't really know until we scout it out."

"The houses are all right down on the sand, and built really close together. Assuming it's the same, Dedushka will be able to walk directly from his house onto the beach. There's no seawall or anything."

Adan nodded. "We'll need to let him get well clear of the house before we make a move."

"Right. We don't want him retreating to the house if something goes sideways. The beach is wide-open, but confined. There are houses along one side and the ocean on the other."

"Yeah, but that's not an advantage. The ocean is a hard boundary for us, but not for the spirit."

"I agree. We have to take him on the beach. If we let him into the water, the job's over."

"I've got the sniper rifle. I could take a position on the roof of a nearby house."

"That's what I had in mind when I asked for the rifle. By the way, can you actually use that thing? It's pretty high-tech." It wasn't, really, even by early twentieth century standards, but it was a hell of a lot more sophisticated than Adan was used to.

"My father was giving me instruction before he left. Anyway, the rifle is a magical artifact and I have plenty of experience with those."

"Okay, you and the rifle are backup, though." Adan started to protest but I shook him off. "No, look, the spirit's going to have bodyguards around him, so it might be tough to get a clean shot. More importantly, we don't know what this guy can do. We don't know how tough he is. If you shoot him and he doesn't go down, it's game over. He can be in the water in seconds."

"You're going to try to get close," Adan said.

"That's the only way to do it right."

"What makes you think he'll let you get close?"

"I'm feeling a lot better now that I got some sleep. I figure I'll use my glamour."

"Absolutely not, Domino. I know you're stubborn but you're not stupid. There's too much on the line and you're too important to risk your life playing with somebody else's magic."

I didn't argue. I was secretly relieved. When I'd used the glamour to shapeshift, it had been worse than any pain I'd ever imagined possible, let alone experienced. It had felt *wrong,* like a cancer spreading through my body. I wasn't looking for a chance to return to that place. If I had a choice, I'd never go there again.

"What then?" I said. "Maybe Honey can dust me. It doesn't have to be complicated. Just an invisibility glamour. Just enough to let me get close."

"I'm sure she could, but like you said, we don't know what this guy can do. What if he sniffs out the glamour? I don't know for sure but I've heard some of the vodyanoy can."

"Maybe you should ask the piskies," Honey said. She and Jack flew in from the Enchanted Forest and landed on the coffee table.

"To answer your question, no, a vodyanoy probably can't sniff out piskie glamour."

"Cool," I said, "then you can—"

"But it *will* sniff out you," Honey finished. "He has a nose for human magic, Domino. Most of us from this side do. And remember, that's all you are in the Between."

"Damn it, how am I going to get close if he can smell me even if I'm invisible?"

"You have to let us do it," Honey said.

"Us who?"

"Jack and me. We're piskies. We don't smell like you."

"Thanks," I said, "but no way. This is my job. I'm not putting you in it."

Honey's face flushed and she put her hands on her hips. "Domino, I fought beside Oberon upon Gastonbury Tor in the days before your people discovered gravity. Before our return to Arcadia, Jack was one of the King's Knives."

I looked at the piskie. "He's about the right size, I guess."

Honey threw up her hands. "The King's Knives, Domino.

Jack's an assassin. He crossed into the lands controlled by Queen Mab, behind enemy lines, and executed the Unseelie enemies of the king."

I was suitably impressed but I couldn't help remembering their glamours had bounced off Abe Warren easy enough. I didn't want to piss off Honey any more than she already was, though. I decided to raise my concerns delicately. "He's probably protected against fairy magic…"

"I *knew* you'd bring that up! For your information, we didn't use any lethal glamour against the ghost-hunter. We *thought* you wanted to talk to him. There wasn't a whole lot to your plan, as I recall, but you did say 'grab him' not 'kill him.'"

"That's true," I allowed, "but this guy might be protected against your deadly glamour, too."

Honey blurred and suddenly my head was jerked backward. The piskie was perched atop my skull holding a fistful of my hair. The other hand held her silver sword in a downward grip, the point poised just above my left eye. "If our magic doesn't work," she said calmly, "we'll poke holes in him until he stops moving. Sound good?"

"I admire the simplicity of it," I said. "What about the bodyguards?"

"Probably just ghosts," Jack said. He shrugged.

"We'll come at him from above," Honey elaborated. "The vodyanoy will be dead before he realizes what's happening."

"We could cover them with our guns from the houses, Domino. If the bodyguards get in the way, we take them out. Even your pistol should have enough range for that."

I felt like I should stand up for Ned, but I let it pass. "It could work," I said. "It's a pretty damn good plan, Honey."

"Thanks!" she said brightly. She let go of my hair and landed on my shoulder.

"There's one more thing I have to do before we can clip Dedushka, though."

"What's that?" said Adan.

"It's the zombies," I said. "The math is a real problem. There can't be that many Xolos. I'm worried that by the time we rescue them, there will be too many zombies for them to handle. If there are too many zombies and they're all creating more zombies, the Xolos will never catch up and we're all screwed."

"You need Oberon," Honey said.

"I need everyone," I said. "I'll have Chavez put the other outfits—our allies—on zombie patrol, but we don't have the manpower to stay ahead of this thing. There are already more zombies than gangsters in L.A. and they're making more faster than we can put them down. Oberon has the manpower."

"The question is whether he'll give it up," Honey said.

"I'll ask nicely."

I called ahead to the Carnival Club and Titania told me Oberon was in the field. The queen gave me the address and I used the traffic spell and two freeways to get to Chinatown in about fifteen minutes. I spun the parking spell and pulled into a spot just across Yale from Castelar Elementary School. Oberon stood on the sidewalk outside a nondescript apartment building watching the front entrance of the school. A waifish female sidhe with dark hair and pale skin stood at his side.

Oberon nodded when I got out of the Lincoln and approached. The woman glanced at me and then turned her attention back to the school.

"What's going on?" I said.

"Catriona tells me it started with a janitor," Oberon said. "He came to work this morning—already dead, one imagines—and then turned. There are seven hundred children inside."

I took a moment to let it sink in. I looked at the cream-colored school building with pink trim, and then turned to the woman. "You're Catriona?" The woman nodded but didn't speak. Her skin was *really* pale—it almost looked bleached—and her eyes were very dark, nearly black.

"I've been using the bean-sidhe to locate targets," Oberon said.

"Banshees are fairies?"

"We are sidhe," Catriona said, and the corner of her mouth quirked up. "We have a particular skill for finding death. It is our privilege to serve our king."

"I have a squad inside," Oberon said. "We don't know yet how many of the children are still alive."

Population clusters. The Stag geeks had told me this is how it would go. It wasn't going to be limited to shopping malls and movie theaters. "Goddammit, I need you to get a handle on this shit, King."

"We are doing what we can," Oberon said. "There are a great many zombies loose in the city already, and more being created by the minute. Perhaps if we had caught it sooner…"

"I don't care how many there are," I said. "You have a kingdom behind you."

Oberon looked at me and raised an eyebrow. "A kingdom, yes, in Avalon," he said. "Here, I have only a tiny few who can assist in this effort."

"Bring in more. I don't care how many it takes."

"I cannot do that," Oberon said, shaking his head regretfully.

"You can't or you won't?"

A shadow crossed the sidhe king's features. "I believe I said what I meant. I cannot bring more of my people to this world. I do not control sufficient territory for them to survive here."

"You need more juice," I said.

"I do. There are thousands of zombies in the city, Domino. To sustain the numbers I would need to contain them, I will need far more juice than I can tap from Hollywood."

So that's how it was. Oberon was going to use this crisis to expand his territory. Or, he'd let the zombies wipe out half the city's living population, and *then* he'd move in. He was a cunning motherfucker, no doubt, but I also had the idea he was telling the truth.

"You can pull more juice from my turf," I said. "I'll give the word. You can put your taggers on my streets. But, King, let's be real clear. This is a temporary arrangement, feel me?"

"I do, indeed," he said. "Inadequately temporary, I'm afraid. I will not ask my people to come to this world, save your people in this time of peril, and then go back where they belong once you've no further need of them. My kingdom must be large enough to welcome all those I ask to serve."

I clenched my jaw and glanced at Catriona. She was smiling. The sidhe were the only game in town and I needed tickets. They both knew it. "Fine," I said. "You get Mobley's turf when this is all over. I'm not sure how your snow-white Irish ass is going to run those neighborhoods but that's your problem." I also wasn't sure how Terrence was going to feel about it when I served up some more shit for him to eat. Of course, there was a good chance he wouldn't survive the war with Mobley anyway.

"Done," Oberon said, inclining his head. "That should be sufficient to support a few hundred of us. We shall do our best to stem the tide."

The sound of breaking glass drew my attention back to the school building. A small boy—perhaps seven or eight years old—crashed through the front doors and sprawled on the sidewalk. He crawled to his feet and looked around, his head darting wildly from side to side. The boy's face and hands were streaked with blood, and despite his tumble through the glass doors I was pretty sure most of it wasn't his own. His eyes latched onto us and he started across the street, a wide, bloody grin twisting his face into a terrible mask.

I pulled juice from the street and prepared to spin my ghost-binding spell. "There's just one more thing, Your Majesty," I said. "Sooner or later, you're going to be up against a wall and you're going to come to me for a favor. Rest assured, I'll offer you the same friendship you've shown me today."

"Are you threatening me, Domino?" Oberon said.

"Not at all, King. You're my ally and I'm grateful for your assistance. I'm just saying, when that day dawns don't forget your wallet. I don't come cheap."

The vodyanoy's beach house was a modern two-story affair of redwood and beige cement wedged between a white cube with round windows on the right and something that looked vaguely Art Deco on the left. All of them had the faded, sepia tone look of an old photograph, and it made for an eerie accompaniment to the air of nostalgia that hung over the secluded beach. No ghosts roamed the strand and no gulls wheeled overhead. The light surf rolled silently against the shore.

There weren't many access ways down to the beach through the tightly packed homes, and we didn't want to cross in front of the vodyanoy's house. This might have presented a minor obstacle in the real world, but fortunately, we didn't mind trespassing. We chose an older wood-frame beach house a few doors down to the east. When we were as sure as we could be it was uninhabited, we went in through the front door.

The house was narrow but had three floors. The upper floors had wide covered balconies that ran the entire width of the beachfront side. The balcony on the top floor was crowded with boxes and spare furniture. Whether its current owner or one long dead, someone seemed to have used the balcony for storage. The neighbors probably wouldn't care much for the untidiness, but the junk made a convenient concealed position for a couple of snipers.

We all sat on the deck and huddled around, waiting for showtime. Adan was working the bolt of his rifle back and forth and sighting along the barrel. Honey and Jack sat cross-legged facing each other, whispering in their own musical language. I just sat quietly and watched them. None of them had to be there. Even Adan could have stayed behind to run the business side of the outfit. We still needed juice, after all—now more than ever. They weren't there because they were getting paid. They weren't there for power. I knew why Honey was there—she was my friend.

If I'd been a normal person, it would have been an easy thing to take for granted. Well, if I'd been anything like normal, I probably wouldn't have been sitting in a beach house in the spirit-world version of Malibu waiting to do a hit on a Russian river spirit. That aside, friendship wasn't something I could take for granted because I'd never really had it. Chavez was the closest I'd really come to it and even then the outfit was always between us. We were probably as close as two gangsters could be. Maybe someday, on the other side of this war and with the outfit behind us, we could have a real friendship, a normal friendship. Of course, I knew the chances weren't very good that either of us would live that long.

And that made me think of Adan again. It seemed like just about everything made me think of Adan. He was a gangster now, too. So what made me think he was my friend? He'd been given power and authority within the outfit, but he had little if any support. He needed to make his bones, prove he had juice. He needed to win friends and influence people, and from what I'd seen, he wasn't all that good at it. He was smart, but he didn't know the outfit. He didn't know the underworld, didn't belong to it. Adan didn't have a history in my world. He needed to form alliances and win the respect of the big hitters and their crews to consolidate his power.

If I looked at it with a clear head, that's why Adan was here. The wartime captain is in a tight spot, here's Adan to step in and save the day. He wasn't my friend. He was playing an angle, just like everyone else.

Adan wasn't the changeling. He looked the same, talked the same, had all the same mannerisms and body language. At the club, he'd even smelled the same, like apples and cinnamon, though I couldn't be sure if that was Adan or the fairy mojo Oberon had put on us. Since squeezing the changeling, I had defenses against fairy glamour, but I'd either let them down or Oberon's magic was powerful enough to defeat them. What about Adan's glamour? Why *had* he smelled like apples and cinnamon that night? Was it possible he knew the effect it would have on me? Might he have used his glamour to seduce me?

There was a fine line between healthy suspicion and paranoia, and it was especially fine where fairies and victims of fairy abductions were concerned. Fortunately, I didn't share Adan's weaknesses. I knew the underworld, I knew the outfit and I knew a thing or two about exposing rivals and forging alliances. The key to both was to slow the fuck down. Don't make assumptions. Don't jump to conclusions. Sit back, watch and learn. You couldn't always know what was in another gangster's heart, but if you had some patience he'd show you soon enough.

I glanced up and caught Adan staring at me. He smiled and went back to playing with his rifle. All I needed was a little patience. Lie back in the weeds and let this guy reveal himself. Maybe he'd prove himself an ally, a partner, even a friend. That would be nice. And maybe I'd find out he was just playing the game. That wouldn't be so nice, but it wouldn't be the first time and at least I'd know how it was. The ball was in Adan's court, and I could play it either way. The truth was, he needed me more than I needed him. I liked it that way. I always had.

"It's time," Adan said.

I sat up and looked down the beach. An old man with a close-cropped white beard walked toward us along the high-tide line, surrounded by half a dozen ghosts. He wore an old felt hat and a bright red track suit—what was it with Russian gangsters and track suits, anyway? His bodyguards looked like disposable muscle, except that some of them had obviously drowned. Their bodies were pale and bloated and their clothes hung in damp tatters. A couple were even sporting long strands of seaweed like feather boas.

Jack pulled Honey to him and kissed her, long and hard. Then they both nodded to us and disappeared. Adan and I lay flat on our bellies, aiming our guns through the slats in the balcony railing. I'd cautioned Adan to stay back—you wanted to sight through the railing, but you didn't want the barrel extending past it. It was the kind of thing a trained bodyguard could spot, more easily than you'd expect.

It was still daylight, though it was late enough I imagined the sun would be setting into the sea in the real world. The light in this place was indistinguishable from midday, and we'd have good visibility—by the standards of the Between—if we needed to use our weapons. The plan was for the piskies to attack when the group drew even with our position, to give us the widest possible field of fire. We waited and I watched Adan out of the corner of one eye. He was calm, breathing deeply and easily, his finger resting lightly on the trigger of the rifle.

The piskies' initial attack went just as they had planned it, and it failed completely. One moment the vodyanoy was walking leisurely along the beach and the next moment his throat had been opened from ear to ear. Juice the greenish-brown of stagnant river water sprayed across the sand and spattered the nearest bodyguards. The old man clutched at his throat and fell to his knees. The ghosts drew weapons and closed ranks, looking around in panic, but the piskies didn't show themselves. Then the vodyanoy reached into his jacket pocket with one bloody hand and withdrew something small and white. I couldn't be sure, but it looked like an egg. He slammed it down on the beach, crushing it, and golden light poured from within.

"It's a true-seeing charm," I hissed, and Adan nodded.

The light revealed the piskies, hovering in the air above the vodyanoy's head with their swords bared and wet with the creature's juice. When they became visible, the ghosts attacked, opening fire with a variety of weapons that ranged from revolvers to Thompson submachine guns. The piskies spun and darted and most of the bullets missed completely— it was a lucky break none of the ghosts was packing a shotgun. The piskies sang their ancient songs and their defensive glamours withstood the few rounds that found their targets. Silver fireworks flashed in the air as the bullets exploded against the fairies' shields, and pixie dust cascaded down on the attackers like emerald-green confetti.

When the glowing dust touched them, the ghosts dropped their weapons and began clawing at their eyes and bare skin. First their clothes and then their spectral flesh began to disintegrate under the magic's touch and the ghosts came undone like crematory ash carried on the wind.

While the piskies dealt with the bodyguards, the vodyanoy was changing. His mouth widened and his skull expanded, seeming to bulge and bloat. His body became squat and obese, while his arms lengthened and thickened, and his hands contorted into webbed claws. His eyes grew large, and round and yellow, and his hair fell from his skull in clumps. Finally, the track suit split at the seams, revealing amphibian, gray-green skin that glistened in the wan light.

"Son of a bitch is a frog," I said.

"Fishtail," said Adan. I looked again. The vodyanoy's legs and feet had transformed into a mermaid's tail that darkened from pale gray to near-black at the fins.

"Okay," I said. "Son of a bitch is a frog with a fishtail."

The vodyanoy opened its maw wide and made a noise that was something between a roar and a croak. It sounded a little like a foghorn but with a sickly organic quality that made me a little nauseous. Swamp-water juice covered its bulging throat and pale, flabby chest, but the wounds appeared to be closing.

The piskies attacked again. They darted in and slashed with their silver swords, opening long wounds in the soft flesh that gaped and oozed. Honey circled around and dived at the thing's head, her sword reversed and gripped in both hands as she went for one of its unblinking yellow eyes. At the last instant, the monster's head snapped up and a sinuous amphibian tongue flashed from its mouth. The disgusting appendage struck Honey in her center of mass and held her fast, then reeled her in to the yawning maw with dizzying speed.

Just as a scream began to bubble up in my throat, Jack was there. He darted between the vodyanoy and Honey and severed the creature's tongue with a powerful two-handed slash. Honey tumbled to the sand, pulling the limp, rubbery flesh from her body.

I knew what was coming before it happened, but there was nothing I could do about it. Jack had gotten too close. One of the vodyanoy's webbed claws flashed out and snatched him from the air. The monster tightened its fist and squeezed, and Jack screamed. Then the vodyanoy slammed him down into the sand, silencing the piskie warrior.

"Cover me," I said, and I was over the railing before I had a chance to think about what I was doing. It must have been at least thirty feet to the stone-tiled patio below the balcony. I whispered Honey's mantra as I fell: "Magic and mind, magic and mind..."

I landed in a crouch with the fingers of one hand braced against the stone to steady myself, and then I was running for the beach. I was a hundred feet from the vodyanoy when I started firing Ned on the run. Honey was still down, struggling to free herself from the sticky, severed tongue, and the creature was dragging itself across the sand toward her, pulling with its powerful arms and slapping the sand with its fishtail.

In the real world, with a normal gun, you wouldn't have high expectations for any shots you fired at a dead sprint. This wasn't the normal world, though, and Ned definitely wasn't a normal gun. A burning blue wound blossomed in the vodyanoy's side and another where the thick tail merged into his torso. He let out another watery foghorn blast but kept crawling toward Honey as the sapphire energy chewed his blubbery hide. The piskie pulled frantically at the clinging strands and tried to scramble away, but the vodyanoy was covering a lot more ground than she could.

I knew I wouldn't be able to get there in time. I could keep firing and hope for a lucky shot that would put the creature down or I could stop and aim. Indecision gripped me and I barreled on across the sand by inertia, fanning the Peacemaker's hammer and silently praying for a kill-shot. The vodyanoy opened its mouth and screamed again, drowning Honey in a deluge of mucus, spittle and bile. It reached for her with one clawed hand, its long, knobby fingers twitching eagerly.

Then I heard an echoing crack like thunder rolling overhead, and the vodyanoy's head exploded, splashing greenish-black juice across the beach. The monster's fat body dropped and jerked a few times before collapsing into a pool of evil, foul-smelling magic that quickly soaked into the sand.

I ran to Honey and helped pull the last bits of tongue from her. Then we both looked over to where Jack had fallen. He lay there unmoving, his body limp and broken. A tortured cry tore itself from Honey's lips and she half ran, half flew to his side. She cradled him in her arms, tilted her head back and wailed at the sky. I dropped to my knees beside them just as Adan ran up, holding the rifle lightly in one hand.

Jack coughed and opened his eyes. He blinked. "Good fight," he said.

Honey made fists of both hands and began flailing at him, pummeling his chest and stomach. She was laughing and crying, and Jack finally defended himself by grabbing her and pulling her onto the sand with him, rolling over so she was pinned beneath his body.

"Do not cry, my love," he said, and I noticed the slight brogue in his voice for the first time. "The gods gave us victory this day and there is life in us still." Honey pulled him closer and kissed him fiercely.

I looked at Adan and cleared my throat. "Maybe we should…"

"Yeah," he said, and we turned and walked back toward the beach house.

"Nice shot," I said.

He shrugged. "Frog-boy had a big fucking head."

"Yeah, he *did*."

Adan glanced at me and lifted an eyebrow. "What's the problem?"

"I was supposed to bring it to the Burning Man."

nine

I was prepared to tell the Burning Man to grab a shovel and scoop up some sand if he insisted on having Dedushka's head. As it turned out, news of the hit beat us back to Van Nuys and the spirit wasn't inclined to jack me up on a technicality. He'd arranged to escort Adan and me to the Mocambo later that night. It seemed the piskies weren't welcome—La Calavera had a problem with the way the fairies had moved in and used her turf as a rest stop on the way from Avalon to Arcadia.

I also considered asking Adan to stay behind. I knew the only way to stop the zombie outbreak was to rescue the Xolos, but in the meantime there were zombies running loose in L.A. Still, if Oberon, Terrence and Chavez couldn't keep a lid on things, Adan probably wouldn't make much of a difference. I didn't really know what I'd be walking into—except that it was an underworld nightclub in the Between run by the Lady of the Dead. Even if I couldn't be sure where I stood with Adan, I needed backup. I also needed to keep an eye on him.

We grabbed some dinner in my condo and then crossed back over into the spirit world a little after ten. We met at the warehouse in Van Nuys and I was surprised to see the Burning Man had left his gangbangers at home. When I asked about it, he explained that the Mocambo was considered neutral ground in his world, and besides, there would be enough "dangerous men" in the club that a couple ghosts wouldn't make much difference if things got ugly. I didn't have a problem with it—the Burning Man was my ticket in the door, but he wasn't my friend. Whether he had muscle or not, it wasn't likely to change my fortunes either way.

We walked into the mist and emerged on the Sunset Strip in West Hollywood, circa 1949. I didn't recognize most of the old buildings that lined the street, and I figured all but a few had been demolished to make way for the chic boutiques, shops and street-level malls that hugged the boulevard in my world.

This was also the first time in the Between I really missed cars. You didn't need them with the mist to transport you instantly wherever you wanted to go. But this street, in this time, had been a kind of drive-through shrine to the automobile. I should have seen Cadillac convertibles, Packard coupes and Lincoln Cosmopolitans cruising the boulevard. Instead, the street was empty but for the few well-dressed ghosts with somewhere to be.

The Mocambo club was a two-story stucco building with a Spanish tiled roof and a row of faux-shuttered windows running along the top floor. There was a small marquee and a short canopy covering the entrance. The marquee was blank. I didn't know if that was an oversight or some kind of existential statement.

The ghosts flanking the front doors were nothing special to look at, but malevolence rolled off them in waves. I wondered about the things they'd done in life to earn their juice in the shadow world. The Burning Man ignored them and they didn't challenge us as we passed.

We followed our host down a short, dark hallway past a coat check and then stepped out onto the main floor of the club. The place made the Carnival Club seem a little staid and conservative by comparison. The central bar was designed like a carousel, featuring polished brass poles and a canopy with a red and white pinwheel design overhead. Candy-striped pillars were scattered around the floor and each was crowned with concentric, irregularly shaped hoops that gave them the appearance of huge, fanciful umbrellas. Behind the bar and adorning the walls were dozens of plaster figurines. There were weird, anthropomorphic animals in opulent, old-fashioned clothes, a variety of mythological creatures leering down at the crowd and vaguely human figures so bizarre as to be near-abstractions. Glass cases were set into the walls running up toward the stage. Ghosts were locked inside the cases, and they were of varying ages and vintages to judge by their clothing.

We were greeted by a hostess and escorted through a maze of round tables with white tablecloths to a booth with red-and-white-striped upholstery. Ghosts hung on the walls between our table and the adjoining booths like captive thieves. The Burning Man ordered champagne and waited until we sat, and then he went to make the rounds. I looked at the champagne but I wasn't about to drink any. It couldn't actually be champagne in the Between and I didn't want to know what it really was.

The back wall of the club was draped in rich gold curtains that were pulled back from the stage and bandstand. A female ghost stood in the spotlight singing a Billie Holiday number to the accompaniment of the house orchestra.

I realized all of the staff were ghosts—the bartenders,

waiters and cigarette girls, as well as the entertainment. The patrons were something else entirely. I'd never imagined a place where the Burning Man would appear ordinary, but the Mocambo was that place. Most of the clientele looked at least somewhat human and all were impeccably dressed. But even when they lacked the Burning Man's special effects, they clearly weren't mortal. Some were impossibly tall and gaunt, and others were obscenely fat. I saw a woman in a crimson evening gown with barbed wire woven into the flesh of her throat and wrists. I saw a man in a tuxedo with a mask of human skin not his own.

It wasn't hard to pick out La Calavera. She stood by the bar attended by a small army of waiters and sycophants. She was beautiful, with dark hair, pale skin and a lean, sinuous body. She wore a white cocktail dress with cascading ruffles and a wide black belt, black pumps and a huge floppy black hat with an elaborate bow. Her face and mouth were painted white to mimic a skull, with blacked-out eyes and nose and dark lines on her lips suggesting teeth. When I turned my head to point her out to Adan, the makeup job faded and I saw a fleshless human skull beneath the oversize hat.

"There's our girl," I said to Adan. "When you look at her out of the corner of your eye, you get the full *calavera* effect."

"What does *calavera* mean, anyway?"

"Look at her like I said and I'll bet you can tell me."

Adan looked over at the bar, turned back to me and then did a double-take. "Goofy hat?" he said.

"Try again."

"Skull."

"There you go," I said. "*La Calavera Catrina*—the elegant skull. What else do you see?" I knew my world better than Adan did, I knew the underworld, but he'd had more experience with this place.

Adan was silent for a moment, watching her intently. "She's straight out of the Beyond," he said. "Not Avalon—somewhere else. She's a spirit but not born of the earth, like your jinn. An outsider."

"She's got juice."

He nodded and looked around. "You can tell that much even without the sight. Every player in the club is afraid of her. I've seen worse, but not usually in the Between. She needs a lot of juice to sustain herself here. She can pull some from the Beyond but she's got a lot of local sources, too."

"So this thing with the Xolos, it's producing for her."

Adan nodded. "She needs a lot of rackets. And her operations must have taken a hit when Oberon moved into Hollywood."

"So La Calavera has a beef with Oberon. He's a threat."

"Yeah, but you have to look at the other side, too. She's a threat to him. He's got a rival gang boss operating just on the other side of the veil."

"I can't see a way to connect Oberon to this, but I don't like the fact I just coincidentally find myself in conflict with one of his enemies. The king should be on this job."

"You think he played us?"

"I don't know," I said. "There's no reason to think Oberon knew anything about what was causing the zombie problem, or that La Calavera had anything to do with it. It's just awfully fucking convenient for him and that makes me suspicious."

"So how are we going to do this?"

"We try to get close. It's a dogfighting ring, which means there's wagering. We want in on the action. If we can get inside this thing, that's our best chance to find the Xolos and free them."

"And to find out if King Oberon knew about the racket and put us between him and La Calavera," Adan said.

"Showtime," I said. The Burning Man had stopped by the bar and was deep in conversation with La Calavera. She looked in our direction and we made eye contact. Just for a second, I saw the naked skull again. Then she smiled.

She stood and took the Burning Man's arm, and they walked over to our table. "La Calavera Catrina," he said, "may I present Adan Rashan and Domino Riley." Under different circumstances it might have hurt my feelings that he introduced Adan first, but I knew his sense of propriety was stuck in 1949, just like the rest of the club.

"Master Rashan," she said, "your father's name is well-known here. Welcome to the Mocambo." Her smile was dazzling.

"Thank you," Adan said, and gestured to the space beside me. "Would you care to join us?"

La Calavera seemed to notice me for the first time since our little stare down. I smiled and tried to force as much warmth into it as I could, which probably wasn't much. "I think not," she said, returning her attention to Adan. "I adore this performer and I would rather like to dance. I'm sure your companion won't mind."

I was expecting deer in the headlights, but Adan was smooth. Maybe too smooth. "I'd be delighted," he said, smiling. At least he slid the other way out of the booth so I didn't have to get up. They walked together to the dance floor and every eye in the club followed them.

The Burning Man nodded to me once and wandered off. Even without the burning I wouldn't have wanted to dance with him, but he could have asked. Instead, I got to sit there, alone, with the champagne I couldn't actually drink because it was probably pureed human soul or something, and watch Adan and La Calavera cut a rug.

The ghost who had taken the stage looked and sounded just like Frank Sinatra early in his career. It couldn't actually *be* Sinatra—from what I knew about the guy, he might not be in heaven but he probably wasn't still playing the Mocambo. He did "Close to You" and followed it up with "Almost Like Being in Love." There'd been some daylight between Adan and La Calavera when they started, but they were wrapped up pretty tight by the time the blue-eyed bastard got to "Some Enchanted Evening." I considered whether it would be an unforgivable breach of etiquette to shoot the entertainment.

Eventually, they made their way back to the booth, walking arm in arm and laughing. Adan stood aside and allowed La Calavera to sit first, and then he slid in beside her. She took a long drink of champagne and her shadowed eyes glittered as she watched me over the rim of her glass. She set the flute back on the table and licked her lips.

"What brings you to the Mocambo tonight?" she asked. "Surely, it wasn't just to share." I saw her arm move and Adan swallowed hard. She'd put her hand on his thigh. At least I hoped it was just his thigh.

"We heard there was action here," I said. It probably wasn't the best choice of words.

La Calavera laughed and leaned into Adan. "More action than you'd like, perhaps."

I grinned and shook my head. "Okay, let's get this out of the way. I'm a guest in your club so I don't want to disrespect you. On the other hand, there *is* a limit to how much shit I'll eat just to be polite, and I'm filling up pretty fast. As far as Adan goes? Between you and me, sister, I don't think he likes it cold. But if he's buying what you're selling, by all means, get your nasty on so we can stop pulling each other's hair and get down to business."

I got another flash of the bony hag behind the pretty face, and then La Calavera smiled. "I do believe I'm going to like you, Miss Riley."

"Call me Domino."

"Very well, Domino. You can drink the champagne, by the way. It's just juice. You'll like it."

I was more worried about where the juice had come from and how it had gotten into the bottle, but I picked up my glass and took a drink. I probably wasn't going to get an invitation to the dogfights if I was afraid of a little Between-style bubbly. I drained off half the glass and put it back on the table. It *was* pretty tasty.

"So what business do we have, you and I?" La Calavera had gone from hanging all over Adan to pretending he didn't exist. For his part, Adan seemed relieved by the abrupt shift in focus.

"We heard you were running a game—not the kind of action we get on our side of the tracks."

"It's true," La Calavera said. "I do provide certain amusements for the denizens of this place. Just as you do, I'm sure, in the mortal city. But I have to say, we don't enjoy the patronage of humans very often—even of human sorcerers. We play big, as they say, and the stakes can be intimidating to those on a more limited bankroll."

"Juice," I said. "You play for juice."

"Of course. Gold can be useful to those of us with dealings in the mortal world, but juice is the only currency that has real value here."

"Our bankrolls are petty deep. We run an outfit—"

"I know who you are, Domino, and I know you have

the juice to play with us. I simply don't want there to be any unpleasant misunderstandings later. You're new here and you might be excused for thinking we run a *friendly* game."

"No game worth winning stays friendly very long."

La Calavera smiled. "Isn't it so?" she said. "Very well, where do your particular interests lie? Poker is quite popular right now and dice are always in fashion. We do have more...exotic...games, as well."

"We're here for the dogfights," I said.

La Calavera's eyebrows jumped. "I must say, I'm surprised you've even heard of the dogfights. I wasn't aware your friend the Burning Man knew of them."

"He's not my friend, just a guy I went to see about a gun."

"I have made every effort to maintain a certain exclusivity where the dogfights are concerned. The investment required to offer this kind of entertainment is substantial, and the stakes reflect that commitment."

"I'd like to think it won't be any less exclusive when you let us in on the action," I said, and smiled.

La Calavera nodded. "No, indeed. You and your friend are rarities here, as I said, and I'm sure the others will welcome the novelty. They will relish the opportunity to wager against such a...delicacy."

"Great," I said, even though I didn't really think of myself as a delicacy. "When is the next fight?"

"Tonight," said La Calavera. "Enjoy yourselves until the party winds down. For the convenience of our players, we hold the fights on the premises. And now, if you'll excuse me, I really must attend to my other guests." She stood, glanced once at Adan and walked away.

"I feel so used," Adan said. "Hold me, Domino."

I laughed. "You're a good dancer."

"Oberon taught me. He said you had to be able to fight, dance and lie to survive at court, not necessarily in that order."

"You're a good fighter, too."

"Yeah, honesty is my downfall."

"Spoken like an expert liar," I said. "So what was your relationship to Oberon, exactly? He abducted you."

Adan nodded. "I was his ward—somewhere between his son and his hostage. We weren't blood, obviously, and that means a lot in the Seelie Court. But he was responsible for me. He took it seriously."

"What was it like? Growing up with fairies, I mean."

"It's like a dream now, even after a few months. Like Oberon's party. It's hard to remember details. I think it seemed normal at the time—I didn't know anything else."

"You don't remember anything?"

"Impressions," Adan said. "It was…cold. Not the climate—it was always summer in our part of Avalon. But love, genuine warmth, is a rare thing among the sidhe. That's one thing that makes Oberon and Titania unusual—they've got it. But for the rest of them, there's blood, honor, duty, loyalty… There are a lot of good things in Avalon, but kindness and compassion aren't among them."

"It sounds like the barrio, only worse."

"A lot worse, I think. Even in the barrio, I'll bet there was at least some sense of community. Some basic human decency despite the poverty and hopelessness."

I nodded, thinking of my mother and thousands of others like her. "There are good people in the barrio. The poverty and hopelessness just makes them stronger."

Adan got a faraway look in his eyes. "I do remember something. I remember the first time Oberon took me with him on a hunt. We were hunting wild boar in the woods, maybe a day's ride from the city. I must have been about ten years old. We were mounted and we had these short, heavy spears with broad, silver points. The dogs—your barghests—would flush the boars out of the bush and we'd spear them. I could barely even lift the spear."

He laughed and looked at me. I just nodded.

"These boars—they weren't like normal animals, obviously. They could get as big as the barghests, and a lot heavier, a lot more powerful. They had thick, coarse fur and tusks as long as my forearm. Their hides were so tough and they were so fierce, it always took a few good throws to bring them down. Anyway, you probably know how this story goes. I was a decent horseman for my age and size, but you've seen the sidhe horses. I got thrown and a boar charged me. I lost my spear when I fell. All I had was my sword and a short, wide-bladed knife. The rest of the sidhe—including Oberon—just sat their steeds and watched."

"Jesus Christ. What happened?"

"I killed it," Adan said, and shrugged. "I don't remember how. When it was over, my sword was broken off in the boar's chest and my knife was buried to the hilt in its eye. And I was covered in blood, like someone had dumped buckets of it on me. Not all of it was the boar's."

"And they didn't do anything to help?"

"They just watched. They didn't even say anything—no cheering, no encouragement, no advice. They just waited to see what would happen. But that's not really what the story's about. I'll never forget what Oberon said to me when it was over. He said, "The horse sensed your fear. Master your fear and you'll master the beast. You've proven yourself a man, now, so don't expect any more coddling.""

"Coddling? Son of a bitch!"

"Yeah," Adan said, laughing. "That's what I thought—someone must have neglected the coddling part. He was true to his word, though. After that I was always on my own. I could have just about anything I wanted, as long as I was strong enough and clever enough to take it for myself."

Oberon as Adan described him reminded me a lot of Shanar Rashan—maybe that's why they hated each other. My boss had taught me a lot and I'd always be grateful to him for it. But he'd also been more than willing to let me learn the hard lessons on my own. And if I didn't survive one of those lessons? Well, I guess in six thousand years you see a lot of people die. Adan and I were a lot alike, too, with one big difference: I'd always had my mom. Adan never had anyone. Even now, after he'd returned from Avalon, the first thing his father did was go on vacation.

"What do you think of the mortal world so far?" I asked.

Adan nodded and gave me a little smile. "Honestly? So far it seems a lot like Avalon. Our little corner of it, anyway."

"The more things change…"

Adan just looked at me, waiting for me to finish the thought.

"Uh, the more they stay the same. It's just a saying. Adan, how is it you know Jude Law movies but you don't know shit like that?"

"It was a good movie," he said, laughing. "No, I hear you—it's weird. The Seelie Court has been watching this world a long time. That isn't news to you—Oberon had to know what was happening here in order to set his plans in motion. But watching a place isn't the same as living in it. Think of a place you know a little about but have never visited, a place you've never lived."

I nodded. "Like Japan. I know a little about the popular culture, and I maybe have an image of what it looks like—Tokyo, anyway—but I'd be fucking clueless if I actually went there."

"Yeah, that's what it's like for me. Parts of this world are familiar to me. Most of it is alien."

I held up my glass. "Well, here's to two well-adjusted individuals who survived lost innocence and childhood trauma to lead healthy, happy and productive lives."

Adan raised his own glass and touched mine. "They sound like amazing people," he said. "I'd like to meet them someday."

We laughed and drank. We finished the first bottle of champagne and ordered another. It was definitely juice—I got the same buzz off it I got from spinning spells. We couldn't be sure who was listening so we avoided talking about zombies, Xolos or demons. We talked about the outfit, instead, and I realized it was because neither one of us really had anything else going on in our lives. There just wasn't much else to talk about. I didn't mind. It was nice just to talk to someone.

There was never a last call in the shadow world, but eventually the crowd thinned and the staff turned from serving to cleaning up. There were only about a dozen spirits left in the club, and they huddled together in small groups, no doubt discussing the forthcoming entertainment. Before long, La Calavera reappeared and ushered us all through a door by the stage to the back room where the fights would be held.

In the real world, underground dogfights were usually held in vacant lots or buildings, and rarely in the same place twice. The "pits" were really nothing more than small, portable enclosures built from plywood that could be pulled out of the back of a van or truck and set up in a few minutes. La Calavera had done some redecorating and her pit was the real deal. The room behind the stage was like a small amphitheater, with rows of low stone benches encircling the pit. The pit itself was only about four feet deep and fashioned of cut, pale stone mottled with dark-brown stains. There was an open space between the stands on the far side of the room, and half a dozen cages were placed there, side by side. Inside the cages were the Xolos.

They didn't look anything at all like Caesar. In the Between they were made of light, like a master artist had sculpted a sunrise in the shape of a dog. They were beautiful, magnificent, and to look at them was to know peace. And they'd been driven mad.

One of the Xolos threw itself at the bars of its cage, over and over, until white-gold light spattered the insides of the cage and the stone floor like blood. Another sat on its haunches and howled, a mournful lament that worked its way into the center of me and filled me with despair. Another Xolo lay on the floor of its cage, its eyes wide and staring, its light dull and dim. One of the creatures turned in circles inside its cage, first one way and then the next, whimpering quietly.

It took everything I had not to draw Ned and start shooting. I glanced at Adan and saw the muscles of his jaw clenching and unclenching. The spirits in the room didn't even look at the Xolos. They talked quietly in their little groups and drank champagne. They laughed. I saw the woman in the red dress and barbed wire and the man with the skin mask. The others I didn't recognize, but I vowed to remember them.

La Calavera walked over and stood in front of the cages. She raised her arms and the other spirits quickly took their seats. Adan and I sat close together on the stone bench. I took his hand and he held it tightly enough that I couldn't reach for my gun.

"Welcome, friends," La Calavera said. "Most of you are regulars here, but we do have some newcomers—Domino Riley and Adan Rashan, who come to us from the mortal world—so allow me to explain the rules of our little game. There will be three fights—two dogs in each fight pitted against each other. All of you must place a wager on each fight, but you are, of course, free to choose the beast on which to place your bet. You may not place a wager smaller than the last bet on your chosen beast. The order of betting will be determined randomly. Each fight will continue until one dog is unwilling or unable to continue. At that point, all wagers will be settled and the winners will be paid by the losers in proportion to their original bet. The house takes any remainder. If there is anyone here who does not understand these rules, let him speak now."

It was a clever betting scheme. There were no odds, but the rule that your bet must equal or exceed the one that came before it created an incentive to bet on the weaker dog since betting on the favorite would quickly escalate.

"How are the bets placed and the winnings recovered?" I asked. I didn't really want to draw attention to us, but the spirits were all eyeballing us anyway and the only stupid question is the one you don't ask.

"That shall be demonstrated shortly," La Calavera said, and everyone laughed. Everyone except Adan and me. "I will allow your names to be placed aside and drawn last for the first fight, so that you may see how the others wager."

Given that the betting was going to escalate, betting last wasn't an advantage—just the opposite. "You are kind, La

Calavera," I said, "but that won't be necessary. If one of us is chosen first, just tell us what to do."

La Calavera inclined her head. "As you wish. If there are no further questions, let us begin."

The dogmen—both of them ghosts—went to the cages and looped heavy silver chains over the necks of the first two fighters. The Xolos were dragged to the pit and thrown inside, restrained by the dogmen behind the scratch lines carved into the stone. The Xolo on the left was the one that had been lying on its side in the cage. When its handler lifted it and dropped it into the pit, it collapsed again. The other Xolo strained against the chain around its throat, baring its teeth and growling.

"Jesus Christ," I whispered to Adan, "I'm not sure I can do this."

"We have to," Adan said, squeezing my hand. "If we're going to help them, we have to get through this."

"How about we kill all these motherfuckers instead?"

"Then we'll probably die, and even if we don't we'll never find the other Xolos. There are only six of them here."

"Okay, but promise me I can kill them later."

"Promise," Adan said. "I'll help."

Another ghost brought a golden bowl to La Calavera. She reached inside and drew out a small, white card. "The first to wager is Valafar," she said.

A remarkably fat, middle-age man in a charcoal suit and lionskin cloak stood and waddled over to the pit. The other spirits groaned. The pelt taken from the lion's head and mane draped over the man's shoulders, and golden fur cascaded down to his ankles. Other than the cloak and his substantial girth, I couldn't see anything particularly unusual about him. Then he turned to the spectators and smiled.

His eyes were on fire and a serpentine tongue licked out between yellow, jagged fangs.

Valafar stepped into the pit and walked over to the Xolo that was straining against its chain. He knelt awkwardly as only a truly fat man can and grasped the chain around the dog's neck in both hands. Then he leaned in and bared his throat to it. The Xolo snarled and savaged him, shaking its head from side to side and spattering the stone with black juice. The man craned his neck and watched me, still smiling, as the Xolo consumed him.

It went on for quite a while. Finally, Valafar tore his throat away from the dog and wiped the spatters of black magic from his cloak and suit, licking it from his fingers with his forked tongue. Then he struggled to his feet and returned to his seat, still smiling. The flesh of his throat was whole again, but I could see he was diminished even without using the sight. He'd placed a big bet.

The betting continued and I realized it was a perversion of the Xolos' sacred gift, the ability to tear the divine spark from an earthly vessel whose time had come to move on. This was why La Calavera needed Xolos for the fights. Other creatures, like the barghests, could chew on you all day and they'd never be able to take that part of you into themselves, to hold it and keep it safe. Only the Xolos could do that. La Calavera had used that and made it an abomination. It was something only a truly evil mind could conceive.

Mine was the seventh name to be called. All of the betting had so far gone to the same Xolo, the one that was as close to a sure thing as you could probably get. The wagers had escalated quickly, but I could see why the other players would prefer to risk a large bet on a heavy favorite. Maybe I didn't want to play that big or maybe I just have a thing about the underdog, but I put my juice on the nearly catatonic Xolo. I knelt beside him, stroked his sides and scratched behind his ears. He flinched the first time I touched him and then lay still.

He didn't stir when I leaned in and showed him my throat. I heard a scattering of laughter from the spirits in the stands. I bent down until my lips were next to his ear. "We both have to do this, puppy," I whispered. "We have to get through this, we have to stay alive, and then very soon I will make it better. I don't know if you can understand me, baby, but I promise this to you."

I heard a soft whine and felt a tongue on my face. My vision blurred, though I didn't have any tears in the Between. "Do it, puppy," I said. "You won't hurt me." And it was true. It didn't hurt. The Xolo was gentle and he lacked the strength to take very much. When it was over, I kept petting him for a few moments. He didn't feel like a dog— touching him was like touching warm sunshine. "Stay alive, puppy," I whispered. "Remember what I said. Just stay alive."

I returned to my seat in a daze and shut down my mind for a while. I was aware enough to hear the sounds the Xolos made when they hurt each other. I knew when it was over and my dog lost. It didn't take very long. The players weren't happy with the meager sport, and I heard their curses. I knew what was happening when the winners went down to claim their take from my Xolo. They did it just as the dogs had taken the bets from us, only with far more cruelty. I remember thanking a God I didn't really believe in that I hadn't won.

I'd done a lot of bad things in my life. I wasn't an innocent. I didn't dwell on it, I didn't cry about it, but I knew there was evil inside me. Maybe it had always been there or maybe I'd had a choice somewhere along the line and I'd done it to myself. It didn't matter—it was there all the same. I'd thought I could give my life some meaning, some purpose, by turning that darkness against a darkness greater still. I couldn't change what I was but I could be the lesser of two evils. I could be the devil you know.

But here's the thing about doing battle against the forces of evil. It's not always a clean fight against a cackling villain or fanged horror. Sometimes fighting the darkness means you have to get all the way down in it, and it clings to you like tar, it stains you, and it never goes away. There might be a reckoning later. You might exact some measure of justice. But once you go down into that pit, you leave a little bit of yourself there and you bring some of the pit back out with you. I could live for six thousand years, just like my boss, and I knew I'd never be able to forget what I saw that night.

Adan and I both placed our bets carefully and we managed to go oh-for-three on the night. When the games were finished, there was more champagne and casual mingling. I fed on my hate, and the spirits took the light in my eyes and the evil smile on my face for enjoyment. They consoled me on my losses and congratulated me on always playing the long shot. They said I had style.

The players were beginning to depart when La Calavera came to us. "How did you enjoy the evening's sport?" she said.

The fire inside me flared and my smile sharpened. "I can honestly say I've never experienced anything like it," I said.

"It was...inspiring," said Adan.

La Calavera threw back her head and laughed. "It does have that effect, doesn't it? I suspect the mortals will sleep uneasily tonight and they'll suffer worse than nightmares if some of our players manage to break through to the other side."

"When will you hold the next one?" I asked. "And is it always the same six dogs?" I tried to sound more eager than curious.

"Three nights hence," said La Calavera. "And no, my kennels have become quite substantial. We have about a hundred beasts in all. The training is quite arduous, you understand, and attrition is high once the beasts are ready to campaign. Still, our stock should be sufficient for quite some time. And, after that, we shall simply have to think of something else."

"Kennels for a hundred dogs? I didn't see anything like that around here."

"Not here, no, but rather close. The kennels are at my estate. You must come and visit sometime, it's quite spectacular. It was Jayne Mansfield's home in Beverly Hills."

The Pink Palace had been torn down years ago in my world, but the Mocambo club was proof enough that didn't mean much in the Between. I knew exactly where it would be. "I'd love to visit," I said, "very soon."

"Splendid! There's no need for formalities—drop by anytime."

"It's a promise."

"I'll bid you good night, then," she said, and kissed me on both cheeks. I was sure I felt the scrape of bone against my skin. She walked us to the door of the pit room, where two ghosts met us and escorted us from the empty club.

A Xolo's howl filled the night as Adan and I walked across Sunset Boulevard into the mist.

ten

"I've never wanted to kill anyone as bad as I want to kill her," I said when we were back in my condo. "I mean, I'm willing to make it a cause. I'm ready to dedicate my life to doing that evil bitch."

Adan went into the kitchen and came out taking a long pull from a bottle of tequila. He passed it to me and then looked at his hand. It was shaking. "I want in," he said. "I was ready to give it a shot when she told us where the dogs were."

"I'm glad I didn't know what you were thinking. It would have been enough to push me over the edge. She had too much security and that fat, snaggletoothed creep Valafar was still hanging around. It's better if we come up with a plan and make it count. We get the dogs out first, then we go back and make things personal with La Calavera."

I called Lowell and Chavez and brought them up to speed. I told Chavez to brief Oberon, but to hold off with the other outfits. I was pretty sure La Calavera had informants on our side of the wall and I didn't want anyone cluing her in that we weren't going to be BFFs.

"What's going on?" Honey said. She flew in from the

Enchanted Forest with Jack at her side. "Did you find the dogs?"

I looked at Adan. We didn't exchange any words, but I knew we'd never tell anyone about what we'd seen that night. What we'd done. "We found them, Honey. We're going to need your help to get them out of there. You, too, Jack, if you're up to it."

"He's up to it," Honey said, and giggled. "He recovers fast."

I smiled. "That's good, Jack. You were the fucking man in that fight."

He inclined his head. "A wee fighter takes a big beating," he said. "You get used to it."

We all shared a laugh at that. I brought shot glasses from the kitchen and Honey fetched weed from the balcony. We drank and smoked and talked about nothing in particular, and we forgot about the darkness outside our doors for a while. We made a racket and must have sounded like we were having a pretty good time, because some of Honey's sisters even came out and joined us. I noticed Honey kept them well away from Jack. I didn't blame her—you never want to share the good ones.

By the time we were finished we were all pretty well loaded. I was going to need Alka-Seltzer and a purification spell if I expected to kick any ass in the morning. The sisters had buzzed unsteadily back to the Enchanted Forest, and my friends and I sat quietly together on the sofa, lost in our private thoughts. "Let's get some sleep," I said finally. "We do this tomorrow. Honey, Jack, I can't know all the battles you've fought. But for my part, this is going to be the most important thing I've ever done. It matters to me."

Honey looked like she wanted to ask me something, but she just nodded. "Then it matters to us, Domino." Jack touched his hand to his heart and nodded once. Then the piskies flew away and left me with Adan.

"I guess we've got the couch again," I said. "Mrs. Dawson's going to be camped out in my bedroom for a while."

"I like your couch," Adan said. He reached across the distance between us and brushed a lock of hair from my face. "Tomorrow will be a better day, Domino. Take hold of that and don't let her into your dreams." Then he smiled at me and stretched out on his end of the sofa, turning onto his side and tucking a throw pillow under his head.

I tried to do as he said. It didn't work.

When I woke up the next morning, Honey and Jack had built a scale replica of the Pink Palace on the table in the dining nook. The Mediterranean villa sat on more than three acres of prime real estate in Beverly Hills. The house and the brick and stucco walls surrounding the estate had been painted a soft pink mixed with powdered sandstone. That had been Mansfield's touch—she and her new husband had given it the nontraditional paint job when they bought the place in the late fifties. Long after it had been demolished in the real world, this seemed to be how the shadow world remembered it, and the Pink Palace it remained.

"You did some recon," I said when Honey and Jack flitted into the room.

"Yeah," said Honey, "we were bored. You and Adan were still sleeping, and we figured this would help us make a plan."

"It's great," I said, circling the table and studying the model. "Nice work."

"You should see the inside," Honey said. "Her bathroom has wall-to-wall and floor-to-ceiling pink shag carpet!"

"Truly evil," I said. "These are the kennels?" There was

a kind of shantytown built of scrap wood and corrugated metal sheeting along the back wall of the estate.

"Yeah," Honey said. "The place is a warren. They just kept adding on when the ghost-hunter brought in new dogs. There are at least a hundred of them there."

"And you were able to get inside? No problems with wards or anything?"

"There are no wards," Jack said. "The place doesn't need wards. It's evil. It hurts to be there, and not just because of all the pink."

"We'll need to do this fast, Domino," Honey said. "We'll be weak there. If we stay too long, it would probably kill us."

"Let's do it. Where's Adan?"

"He went home to change clothes," Honey said. "And anyway, we can't go during the day."

"Why not?"

"Vampires," Jack said. "She uses them as security. We saw two of them on the grounds and one in the house. There are worse things there, too—La Calavera and her ilk. At night, the vampires will be gone and most of the spirits will be at the club." Vampires were active in the real world at night and in the Between during the day. They were tougher in the shadow world and it would be best to avoid them if we could.

"So we'll only have to deal with ghosts," I said, nodding. "Okay, I guess it can wait a few more hours."

The front door opened and Adan walked in wearing black military fatigues with a sword belted at his waist. "Did you run off and join a SWAT team while I was sleeping?" I asked.

He shrugged. "It's practical. It would be easier if I could cross over like you, but I have to do it the sidhe way. Did they tell you about the vampires?" he said, nodding at the Pink Palace.

"Yeah, so we're going tonight. There's no dogfight, so all the Xolos should still be in the kennels."

Adan nodded. "How do we get the dogs out?"

"I haven't really thought about it. According to Caesar, the Xolos can cross to the Between and back at will. I figure if we let them out of their cages they'll hightail it out of there."

"Maybe, but something is holding them. They don't try to escape. They don't try to leave the dogfighting ring. Some of them probably aren't in very good shape. It might not be as simple as just opening the cages."

"Well, what's holding them, then? It doesn't do much good to poke holes in my plan unless you have a better idea." Right about then, my cell phone beeped. I had a text message.

the elegant skull turns the center
a dead stone in the city of smoke
cages of old sorrow and torn memory
death's lightness bound in brittle spite

"What is it?" Adan asked when I finished reading.

"Someone's telling me we need to clip La Calavera," I said. "She's holding them there, somehow. It doesn't really matter how—if we take her out, we'll be able to free the Xolos. So we hit the place after dark, when the vampires are on this side, but before La Calavera heads out for a night on the town."

"Who sent the text?" Honey asked.

I checked the call log but the number was listed as "Unknown."

"Could be three Pakistani women in federal custody," I said. "Could be Hecate."

"The goddess?"

"That's what the Feds call her."

"A goddess is sending you text messages?"

"I don't know it's a goddess. It's like a signal in the ectoplasmic flow."

"That doesn't make any sense, Domino," Honey said. "What the hell is an ectoplasmic flow?"

"Magic. It's what the government nerds call magic. Look, it's hard to explain. I don't know what Hecate is. I don't know why it's sending me text messages."

"But whatever it is, it's telling you to kill La Calavera, so that's what you're going to do."

"It's not telling me that, exactly. 'The elegant skull turns the center.'"

"It's gibberish," Honey said.

"Yeah, that's what I thought at first, too. But it was right about the Xolos."

"It told you about the Xolos?"

"Sort of. 'Claimant and messenger, lost. Stone circle, grasping the harmonic motion.' Hey, the stone circle bit could be talking about the dogfighting pit."

"What's a harmonic motion?"

"I don't remember. Something about a pendulum, maybe."

"It's gibberish, Domino!"

"What about 'death's lightness bound in brittle spite'?" I said. "It's clearly talking about the Xolos and how La Calavera has them bound in her...brittle spite."

Honey arched an eyebrow and looked at me.

Adan spoke up. "Even if we can't be sure about the reliability of the intelligence," he said, "it's still not a bad plan.

Maybe killing La Calavera won't free the Xolos, but freeing them will be easier with her out of the way."

"Yeah," I said, looking at the cell phone screen. "She's a 'dead stone in the city of smoke.'"

"That could be a reference to the Pink Palace," Adan said, looking over my shoulder. "Or it could be talking about the dogfighting pits again."

"Why is it mortal sorcerers are always so eager to swallow anything some old spirit dishes up?" Honey said.

"They're gullible," Jack said, and shrugged.

I looked at them and scowled. "Spirits aren't *always* lying, Honey," I said. It was mean, but I was losing patience with all the second-guessing.

"Only when our lips are moving," said Jack, grinning. She probably hadn't told him about our history. Not all of it, anyway. Not the part about how she'd lied to me, betrayed me, to protect her family.

"Some spirits are your friends, Dòmino," Honey said softly. "You don't even know what this one is or what it wants."

Now she was going to guilt-trip me. I probably had it coming. I smiled at her and nodded. "I'm not going to trust this Hecate—or whatever it is—like I trust my friends. Maybe it's playing an angle. It makes sense to hit La Calavera either way."

"It's like déjà vu, Domino," Honey said. "This spirit may not be that easy to kill. And you still can't fight worth a damn in the Between."

"Thanks," I said. "But this time we've got Adan and Jack backing us up."

"How do you want to do it?" Adan said, walking over to the Pink Palace.

"The gangster way," I said. "We're not going to assault

the castle, Adan. You want to hit a guy, you wait until he comes out and you gun him down on his front porch or in the street." Actually, nine times out of ten when you clipped a guy it was someone you knew, probably someone in your own outfit. Getting close wasn't a problem. This wasn't that kind of situation. I pointed to the front wall of the estate where the private driveway opened onto the street. "I think we wait for her here, at the gate. There are no cars, so she'll come out on foot when she goes to the club."

Adan nodded. "Like the vodyanoy. I like this terrain better. More places to hide."

"And no ocean to worry about," I said. "We just have to put her down before she can get into the mist."

"All this scheming and plotting and ambushing," Jack said. "It reminds me of Avalon."

"Yeah, well, I'm not a knight in shining armor, Jack. I'm a gangster."

The piskie shook his head. "That is only a choice. To fight with honor—that is also a choice."

"Weren't you an assassin, Jack? Seems like you wouldn't have any objection to a nice ambush."

Jack shrugged. "Sometimes assassination is the right choice."

"Exactly. My choice is whichever way is most likely to end up with La Calavera dead. Honor isn't going to set the Xolos free."

Jack just shrugged again, having apparently run out of words, but Adan picked up the argument. "Are you sure, Domino?" he said. "The Between isn't Arcadia. La Calavera's evil binds the Xolos to that place. We don't know exactly how. It may be necessary to defeat that evil, to challenge it, confront it, and ultimately to overcome it, in order to free the Xolos. Ambushing the spirit at the front gate may not break that evil spell—it may only feed it."

"So what am I supposed to do exactly? Call her out for a showdown at high noon on Sunset Boulevard?"

"No, we should still wait for sundown," Honey said. "If the fight doesn't go her way, she'll double-cross us. We can handle the minions, but we may as well wait until the vampires have returned to the mortal world."

"Honey, the last time this came up you tried to talk me out of fighting a spirit. You said I'd probably get my ass kicked."

"This is important, Domino. That time, you were just trying to protect Adan and I didn't think he was worth it."

"Hey…" said Adan.

"It wasn't really you, Adan," Honey said. "The changeling was a loser."

"Thanks, I think."

"I just think Jack's right about this, Domino," the piskie continued. "In Avalon or in the Between, fighting isn't just about violence. It has power. Think of it as a ritual. You can't just skip ahead to the last step. You have to do it right. Maybe that's what this Hecate is trying to tell you."

I knew the truth when I heard it and I wasn't afraid to face La Calavera. I was afraid I'd fail. Nothing much had changed since Honey had tried to train me in the kung-fu magic at the L.A. Coliseum in the Between. I still sucked at it. How would it help the Xolos if I called out La Calavera and she put the beat-down on me?

"If we have to go mano a mano," I said, "why does it have to be in the Between? I can summon her into this world and wipe the floor with her."

"For the same reason we can't just bushwhack her,

Domino," Honey said. "You have to defeat her in her place of power to free the Xolos."

"I'd like to have some time alone with whoever came up with these stupid rules."

"It doesn't have to be you, Domino," Adan said. "I'll do it."

It was almost startling to discover it didn't piss me off. I knew why he was offering. I knew he wasn't challenging me. "That would probably be the smart thing to do," I said, "but it has to be me. I'm the wartime captain, Adan. I'm Rashan's champion. I can't keep the title if I can't do the work."

"She's right, though," Honey told Adan, "she's a really bad fighter without her spells."

Adan looked at me and nodded. "That's okay," he said. "I was, too, at first. We've got all day to work on it. You'll be ready, Domino."

We all make a lot of choices in life. Most of the time we can't see with perfect clarity where those choices will lead. It's only with hindsight that we can look back and judge the wisdom—or lack thereof—of the decisions we made. We choose that path less taken and when we find ourselves all alone in the middle of the woods at night, only then do we ask, "What the fuck was I thinking?"

On rare occasions, though, we make choices that are so foolish it's obvious even in the heat of the moment. We make them anyway because we seem to have eliminated all the options. I didn't believe in fate. I didn't believe in some magic in history that pushes us along in some preordained direction. But every now and then you really had to wonder. I couldn't figure out exactly how we'd gone from "free the Xolos" to "kill La Calavera" to "one-on-one, toe-to-toe honor duel with La Calavera at the front gates of the Pink Palace."

Gangsters don't do honor duels. We have fairly elaborate rules in place to make them unnecessary. You follow the rules, you don't have to worry too much about getting clipped—unless someone else decides to break the rules. And if you do break the rules you don't feel entitled to any honor duel. If you've earned it, you might get enough time to put on your best suit and there might be a pleasant car ride out into the desert, but that's about it. Mostly, you're just hoping they send a professional and the work will get done fast and clean.

There was a kind of logic to what I was doing and it was even a kind of logic I was familiar with. It wasn't the logic of the ordinary world—it was the logic of magic. With sorcery, actions had little significance in themselves. There was no magic in the quotations I used for spellcasting; there was no magic in the web surfing I did for divination magic. The magic—the significance—was behind and beneath those actions. The magic was in the symbolism. Honey had it right when she said I had to see the showdown with La Calavera as a ritual. The act of killing the spirit was just a symbol, and for that symbol to have magic I had to do it right.

The true goal wasn't just to kill La Calavera. It was to break her power. And that's why I was standing alone at the front gate of the Pink Palace just after sundown with only Ned at my side to give me comfort. I knew why I was there. I knew what I had to do. Maybe it was fate. Or maybe that was just a word for actions noble, necessary and really fucking stupid.

"I've got a bad feeling about this," I muttered. Then I tilted my head back, cupped my hands around my mouth and shouted into the cerulean darkness. "La Calavera

Catrina," I yelled, "I'm calling you out!" I couldn't cast spells in the Between but I put some juice into it, just as I had that first time I called Honey.

Then I waited. Being the glass-half-empty type, I'd given some thought to what I'd do if she simply ignored me. I couldn't say I'd come up with anything that really broke new ground, but I had some good insults at the ready if it came to that.

Fortunately, La Calavera was ready to play. With a ghostly creaking, the gates began to open of their own accord and I saw her walking alone down the winding, wood-lined driveway. The dress was black and white vertical stripes this time and the hat was smaller, more of a derby, with a wide silver band. She glided, swaying, and she reminded me of a lioness moving nonchalantly toward the antelope at the edge of the herd.

She stopped and cocked a hip like she'd reached the end of the runway at a fashion show. "This is rather a surprise, Domino," she said. "The usual custom is for my callers to ring the doorbell."

"This isn't a social call," I said.

"What, then? I'm afraid you've caught me at an inconvenient time. I'm to entertain at the club this evening."

"I need you to free the Xolos. You could do it as a favor to me, if you're so inclined. If not, I'm here to make you do it."

La Calavera laughed. "You're not particularly skilled at asking favors."

"I'm not asking. But you could look at it that way, if it makes it easier for you."

"Why would I want to free the Xolos? Really, you've no idea the trouble I went through to acquire them."

"They don't belong here, La Calavera, and they're needed

on my side. The dead walk in their absence. You might have noticed that if you weren't so self-absorbed."

She brought a finger clad in black silk to her lips and considered it. "The dead walking sounds splendid, but I take it you find this somewhat objectionable. Perhaps we can arrange a trade."

"Right," I said. "You give up the dogs. Or I take your life and then I take the dogs. That's the deal."

The spirit gave me a brief glimpse of the full *calavera*, probably to make the point that her patience was limited. "Your negotiating skills are somewhat rusty as well, dear."

"So what's it going to be?" I let my hand fall to Ned's walnut grip. I guess I was giving *her* the full *calavera*.

"Hmm. The dogs or my life," she said. "Here is my counterproposal. When you beg me to kill you, I'm going to throw what's left of you in the pit with the worst of my Xolos, the ones so maddened by pain and blood they—"

In one swift motion, I drew Ned and shot La Calavera right between her black-rimmed eyes. A ragged hole opened in her phantasmal flesh and blue fire licked at the edges. A trickle of black juice ran down the bridge of her nose and onto her flawless, pale cheek. She wiped at it and then studied her finger. The juice pulsed against the silk, black on black. She put the finger between her lips and sucked it clean. La Calavera shuddered. Then she smiled.

The flesh melted from her face and body in an instant. Her fashionable clothes aged decades before my eyes, falling to rags and dusty tatters as I watched. She raised a hand and pointed at me, and bony claws extended from the ragged fabric of her gloves. A chill wind blew up from nowhere and I felt a touch, light and cold as the Beyond, on my cheek. I looked up and saw motes of blue-lit ice falling from the darkening sky like manna. It was snowing.

"My turn, bitch," the spirit said.

The force magic hit me full in the face and knocked me across the street and into the pole of a streetlight that didn't seem to have much of a purpose in the Between. The impact sheered the pole in two and it crashed into the street, spitting sparks that periodically cast a hard, white edge on the battle. I kept going, into the high stone wall partially concealed in the trees and shrubbery that lined the boulevard. The masonry crumbled when I hit it and I was swallowed up in a cloud of fine, choking dust.

I came out of the dust cloud with Ned leveled at La Calavera, my other hand fanning the hammer. The spirit moved so fast it left a ghostly afterimage in her wake and my fusillade burned away uselessly into the night. La Calavera had moved to the edge of the driveway, by the gate, and the metal shrieked as she tore a wickedly spiked, wrought-iron bar from it. I had time to notice it was pink before the spirit turned in a fluid motion and hurled it at me.

I caught the deadly missile in my off hand and let the momentum spin me in a tight circle. As I came out of the spin, I twirled the spear around so the business end was pointing the right direction, and then I chucked it back at La Calavera. It struck her in the chest and pinned her to the brick pillar supporting the gate. You might think a skull wouldn't have the goods to look surprised, but you'd be wrong. La Calavera looked down at the pink spike impaling her and her lower jaw dropped open. She looked back at me and cocked her namesake to the side.

"You missed the training montage," I said. Then I leaped across the street, tore the spike out of her chest and slammed it home again. Black juice bubbled from the skeletal grin and ran down the bony chin onto her ruined dress.

The spirit laughed, her desiccated jaws and black-stained

teeth rattling with the effort. She grabbed me by the ears and head butted me, and I felt the impact shatter my nose. She brought up a knobby knee and kicked me in the groin, and then the force magic pummeled me again and I tumbled into the street. I rolled to my feet and watched as she jerked and lurched forward, wrenching her body off the spike that impaled her. When she was free, she stepped into the street and turned to face me. Black juice flowed freely from her mouth and chest. It sizzled and smoked when it struck the snow-covered pavement.

I have to admit, I was expecting her to take advantage of the break in the action and serve up a nice villainous mono-logue. Instead, she shrieked and launched herself at me. I got Ned up and fired a shot that tore away the side of her skull, but she kept coming. She tackled me and we went rolling across the asphalt. She came out on top. She grabbed two fistfuls of my hair and slammed the back of my head into the street. Then she leaped straight up and hung in midair for a second, her hand drawn back and contorted in some kind of kung-fu death claw. I saw black flames licking along the edges of her bony fingers.

When she came down, I wasn't there. I did a smooth little backflip and launched myself through the air, landing in a crouch by the downed streetlight. I picked it up and swung it in a full circle before hurling it at her. There was a resounding *gong* when the streetlight smashed into her. It carried her through the open gate and slammed her into a tree that spread its naked branches over the driveway. I grinned and went after her.

This, it turned out, was a mistake. As soon as I crossed the threshold, I felt the strength drain out of me. It hap-pened all at once, like I'd been running on borrowed fuel and the marker had suddenly come due. I sank to one knee and gasped; I didn't breathe in that airless world, but I struggled to draw some strength back into my leaden arms and legs.

Whatever power I'd lost, it seemed to flow into La Calavera. Her broken body straightened and she rose to her feet. She picked up the streetlight and lifted it above her head, and then swung it downward like a club. I tried to summon the will to move—and will, I had finally learned, was all I really needed in this place. But I was too slow. The streetlight came down on my back and a spiderweb of cracks blossomed in the asphalt as I was hammered flat into the driveway.

I heard a sharp crack and turned my head enough to see La Calavera walking toward me with a splintered branch she'd torn from the tree. She raised it above me and drove it through the wrist of my gun hand, pinning it to the ground. My fingers spasmed and she kicked Ned away.

"Are you ready now, dear?" the spirit said. "Beg for your death and I will show mercy. I will throw you to the dogs."

If I'd been in better shape, I might have challenged her peculiar understanding of mercy. Instead, I clenched my twitching fingers and then extended the middle one vaguely in her direction. La Calavera laughed and straddled me, sitting on my back. She grabbed my hair and pulled my head back toward her.

"Have you guessed how I will finish you?" she said. "How I will take your power and make it my own? It's not so different from what happens in the pit." She leaned down and ground her teeth together next to my ear. It sounded like old stone crunching underfoot. "This is how we do it on the other side of death." Then her teeth tore into the side of my face. She ground them together, chewing, gnawing, and pulled a large chunk of flesh free with a savage twist of her neck.

"Oh, no, you didn't," I said, spitting the words through teeth clenched against my pain and revulsion. I reached across my body with my free hand and snapped the branch that impaled my other wrist. I twisted under her and grabbed the spirit in a headlock, knocking her hat loose, and then I drove the sharp, splintered wood underhand into La Calavera's mouth. The point burst through the back of her skull, dripping black juice. I twisted it, pulled it out and shanked her again.

The flesh-eating zombie bitch still didn't die. She grabbed the end of the stake and wrenched it from my grip, pulling it out the back of her own head. Then her body disintegrated, collapsing into a squirming heap of plump, white maggots. I jumped back and brushed a few of the disgusting creatures from my clothes and hair. The maggots churned and a form began to take shape from the wriggling mass, growing and solidifying. Then La Calavera was standing there again. She bent down and retrieved her hat, placing it at a jaunty angle on the remains of her skull. Snowflakes fell and stuck to the black magic that drenched her face and chest, and they winked like glittering diamonds from the ruin.

The spirit clenched her hands into gnarled claws and I saw the black fire dance along her fingers again. "You cannot defeat me here," she said. "I will kill you now."

She shrieked and launched herself at me, and I let her come. I extended my hand to the Peacemaker lying at the edge of the driveway. "Ned," I called, and it leaped into the air, tumbling end over end until the smooth, polished grip settled in my palm. La Calavera crashed into me and I enfolded her in an intimate embrace. I felt her bony hands around my throat and the black fire searing my flesh.

I thrust Ned's twelve-inch barrel into her chest and it tore through shattered ribs and gristle until it reached the black pit at the center of her. I held the trigger down and thumbed the hammer, firing again and again as her skeletal body jerked and twisted in my grasp. She raised her face to the sky and screamed, and azure fire burst from her eye sockets, nose and mouth.

Ghosts answered her call. They drifted out of the trees, silent and murderous, and came for me with grasping hands and empty eyes.

"That's game," I said. "I win."

Honey and Jack spiraled down from the darkness, and the pixie dust they dropped on the ghosts was nearly invisible amidst the falling snow. When it touched them, the apparitions hardened and cracked like old china and crumbled to dust. Adan appeared at the gate with his rifle slung over his shoulder and his sword drawn, and he charged to engage the ghosts that made it through the piskies' blanket of destruction.

I leaned in close to La Calavera. "No one," I said, and pushed Ned's barrel up under her jaw. "Tries." I squeezed the trigger and the top of her skull exploded. "To eat." I threw her to the ground and jammed the gun between her grinning teeth. "Me." I fanned the hammer and let Ned kick and dance inside her mouth until the skull began to dissolve into black juice. I pumped a couple more rounds into the center of her torso and it, too, ran liquid, collapsing into a bubbling pool that spread slowly across the asphalt.

A high-pitched, keening wail tore through the stillness and then faded like a bad memory. With it went the feeling of oppression that had weighed on me since I crossed the threshold on La Calavera's estate. The wind died, the snow stopped falling and the night seemed to brighten to a lighter shade of blue.

I regrouped with Adan and the piskies, and we walked up the driveway toward the house. We followed a stone-tile walkway around the side and down a set of wide stairs to the patio that spread out behind the house. The heart-shaped swimming pool was choked with detritus and stagnant water, and we skirted it to the lightly wooded lawns at the rear of the estate.

The ramshackle kennels were lit from within by the soft, golden radiance of the Xolos. As we approached, I realized we wouldn't have to open the cages to free the dogs. One by one, the lights winked out as the Xolos crossed back to the mortal world. My friends had been right. It was La Calavera that held them there, not the pens or the pit.

Still, not all of the Xolos made it back across. The piskies flew through the warren of crates and cages, checking each one and counting the dead. There were seventeen of them. With their lights snuffed out, the dead looked no different from any other dog of their breed. We couldn't think of anything else to do so we laid them out on the grass and dug graves for them. We buried them one by one. This was the spirit world and I wasn't sure how much sense it made to return them to earth that wasn't even real. But for the Xolos, perhaps it was fitting. The Xolo that had fought for me in the back room of the Mocambo club wasn't among the dead. My Xolo had survived, and he came to me and licked my hand before crossing back to the mortal world.

Our work complete, we turned and walked back across the lawn toward the house. Without warning, a deafening roar crashed over us and a jagged line like cracked glass appeared in the air before our eyes. Hateful, red light spilled through the crack and waves of heat washed over us as it widened. Writhing tentacles curled around the edges of the crack and a dark, bulbous shape began to pull itself through from the other side.

"Demon," Adan snarled, drawing his sword. I glanced at Adan and back at the gate. The thing that squeezed through the fracture looked more like an oversize octopus crossed with a hairy black spider than the almost human-looking giant we'd battled at the Carnival Club. Apparently, demons came in all shapes and sizes.

The massive, swollen thing oozed through the crack and plopped wetly into the grass, spider legs twitching and tentacles waving madly. Its maw looked more arachnid than cephalopod, with razor-sharp mandibles that clicked and scraped like fingernails on slate. Pearlescent slime dripped from the evil fangs, and the grass wilted and browned where it struck the lawn. The demon sat back on its bloated hindquarters and a fleshy slit opened the length of its abdomen baring row upon row of small, pointed teeth. Okay, so maybe that was its mouth and the bit with the mandibles was...some other disgusting part of its anatomy.

Honey's musical voice brought me back to my senses as she began singing battle glamours. I opened fire with Ned and scrambled to my right, maneuvering along the demon's flank. Jack dived, twisting in and out of the writhing tentacles like a jet fighter with a bogey on his six. Adan ran at the thing and then leaped in the air, flipping over the grasping tentacles and landing on its back. He slammed his sword two-handed into one of the demon's eyes, and red-orange juice like lava boiled from the wound. The monster screamed and a tentacle snaked in and lashed around Adan's neck. It lifted him into the air and he hung there for a moment, strangling, as he slashed at the tentacle with his sword. Then the demon flicked the tentacle and hurled

Adan through the night to smash into the back wall of the house.

Honey's glamour attacked the monster with cold and ice. Frost appeared on one side of its misshapen head and began to spread. Icicles formed on its mandibles and jaws where the fluids froze solid. The demon screamed and flailed with its spider legs where the cold touched its flesh.

I kept firing and looked for some weakness in the monster's defenses, some vulnerability in its hideous form. I fired again and again, and sapphire flames curled from the holes Ned tore in the demon's hide. Tentacles darted and slashed at me, and it took everything I'd learned from Adan that day to stay clear of them. I leaped and spun in a deadly dance, rolling under tentacles that sliced at my head, and vaulting gracefully over those that grasped at my legs. I kept firing as I jumped and ducked, bobbed and weaved, zigged and zagged.

Until I zigged when I should have zagged. The demon feinted at my head with a tentacle, and I rolled forward, under it, and impaled myself on the spiked talon that extended from one of its spider legs. The barb struck me just below the sternum and I felt it tear through me and out my back. I could feel the coarse hairs, like steel wool, scraping my insides as the leg twisted and twitched.

A dark curtain fell across my eyes and I sank to my knees. Another spider leg shot out and pierced my shoulder, and another lanced into my stomach. I tried to scream but I was choking on my own juice. I coughed and the azure magic sprayed across the grass, glowing faintly in the monochrome gloom. I tried to lift Ned but my arm wouldn't move. A tentacle slowly twined around my hips and another around my neck. They tightened and started to pull, and I felt my body stretch like the saltwater taffy I used to get on the

Santa Monica Pier when I was a girl. It was far more than my flesh could withstand in the mortal world. The torment was like nothing the human mind was meant to endure.

Then Adan was at my side. He slashed at the tentacles and the severed ends fell twitching into the grass. He sliced through the legs that pierced me and stood between me and the demon when I collapsed to the ground. His sword was a silver blur as the pain-maddened monster attacked, and soon the lawn was littered with bits of demon flesh and slick with the black ichor that oozed from its wounds.

As skilled as he was with the sword, Adan couldn't protect both of us at the same time. He was impaled again and again by the demon's spiked talons; tentacles hammered into him and tore at his body. But he was faster than the monster. Each time it hurt him, Adan hurt it worse. The sword spun in his hands and he pressed forward, one step at a time. He butchered the demon as he advanced, slicing through tentacles and severing legs.

For a moment, I thought the monster would run out of appendages before Adan had a chance to finish it off. That's when I noticed the severed stumps were regenerating. I struggled to a sitting position, and my vision dimmed and then steadied. "Adan," I croaked. "It's healing."

I don't know if he heard me, but the piskies did. Honey had maintained her glamour and one side of the demon's head was frozen in a solid sheet of ice. Jack had been working at the other side, bursting black, bulbous eyes and slicing at exposed flesh while the demon focused its attentions on Adan and me. Now the two flew to each other and huddled together. They started singing a new song in a strange and haunting harmony that sounded like a Celtic funeral dirge. They crossed swords and emerald flames licked along the blades. The fairy fire spread up their arms and across their shoulders and chests until their whole bodies were wreathed in the ghostly flames. Jack reached over and pulled Honey to him, kissing her fiercely. Then they dove at their adversary with their burning swords held before them, streaking through the night like tiny falling stars.

When the piskies struck the demon, the explosion made the ground buckle beneath Adan and me and the shockwave knocked us both flat on our backs. A column of green fire erupted into the air and blossomed into a miniature mushroom cloud, bathing the battleground in eerie, emerald ghost-light. The fire was as warm as spring sunshine and smelled like fresh grass.

The cloud burned off and dissipated into the night, plunging the field once again into the blue-lit darkness of the Between. Nothing remained of the demon—not even bits and pieces. It had been vaporized by the blast. Jack and Honey knelt in the grass where it had been. They were kissing.

"Get a room," I muttered as I struggled to my feet.

Adan started laughing. "The Troll King's Lament," he said. "All the years I spent in Faerie, I never got to see it. I thought it was just a legend the piskies fed to buy a little insurance."

Honey and Jack broke away from each other and glared at him. "If it was just a legend," Honey said, "you and the sidhe would all be speaking Troll right now."

I limped over to them with one hand clutching my perforated abdomen and the other gripping Ned at my side. "You might have mentioned you can nuke a motherfucker," I said.

"The legends say it comes at great cost," said Adan.

"It's just juice," Jack said.

"Then why—" I started to ask, but Honey interrupted me.

"A piskie's life is just juice and we're only given so much of it," she said. "It's just juice, Domino, but we measure the cost in *years*."

I shut my mouth and let that sink in. Once it did, I wanted to cry. "Thank you," I said finally. It seemed horribly inadequate. "Please don't ever do that again."

"It is ours to give," Jack said, "and we gave it freely."

Slow applause echoed over the lawn from the direction of the house. I turned and saw Valafar standing on a balcony overlooking the patio and pool. He stopped clapping and rested his hands on the wrought-iron railing. "Most impressive," he said. He spoke softly, but I heard his voice clearly despite the distance. "Of course, that—"

He was rudely interrupted by a hail of unearthly gunfire as Adan and I let loose with our magical weapons. Ethereal lead sprayed the balcony and exploded against the wall of the house behind him. Valafar ducked and quickly retreated into the shadows. We kept shooting until we were sure he was gone. I'd been spared the villainous monologue with La Calavera—I wasn't about to sit through one with Valafar.

"He's a demon," Adan said when it was over.

"That's my guess. Motherfucker has a forked tongue—should have seen that one coming."

"That's how Mobley is commanding the Firstborn he gates in."

"Yeah, he's not commanding them at all. Valafar is."

"So what does that make Valafar?"

"A hell of a lot of trouble."

eleven

We returned to the mortal world and a city on the edge of chaos. I awoke stretched out on the sofa with several generations of Honey's family perched on my body. I rubbed my eyes, dislodging one of Honey's aunts from my forehead, and sat up. The piskies were watching the news on my plasma TV.

"The young ones are out fighting," said the aunt. I think her name was Daisy. Or maybe Petunia. I was pretty sure it was Daisy. She looked at me accusingly, as if she couldn't understand why her daughters and nieces were battling zombies while I was lying on the couch.

I looked at the TV screen. *The apocalypse will be televised.* Live video from a news helicopter followed what was clearly a pack...no, a horde...of zombies that had just broken through the gates in Victoria Park. There had to be a hundred of them and the horde stretched all the way down West Boulevard to Pico. The black metal fence that protected the gated community from the rest of Mid-City hadn't been built with marauding zombies in mind, but it had been barricaded with cars, stacked tires, backyard swing sets and other junk pulled hastily from garages and storage sheds.

A few civilians defended the makeshift wall with shot-guns, hunting rifles, handguns and lawn equipment. They started retreating down Victoria Park Drive when the horde broke through, but they didn't do it fast enough. A blood-drenched woman in a tattered hospital gown leaped at a man in a golf shirt and khaki shorts. He caved in the side of her head with an aluminum softball bat, and then she dragged him down to the street. In seconds, both vanished under the wave of zombies that crashed over them.

"Jesus Christ, we lost it," I said as Adan came into the room with Honey and Jack.

"King Oberon says there are at least a hundred thousand zombies in the city," said Aunt Daisy. I knew she was older than Honey, but she didn't look her age. She looked almost exactly like Honey. In fact, all the piskies in Honey's family looked alike, not to be insensitive about it.

"He was supposed to contain them," I said, an edge of hard bitterness in my voice I hadn't intended. "This wasn't supposed to happen." There was no audio in the coverage, but the news ticker scrolling across the bottom of the screen said BLOODY RIOTS IN LOS ANGELES. The governor had called in the National Guard and declared a state of emergency.

"My daughter says there would be more than a million already if it weren't for the Seelie Court's heroism," Aunt Daisy said.

The ticker kept scrolling. TERROR LEVEL RAISED TO RED...WATER SUPPLY SUSPECTED.

"This can still work," Adan said.

"How? There are maybe a hundred Xolos, Adan. They can move fast through the Between, sure, but they're not going to clean up a hundred thousand zombies anytime soon. In the meantime, the ones they don't get are going to be making more zombies. I kept telling people, this isn't a fucking plague and we haven't found a cure. There are already too many zombies. We're done."

"It's not just the Xolos. We also have the Seelie Court and the other outfits you called in. They've done a good job, Domino. It's been, what, five days since Terrence's nephews crawled out of their graves? Daisy is right—there could be a million zombies by now. If that had happened, we'd be a couple days away from losing the whole Southland. We still have time to contain it."

"It's on the fucking news," I said. "The Stag guys were supposed to keep it quiet."

"Five days, Domino. They weren't going to be able to suppress it forever. Not with a hundred thousand zombies running around eating people. And the news thinks it's a terrorist attack. This can be contained."

I leaned over and put my head in my hands. "I should have moved faster. Oh, fuck me, I went to a fucking *party*."

"If you hadn't gone to that party, Oberon might be sitting this one out. And then it really *would* be game over."

"A hundred thousand, Adan. And who knows how many before we get ahead of this thing—*if* we get ahead of it. A hundred thousand people. How am I supposed to wrap my head around that?" I looked up and nodded at the TV screen. "They've turned Victoria Park into a fucking all-you-can-eat buffet."

"There are more than seventeen million in the Southland," Adan said. "If you hadn't taken the actions you did, they'd all be gone in a couple days. Try to wrap your head around that, instead."

"What do we do now?" I said, staring at the images of carnage and destruction that played across the screen. "I don't know what to do. I don't want to be responsible for this."

Adan sat down on the couch beside me. Honey and Jack alighted on my shoulders. "We're already responsible for it, Domino," he said. "There's no one else. With the Seelie Court, the outfits and the Xolos on the case, we can roll it back."

I got up and walked to the French doors, threw them open and went out on the balcony. All up and down my street, families were packing up their cars and preparing to flee the city. I wondered what the streets and freeways looked like, and if any of them would make it out. Some of the houses and apartment buildings were boarded up. Were there people holed up inside or had they already left?

I suddenly understood why Chavez always had two or three cell phones within reach—I needed to talk to everybody and I didn't have much time. My first call went to Agent Lowell. I heard a series of clicks and beeps before the connection went through. I didn't know if that meant we had a secure line or if it was just the recording and monitoring equipment switching on.

"Lowell," said Lowell.

"You need to evacuate the city. You know as well as I do this isn't a fucking plague. It's the best way to slow the spread."

There was silence on the line for a moment. "We don't have any evacuation plans for something like this. There are plans for evacuation in the event of earthquakes, wildfires and tsunamis, but they're inadequate for this event. Successful evacuations depend on process, and the process doesn't fit."

"I don't buy that. You get the people out of town. It doesn't seem that difficult."

"Which areas are evacuated first? Not the coast and the areas most in danger of flooding, because that's irrelevant. So no one knows where to start. The plan doesn't apply. Where do you relocate people to? Not the safe zones designated in the plans, because they're irrelevant. So no one knows where to put the people they evacuate. The plan doesn't apply. What do you do when the rescue personnel get eaten? What do you do when you load up a bus or a helicopter and a zombie gets onboard? No one knows, because there *is* no fucking plan for that. So instead of everyone following a plan, you need top-down command and control and that's how evacuations turn into clusterfucks. On top of all that, the plans weren't developed for something on this scale. We need one hundred percent regional evacuation. We don't have anything close. We don't have the resources for it. And even if we did it would take weeks. We have days, maybe."

"So you're not even going to try? Even if you only move out a few hundred thousand people, it makes a big difference in the math. That's a few hundred thousand who won't die, and who won't be killing a handful of other people tomorrow, and the day after that. A few hundred thousand today, a million tomorrow, pretty soon you're talking real numbers."

"I know, Domino. But even though we know it's not a plague, the decision-makers are worried about controlling panic and disruption in other cities. A half-assed evacuation would be bad optics at a national level."

"Fucking *optics?* What the hell does that mean, Lowell? You convince everyone it's just a Los Angeles problem, the rest of the country can still go shopping?"

"Something like that," Lowell said. "I didn't make the decision, Domino. And the few of us who know what's really going on, we can't *prove* this thing won't spread. We can't even fully disclose what's causing it—not outside our little community of freaks. We'd be discredited and lose what little influence we have now."

"So the people calling the shots don't even really know what's happening?"

"That's right, Domino, they aren't aware Los Angeles is being overrun by zombies because some ghost abducted all the psychopomps so a creep called La Calavera could run a supernatural dogfighting ring in the spirit world. Maybe you'd like to come to D.C. and testify before a Congressional hearing. Just don't mention my name."

"How much of it do the networks have?"

"Not much. Stag has put some juice into it. There have been urban legends about LSD in the water supply since the fifties, so we have plenty to work with. Speculation is more unconventional on the internet and blogosphere, of course. There are real zombies giving a play-by-play on Twitter."

"Jesus Christ, okay, I'm hearing a hundred thousand. Does that match what you've got?"

"It's a little more…it's moving fast, Domino. That's up from maybe thirty-five thousand twenty-four hours ago. Vigilantism and riots are a big multiplier now. People aren't sure who's a zombie and who isn't."

"Damn it, anyone who walks with a limp is probably getting gunned down. We haven't been able to contain it at all?"

"Your people are doing a good job, but it's getting away from them."

"King Oberon can bring in a lot more…he's got a nation on the other side. But he needs territory to support them. If I keep giving him L.A. real estate, all the outfits will end up working for the fairies."

"I'll run it up the chain of command, Domino, but I don't think I can sell parceling out the sovereign territory of the United States to some fairy king. If it came to that, I think the decision-makers would rather give up L.A. They do still have the unconventional protocols."

"Fire-bombing the city."

"Yeah, but as unthinkable as that is for us, Domino, it's a scenario with a manageable end-state. L.A. is destroyed, it's the worst tragedy in our history, it's crippling to the country…but it's *over*. Oberon is a whole new open-ended crisis that no one knows how to manage. They're not going down that road when there's a clean way out."

"You're talking about murdering millions of people and calling it a clean way out."

"They wouldn't have to murder anyone," Lowell said. "In a few days, there won't be anyone left alive in Greater Los Angeles. They won't call in the Air Force until then. Maybe they'll even lock down the city and put boots on the ground. A couple hundred thousand combat troops should be able to clear it out in a year or two. Most likely, it'll be a combined forces scenario and it'll be over sooner than that."

"We can't let this happen, Lowell."

"I know," he said quietly. "Tell me what you need."

"This is a race. Between the Xolos, the outfits and the sidhe, we can drop zombies faster than they can kill people. Problem is, even if I throw open the door for Oberon, we're outnumbered."

"We need to minimize the zombies' reproductive efficiency," Lowell said.

"Right. If I can get even a thousand Xolos, gangsters and sidhe together, each dropping maybe ten zombies an hour, we can get ahead of it. But we have to control how quickly civilians are getting killed. The single best way to do that is to get them out of town. Just getting them away from the dense areas will help. Spread them out. Fewer live bodies means fewer zombies get made, and more slowly."

"I'll try."

"You're a fucking sorcerer, Lowell. Juice every mother-fucker in the chain of command if you have to, just make it happen."

"Okay."

"Other than magic, is there any good way to put down a zombie?"

"Head shots work, the more extensive the brain trauma the better. Decapitation is best—some animation remains in the corpse, but the zombie is effectively neutralized."

"So it might lie there and twitch a little, but you won't get eaten unless you trip and fall on a head."

"Yeah."

"Then I want troops, Lowell. Send in some army guys with M-16s and machetes."

"I can bring in a black ops task force," Lowell said. "A couple hundred combat personnel. Support elements and maybe a few Black Hawks. Anything more and we can't keep this dark, and Domino, we really don't want that."

"Whatever you can get."

"I'm just not sure how effectively I can deploy my guys. I don't want to send my teams on house-to-house search-and-destroy missions. It's slow, it's dangerous and there are going to be civilian casualties, which doesn't exactly help our cause."

"I can find targets for you."

"How?"

"Banshees. They'll identify targets and coordinate our efforts."

"They can do that?"

"I hope so."

The next call went to Chavez. "Tell me you rescued the dogs, *chola*," he said when he picked up the phone.

"Yeah, but there are only a hundred of them, Chavez. They'll never catch up on the backlog. We have to help them out."

"We're doing our best. All the bosses got their outfits on zombie patrol, except Terrence and Mobley."

"I know, and we have to keep dropping zombies. But we've got to protect civilians, Chavez. The best way to slow down the zombies is to keep the living away from them."

"How you want us to do that, *chola?* If we're herding civilians, that's going to slow us down on the zombie killing."

"I want sanctuaries. You put civilians in every juice box we've got—every crack house, shooting gallery, tattoo parlor and strip club. You tune up the wards on them and put enough shepherds in there to keep the wolves at bay. The rest keep sweeping the streets, dropping bodies. You put them on rotation so everyone gets a rest. Everyone except the big hitters—they all stay on the street. The banshees are going to feed you target locations."

Chavez whistled. "That's good, *chola*. How do we let people know where to go?"

"Yeah," I said, thinking about it, "we can put the word on the street, but the civilians won't know the difference between a juice box and any other business. They could walk into a joint thinking they're safe and get eaten by a stripper."

"We have to mark them. We could decorate the sanctuaries with marigolds." I knew what Chavez was thinking—

marigolds were traditional for the *Día de los Muertos* celebrations.

"We'd need a lot of fucking flowers," I said. "And what's the point of getting all clever about it? These aren't mindless zombies—they'll clue in to the code soon enough."

"That's true, *chola*. What, then?"

"How about you just tag the juice boxes with the word *sanctuary?* If the zombies want to attack our strong points, I say let them come."

"The smart zombies will set traps."

"Oh, yeah. It has to be real tags, then—that's the only thing a clever zombie wouldn't be able to copy."

"The juice boxes already got plenty of tags, *chola*. We can light them up, make them glow like neon. Our taggers can do that, easy—they learn that shit even before they know how to lay down a tag that can actually do something."

"Yeah, that works. The taggers aren't going to be any help killing zombies, anyway. Put them on it. Plus, it fits with the acid-in-the-water story Lowell's pushing. Any reporters see that shit, they'll just think they're tripping."

The line went silent for a few seconds.

"What is it, Chavez?"

"This is it," he said. "We're real soldiers, D. You talked about us becoming an army that could protect the civilians, but it was just talk before. Now it's real."

"I guess it is, Raffy. Are you ready?"

"I been waiting on you, *chola*. This shit feels pretty good."

He was right. Even if no one thanked us for it, wearing the white hat for a change felt pretty damn good.

I'd encountered any number of law enforcement officers in my line of work, but only one of them knew who I was. Only one of them knew *what* I was. All the others got juiced and they wouldn't have been able to pick me out of a lineup even if they somehow got me into one. Detective Meadows was different. She was a sensitive—an otherwise normal human who was tuned in to the supernatural world for whatever reason. She'd tried to put a case on me back in the day. That hadn't worked out for her, but in the course of her investigation she saw enough to realize there were far worse things than me going bump in the night. I'd decided she could be useful to us, but more than that, I'd decided I liked her. Either one would have been enough reason not to put the hoodoo on her.

"Do you know what's happening?" I asked when she picked up.

"I'm murder police, Ms. Riley. I was at a scene and the vic got up and ran off. Is it voodoo?"

"Different kind of zombies. The voodoo kind wouldn't be eating folks. What's the city doing about it?"

"It's better than ninety-two," Meadows said. "Or at least it would be if this was just a riot. The mayor imposed a curfew. The chief declared a tactical alert and activated the Emergency Operations Center. Patrol officers are being issued tear gas and body armor. And Metro Division has been deployed. That's SWAT."

"Thanks, Meadows, I actually know quite a lot about you people. Are they fighting the zombies?"

"Not on purpose. B and C Platoons are on riot response and crime suppression missions. You know, they aren't actually aware that zombies are causing most of the rioting. At least they weren't—there have been some incidents and rumors are starting to fly. The water-supply story is good but it's starting to get pretty thin. Otherwise, LAFD is fully mobilized and they're getting mutual aid support from

LASD. The governor called in the National Guard at the mayor's request, but they haven't shown up yet."

Getting L.A.'s Fire Department and Sheriff's Department involved sounded like a pretty efficient response to a riot. It might even have worked if the actual rioting hadn't been occurring within the context of a full-scale zombie apocalypse. "Everyone who dies is getting back up with a hankering for brains, Meadows. That will include state and municipal government employees. I don't know enough to say whether the response will break even or not."

"There's not much I can do about it anyway," Meadows said, "but we probably come out ahead. Frankly, we're leaving the large concentrations for the Guard. From what I've seen, it's not as easy as you'd think for a zombie to take down a victim, especially if they're armed and trained. Like I said, even the firefighters and paramedics have tactical support. No one's taking any chances and attrition should be pretty low, at least for now."

"Okay, there's rumors going around anyway, maybe we can use that. You want to go for head shots, Meadows. Or decapitation, but cops probably aren't geared up for that. Do enough damage to a zombie's brain, it goes down. It won't destroy it, exactly, but it'll take it out of the game."

"Those rumors have already started, but I'll help them along. It's like the movies."

"I guess, but that's the only part that's like the movies. A zombie—at least a fresh one—will be as smart as it was in life, just a lot crazier. Some will be armed. And this isn't a plague, so don't start shooting each other just because someone gets bitten."

"What are your people doing?"

"We're putting these motherfuckers down, but it's going to take a while. We figured out what caused it and made it right, so if we can get ahead of it everything will eventually be back to normal. But in the meantime, we have to clear out the existing zombie inventory and stop them from making more."

"What caused it?"

"You really don't want to know, Meadows. The outfits are setting up sanctuaries on our territory. You see glowing tags, it's our joint and we can protect you there. Help us put the word out. Most of our action is in the city so this won't help much out in the 'burbs, but the densest areas will also have the biggest zombie problem."

"You'll expose yourselves. You're not going to be able to stay hidden after this."

"Don't be so sure. We'll juice everyone who comes in a sanctuary. Anyone starts making noise, making people ask questions or think too much, we'll put the hoodoo on them, too. And at the end of the day, civilians believe what they want to believe. You tell them it was acid in the drinking water—oh sure, they knew that kinda thing was happening all along."

"Well, might be you're right about that," Meadows said. "Folks don't look too hard at what they don't want to see anyhow."

"Did you get your family out of town, or are they still in Inglewood?"

"What do you know about my family? And how did you know I live in Inglewood?"

"Stupid question, Meadows. If they're still in town, make sure they know where to go, okay? We'll do our best to take care of them. You can trust me on this."

"I do. My husband's a paramedic. Might be what you've told me will save his life. Thank you."

"Okay, do what you can to spread the word the outfits are

on the side of righteousness in this thing. We can do a lot but we'll do it better if Five-oh can give us some space."

"Are we going to make it through this?" Meadows asked. "Tell me the truth, Riley—should I punch out and spend some time with my family?"

I hesitated before answering. "I like our chances, Detective, but I can't say they're a whole lot better than fifty-fifty. There are a lot of them, and as for our plan, we're pretty much making this shit up as we go along. A lot has to go right and a lot could go wrong. The truth is, I need your help, Meadows. But if I were you? I'd be with my family. I'd lock the doors and keep them close and I'd spend every hour like it was the last."

There were still people I needed to talk to, but I couldn't do it on the phone. I went over to the corner of the room where I'd deposited my old black-and-white TV set and switched it on. The tube gradually warmed up and my jinn familiar appeared on the tiny screen.

"Dominica, you're alive!" he said with mock enthusiasm. Then his face relaxed into its usual expression of bored contempt. "Oh, that's right. Zombies are no threat to the brainless."

"I'm laughing on the inside, Mr. Clean."

"I'm caring on the inside."

"I need your help with the zombies."

"I already informed you, I do not know what is causing the dead to walk. I speculated that it might be a viral outbreak, and though you demonstrated a certain lack of enthusiasm for my wisdom, you agreed to provide me with three score egg rolls from Shanghai Lucky Chow."

"It was three dozen." Mr. Clean apparently really liked egg rolls. It was probably the only thing we had in common.

"And yeah, your wisdom was nowhere to be found on that one, but that's not what I want from you. I need to know if you can help me drop some zombies."

"They're humans. I can slaughter them like lost sheep."

"Can you free their spirits?"

"No," said Mr. Clean, "I can slaughter them like lost sheep." He raised a large, wickedly curved scimitar and showed it to me. It gleamed, even in black and white.

"It would be better if you could free their spirits," I said. The jinn shrugged and the scimitar disappeared. "Still, I'm interested."

"What do you offer? The timing is rather inconvenient."

"Fine, why don't you go back to watching *Baywatch* reruns," I said.

"*Baywatch* isn't on. There's nothing but news reports, though I am enjoying the coverage."

I squeezed my eyes shut and rubbed my temples. "What do you want, Mr. Clean? Time is a factor, here."

"I want you to cook for me."

"Fine," I said. "I'll cook naked. I hope you like frozen burritos." I needed to wrap this up, and he could probably spy on me in the shower, anyway.

"I already spy on you in the shower," said the jinn. "This will be a bounty. One meal for every head I bring you."

"One meal for every *zombie* head. I deduct two meals for every head that doesn't blink or try to bite me. And you're back in the box when I say so."

"Done," said Mr. Clean. "You will likely wish to arrange warehouse space."

"What? Why?"

"The heads," said the jinn. "There will be thousands of them." Mr. Clean grinned and the screen filled with static.

★ ★ ★

Traffic in Hollywood is usually insane even without a zombie apocalypse underway. I spun my traffic spell and wove my way slowly through the gridlock to the Carnival Club. I parked on the street and went inside. The club was full and I was the only human in the place. No one was partying—the sidhe were all armed and formed up in orderly ranks, receiving orders from their commanders. I found Oberon sitting with Titania in a booth in the VIP section. I slid into the booth and picked up the bottle of tequila waiting for me on the table. I looked at the simple parchment label and whistled.

"Ilegal Mezcal," I said. "You must want to apologize." I broke the wax seal, uncorked the bottle and poured.

"It seemed appropriate for this meeting," Oberon said. "I do regret the way we left things at the school."

"From what little he's said about it, he was a jerk," Titania said. "But he wasn't lying, Domino. We cannot bring more of the Court across without sufficient magic to sustain them."

"I offered to let him pull juice from my territory. I guess that wasn't enough."

Titania glanced at her husband and frowned. The king looked decidedly uncomfortable. He picked up his glass and gulped the tequila.

"You should sip that," I said. "You can slam Cuervo Gold shots the next time you're at a frat party."

"Why are we here, Domino?" the king said. "Harsh words were exchanged between us, yes, but we reached an agreement. We are fulfilling our part of it."

I swallowed tequila and shook my head. "I'm not sure anymore how I fell into all this," I said. "A few months ago I was just a gangster making sure the outfit's rackets were doing what they needed to do. Now the world is falling apart and I'm trying to hold it together another day. And that's not so bad, except every time I turn around you've got your hand in my pocket."

"I have a responsibility to my people, Domino."

"I get that. I even understand you need to expand your territory. I knew that right from the start. I wish you the best, Oberon, I really do. Near as I can tell, you're no worse than any other politician we got pretending to run the show. But we're supposed to be allies. We help each other because it's in our best interests. If a demon crashes your party, I help put it down. I don't pause to work out a payment plan with you first. You say you owe me for it, I say whatever makes you happy. But then, if my city is turning into zombieland you don't work me over for the best deal you can get. You give me a hug and go drop as many fucking zombies as you can. That's the way it's supposed to be."

"You're asking me to trust you, Domino. It is not an easy thing to trust a human sorcerer."

"Well, then, frankly we're all fucked, King. We can't do this shit the gangster way. It's too big. This act is just getting warmed up and already I'm a couple days away from losing Greater L.A. Seventeen million people. And once the city is dead you'll be too busy picking demons out of your underwear drawer to worry about expanding your territory. Oberon, Titania, I need you to line up with me on this."

Titania reached across the table and squeezed my hand. "Oberon and Titania are your friends, Domino," she said. "And I will not betray that friendship by lying to you now. The king and queen of the Seelie Court can *never* be your friends. They can only be your allies, in this battle and those to come. They are strong and powerful allies, but they will always pursue the interests of their kingdom and they will always seek advantage. This is their duty. Make use of them, Domino, and align your interests with theirs where you can. But you must not *ever* trust them."

I suddenly remembered the story Adan had told me about his first hunt as a child. I pictured Oberon sitting astride his horse, watching as the boy fought for his life. And I pitied Oberon—actually, I despised the king and pitied the man. I pitied Titania and all of the sidhe. I thought I finally understood what it meant to be without a soul.

"I'm sorry, Domino," Titania said quietly.

I nodded and took another drink. "You can have South Central," I said. "Terrence was barely holding it before— even if he survives this thing, he's not going to have enough of an outfit to hold those streets. With Hollywood, Mobley's turf in South L.A. and Terrence's in South Central, you'll be the second biggest player in town."

"Agreed," said Oberon. "That will be sufficient to bring in thousands more, Domino. We are at your service for the duration of this conflict."

"Good, because I need a lot of service." I filled him in on the details of my plan. It took a while. "I need you to open your doors, too, King. Every juice box you got, you bring in civilians and keep them safe."

"Of course," said Oberon. "We've built up our infrastructure substantially since we arrived. Our doors are open to you."

"I also need the banshees. Can we tie them into a divination ritual? I need them to give Chavez the locations of heavy Zed concentrations. Chavez can deploy the troops, coordinate our efforts. I want them to loop me in, too. I want to know where every dead motherfucker in the city is, in real-time." The only ones I wouldn't be able to coordinate were the Xolos, but I was pretty sure they knew their business better than I did.

Oberon nodded. "This is easily done."

"Good. I also still need you with me on the demons. What do you know about a cat named Valafar?"

"He was a low-ranking general of the Fomoire," the king said. "Is he involved in his?"

"Looks that way. He was a big player in La Calavera's dogfights. I figured he was just another spirit—he didn't look anything like the giant we fought here in the club, or like the spider–squid he sicced on us after we set the Xolos free."

"Did he have the body of a man and the head of a lion?" Titania asked.

I shook my head. "He was wearing a lionskin cloak over his suit. I thought it was a little over the top, even for the Between."

"The Fomoire take many forms," Oberon said. "The fire giant we faced is one form, the shock troops of the legions. More powerful demons have some measure of control over their appearance. The lionskin cloak may have been Valafar's best effort to disguise his true nature in the spirit world."

"Yeah, he had a forked tongue, but it didn't seem all that unusual in a place where everybody's on fire or wearing someone else's face."

"If Valafar was involved in the games, it may be he knew the effect the abduction of the Xolos would have on the mortal world."

I nodded. "And maybe he knew the dead walking would make it easier for him to bring his demons across." I shrugged. "Or maybe he was just a whale with exotic tastes in sports betting. La Calavera needed a lot of juice and she definitely catered to her high rollers."

"Perhaps," said the king, "but such a coincidence would seem improbable. Valafar's involvement also explains how this Francis Mobley was able to summon demons to his cause."

"Yeah, the demon convinced Mobley to open the gate for them, but Valafar brought them through and they're under his command. We can deal with Mobley whenever we get a little spare time, but we won't solve the demon problem until we put Valafar down. I'm not sure what kind of juice he's got, but I'm guessing I'll need you with me for that, too."

"We'll be there, Domino," Oberon said. "This is an enemy we share. It shall always be our honor and our privilege to stand with you against the Fomoire."

"This is remarkable, Domino," said Titania. "To be perfectly frank, we have been doing everything we can to contain the zombies, but we believed it was over. What you've managed to put together...it's extraordinary."

"We haven't done anything yet. We have a hundred thousand zombies in the city. By the time the weekend rolls around, all us poor mortals could be lining up for the brains buffet."

twelve

Terrence was running his war out of an old motel he owned on Manchester in Inglewood. It had a vertical, multicolored sign advertising air-conditioned rooms and color TV, and one of those decorative concrete fences they stopped building in the early sixties. The fence and the motel itself were white with baby-blue trim, which didn't exactly complement the red-tiled roof. The paint looked like it hadn't been touched up in a few decades. I drove through the covered entrance and pulled into the small interior parking lot.

The place was crawling with soldiers. There were six of them out in front of the office, and I saw several more standing in the open doorways of motel rooms. I got out of the Lincoln and walked to the office. One of the soldiers was a white guy…more or less. I recognized him. It was Anton.

His skin had gone a kind of yellowish-brown, almost like we were in the Between, but otherwise he didn't look too bad. He was wearing shades, so I couldn't see his eyes. He had a revolver tucked into the front waistband of his track suit and he was holding a machete. His head turned slowly and he watched me approach.

"Anton, I didn't expect to see you here." I couldn't help myself—I pulled him into a quick hug. Under the track suit, his skin felt hard and stiff, like wet leather that had been left out in the sun to dry. I heard his teeth grinding, and he groaned. I released him and stepped back. "Jesus, Anton, are you keeping it together?"

"It is fucking sun, Domino," he said. His voice was dry and cracked. "It is baking me, like fucking mummy."

"Yeah, I can see that, but that's not what I meant."

"I'm sorry, Domino. You are soft and warm. It is hard for me."

"No, you're doing real good, Anton. I'm just glad you're still you." He didn't even really smell—well, he smelled like cheap cologne, but that was better than the alternative.

"Heavy Chevy's a motherfucking rock," said the soldier standing next to him. I didn't recognize the guy, but he was alive and he didn't seem to object to Anton's company. "He ain't even tried to bite nobody."

"I keep all my guys in line, Domino," said Anton. "Like you do it. We fight Mobley's crews only, and we don't hurt the people."

"I'm proud of you, Anton. I'm going to give you a medal when this is all over."

He tried to smile but his withered lips wouldn't really cooperate. "I do not need medal, Domino. I want the nice funeral, with flowers and the good coffin with little pillows inside."

I nodded and smiled, and then I put my head down and hurried to the office door.

Terrence was in a room behind the front desk, sitting cross-legged on the floor. Softly glowing globes the size of basketballs floated in the air around him, images of the gang war flickering within them like crystal balls. Terrence shifted the spectral globes with his hands, repositioning them and studying each one. He curled his hands into fists and dropped them to his knees, and the spheres vanished.

"We just about done here, Domino," he said. "Pretty soon, all my soldiers going to be on Anton's side and he'll be running this outfit."

"That bad?"

"About eighty percent attrition. Like I said, a lot of them hooking up with Anton's crew, otherwise this would be over already. Most don't last long after they turn, though, and Anton got to put them down. I guess you saw the machete he carries around."

"Jesus Christ."

"Yeah, might be it's time for him. The demons are the worst of it, about like you'd expect. Some of them got juice, Domino. I've seen them pull souls out of zombies and eat them. What do you suppose happens to a guy when his soul is eaten?"

"I don't know, Terrence. Maybe they just eat the ghost— I've seen that kind of thing before." I didn't mention it was Terrence's nephew. "Seems like a soul is more than just a ghost." I sat down on the floor facing him.

"Simeon Wale is MIA," Terrence said.

"When?"

"Last night. He took a crew behind the lines, hit a homeless shelter Mobley was using down in Compton. He said they had a demon in there and that was the last I heard. Ain't heard anything from his crew, either. The shelter burned."

"Okay," I said, "you talked to Chavez? You know what we're doing?"

Terrence nodded. "I like the plan, D. Not sure what I

can contribute, though. Ain't really anything left you'd call a sanctuary south of Huntington Park."

"I know, but there's a lot of people here, Terrence. We have to do what we can to protect them. Pull back, let Mobley breathe and focus on civilians for the next couple days."

"I don't have enough soldiers, D. Didn't have that many to begin with. Think I told you I got about eighty percent less than when I started. It's too much territory, and the front line's basically running along the 105, right through the middle of it."

"I'm going to send you some more reinforcements, Terrence."

He looked at me, his face expressionless. "Outfit?" he said finally. "Or fairies?"

I nodded. "I have to give it to him, Terrence. He can't bring in more sidhe unless he controls enough juice to support them—or he won't, anyway. We aren't going to survive this without his help."

"You know that's how he's going to do it, right?"

"What?"

"How he's going to rebuild his kingdom. I couldn't really figure how he thought he was going to do that, you know? But there always going to be something worse, Domino. Today it's zombies, tomorrow going to be something else. And we're always going to need his help. A few blocks here, a few hoods there. When this is over, he's going to own most everything from Hollywood to Compton, D. He'll be coming for you next, looking for Downtown, looking for Chinatown and Koreatown and Huntington Park, over to Crenshaw and Culver City."

"I know, Terrence, and the only way we can stop that from happening is to get our shit together, get strong so we don't need him for every crisis of the day. Plus, there may come a day when Oberon needs *our* help, and when it does I plan to make the son of a bitch pay dearly for it."

"You say so, D. Anyway, I ain't got the muscle to raise much of a fuss about it. I want you to make room for my people, any of them make it through."

"I will, Terrence. I'll find a spot for you, too. Hell, I won't have to find a spot—you're going to have rank in Rashan's outfit when this is over."

"I live to see the day, I been thinking about an early retirement. The game ain't the same after this, Domino. I ain't the same."

"I need you, Terrence. You don't have to make any promises. I'm not your boss. Just give me a shot to recruit you."

The limp body of one of Terrence's soldiers crashed through the office's plate-glass window and smashed into the front desk. Alarm bells sounded and the hair on the back of my neck stood up as wards activated and raw magic swept through the room.

"Intrusion," Terrence said, and leaped to his feet. I followed suit, reaching for my forty-five semiautomatic under my arm.

A pitch-black, vaguely humanoid creature crawled through the front window and onto the ceiling. It looked like a hairless man, except it had four arms and all of its limbs were impossibly long, thin, and articulated like a crab's. It had no eyes, nose or ears that I could see—just a wide, grinning mouth filled with pointed teeth. It clung to the ceiling of the office and its head swiveled around, a black, forked tongue darting at the air.

Terrence chanted hip-hop lyrics and spun a combat spell. There was no obvious effect, but the creature hissed and dropped from the ceiling to the floor, landing on its back with its arms and legs wriggling in the air like a bug.

"Crawlers," Terrence said. "I hit them with anti-magic spells. Doesn't kill them, but it slows them down."

"Crawlers, plural?"

Terrence nodded. "Always packs of them."

The crawler flipped over, crouched, and leaped onto the front desk. Its jaws yawned wide, the thin tongue writhing at us, and the demon hissed. Another one crawled in through the window onto the ceiling.

"Well, how do you kill them?"

Terrence grunted. "Haven't figured that out yet. Maybe you got some ideas."

"Vi Victa Vis," I said, extending my hand toward the crawler demon. It rocked back on its haunches as the force spell flowed around it and blew out the front wall of the office. "Damn."

"Told you," Terrence said, and then he hit the demon on the ceiling with another magic-suppressing spell. It lost its grip and followed the first down to the floor.

"God is a scientist," I said, "not a magician." I dropped my own magic-killing spell on the demon crouching on the front desk. It hissed again and wrapped all four arms around its head, covering its blank face. I brought up the forty-five and shot it in the chest. The demon's skin puckered and rippled, and the bullet was swallowed up like I'd fired it into a tar pit. Another demon crawled in through the broken window and skittered along the wall.

"This is below average, Terrence," I said.

Terrence glanced over at me. "You telling me, Domino. This is what I been doing while you looking for lost dogs."

"Touché," I said. "Sorry about your motel."

"What about it? I can fix the win—"

"Vi Victa Vis!" I shouted, pulling all the juice I could reach out of Terrence's turf. The force spell blew out the front wall, along with the one facing the street. The roof collapsed into the lobby and two of the demons were buried in the rubble. The demon perched on the front desk screamed and sprang at us.

Terrence triggered a spell talisman and a wall of force formed in front of us, shimmering like a heat wave. The demon hit the wall, but it didn't bounce off. It kind of slowed and flowed around it like a fly in molasses. It dropped to the floor, hissed and leaped up to cling to the office ceiling. We turned and watched as it scrabbled to the back of the room.

"Damn it, Domino," Terrence said. "There's other shit I wanted to try."

"Like what?" I said. "Anyway, it's going to be Oberon's motel soon enough." Maybe it wasn't very tactful to bring it up, but Terrence needed to be practical about the situation.

"I'll suppress its magic, you hose it down with the hostile shit." I nodded and Terrence spun his juice-killing mojo again. The demon plopped to the floor and curled up like a roly-poly.

"All power corrupts," I said, "but we need the electricity." Naked current arced from my fingertips and played across its skin. The demon stiffened and screamed, and greasy, foul-smelling smoke curled from its hide where the electricity touched it.

"Hey, it's working!" I said, and then another crawler demon pounced on Terrence from behind. The monster sunk two clawed hands into his abdomen, two more into his face and clamped down on the back of his bald head with its oversize jaws. Terrence stumbled forward under the demon's momentum, but he didn't go down. He reached out and caught himself on the office desk, and then he pushed off and rammed the demon into the nearest wall.

"Hit it, Domino," he gasped, and spun his suppression spell again.

"It's electricity, Terrence, it will—"

"Hit it!"

"Fuck that, Terrence," I said. "All movements go too far." I spun the telekinesis spell and hurled the demon across the room—tried to, anyway. Even with Terrence's spell eating at its magic, the demon still had enough resistance left to counter most of the juice I could put on it. Gritting my teeth and reaching for more power, I slowly peeled it off Terrence, and its claws left bloody furrows across his abdomen and cheeks as it was pulled away from him. When it was clear, I spun the lightning spell again and electricity coursed over it. The demon dropped to the floor and curled up, twitching and smoking.

"I think the suppression spell has more bite than the lightning," I said. The demon's skin was beginning to dissolve, running down its arms and legs like black ink and pooling beneath it. "You okay, Terrence?" He was braced against the wall with one hand, the other clutching his stomach. He nodded. "Let's kill as much juice as we can, both of us together, and try to choke it out."

We couldn't actually suck the juice out of the demon. We'd need a ritual for that, and even then I wasn't sure I wanted to squeeze a demon. What we were doing was really the opposite—pumping as much of our countermagic into the monster as we could to neutralize its own.

It worked. The demon began dissolving more and more quickly as we opened up the tap on the suppression spells. Its liquefied flesh formed a smoking puddle of tar and ran in black rivulets across the linoleum floor. Soon all that was left was its head, and it shifted and shuddered as it dissolved and broke apart, like a fused mass of ice cubes under hot water. We repeated the tactic on the other demon and soon the floor was slick with smoking black tar. As we watched, the tar appeared to evaporate in fast-forward, the puddles receding from each other, thinning, and finally disappearing altogether.

"Still got the ones the roof fell on," Terrence said. "Might be more outside."

Right on cue, some of the rubble shifted and one of the crawlers poked its head out. We pumped countermagic into it until it dissolved and disappeared back into the debris. I used my telekinesis spell to dig out the last one, and we repeated the trick.

"These guys aren't so tough," I said.

"Fuck you, Domino," said Terrence. I looked over at him and saw he was dabbing at the ugly red wounds on his face with a handkerchief.

"Damn, Terrence, sorry. You have any aspirin? I could try my healing spell."

"I've seen your healing magic," Terrence said. "I'd rather stand here and bleed."

I couldn't really blame him. "You any better at it? I can get Honey down here—she'll patch you right up." I knelt beside the soldier who had come through the window. His back and neck were broken, probably in multiple places.

Terrence shook his head. "I can do it. Need some props, though. I'll live."

"You were right, Terrence. The way to hurt these fucking things is to kill the juice. My spell is really defensive mojo. It would work even better if I could modify it into an attack spell."

"Yeah, the problem with the crawlers is there's always a

lot of them. But even with the ones that work alone, killing their juice takes a while. Most of them don't lie down and curl up while you working them over."

"I'll give it some thought on my next coffee break," I said. "In the meantime, it's nice to know the fucking things have a weakness."

I spun my eye-in-the-sky spell and sent it outside. The soldiers who had been standing guard at the front door were dead. There was no sign of Anton. I hoped he'd had the sense to make himself scarce. He wasn't going to accomplish much against a demon with his gun or machete. I didn't know whether the crawlers could eat souls, but I sure as hell didn't want Anton to go out that way.

A fat man in a white suit sat in a red Cadillac convertible parked on the other side of the driveway from the office. The hood ornament had been replaced by a large white cross. The man looked up at my eye—which should have been invisible—and a fleshy smile peeked out between his heavy jowls. He waved.

"There's a preacher parked out front," I said.

Terrence eased forward, trying to stay out of sight, and looked out through the shattered window. "Maybe he needs a room," he said. "But I don't see a hooker in the car."

"I don't know, I think this guy's got some juice. You hang back, I'll see what he wants."

I walked out of the office, picking my way carefully between Terrence's dead muscle. The preacher opened the door of the Cadillac and clambered out, his face flushing with the effort. He stood and straightened his toupee, then smiled that beatific smile again. I was pretty sure he was even fatter than Anton—before he'd become a zombie, even. I checked him out with my witch sight and saw black juice radiating from him in waves, like the stink from a cartoon skunk's tail.

"What the fuck are you supposed to be?" I said, stopping in my tracks and gripping the forty-five more tightly.

"You don't recognize me, Ms. Riley? I'm disappointed." He looked down at his gut—creating a few more chins in the process—and straightened his lapels. "I suppose it's the new suit."

"Valafar," I said. "You're possessing that man."

"Yes," he said, smiling. "Ironic, isn't it? He's hideously fat, don't you think? A true glutton—and not just for food, mind you. Most appealing."

"Thanks for showing up and giving me another chance to kill you," I said. "You ran too fast the last time." I started pulling juice from the parking lot, and I hoped Terrence was doing the same.

"That was neither the time nor the place," the demon said. "Nor is this, if you ask me. But go ahead, kill me if you must. No need for witchcraft—the gun will do nicely." He sighed and spread his arms.

"You'll just possess someone else."

"Well, sure," Valafar said, shrugging. "But you'll ruin my suit. Not that it will last very long, anyway—I wear them out so quickly." One of his eyes popped and flames licked out.

"What do you want?"

"I want…what is it you say? A sit-down, yes, that's right. A parley."

"What do you and I have to talk about? You're a demon, I'm a human, sooner or later we're going to throw down."

Valafar nodded. "Yes, I'm a demon. So what? What does that mean, anyway, a demon? It's just another word for bad guy. You're a bad guy, I'm a bad guy—we're all bad guys to the sheep, stumbling their way through life until it's time for them to be slaughtered. It's semantics."

"You're a psychopath. Born without the knowledge of good and evil. It's not in the cards for you and me to be friends."

"Oh, right, you know that because it's what your own personal demon told you, and of course he would never lie."

"Okay, we're talking. I'll ask again—what do you want?"

"Will you trick me into revealing my secret plan?" the demon asked.

"I doubt it. I figure you're itching to tell me anyway, otherwise you wouldn't be standing here flapping your fat face at me."

Valafar giggled. "I'll tell you the honest-to-God truth," he said. He started to cross himself but seemed to get lost about halfway through and wrapped it up with a vague flutter of his hand. "I don't have a plan. None of us do, not really. Not even world domination. Oh, sure, we do want the world—we want it *back*—but not to rule it. We just want to have a little fun."

"You should try Disneyland." In my defense, I regretted the quip as soon as the words were out of my mouth. My bad, Anaheim.

"I believe I shall," he said. "A whole park filled with people—with children—all for my amusement. It's a lovely concept, these amusement parks. Sadly, I believe the current situation has forced it to close, temporarily. It will have to wait until things die down a little, if you'll excuse the expression."

"So you just want to kill people. I'm still not seeing the point of all this talking."

"Oh, not killing, exclusively," the demon said, "though there is great power in murder, as you know. Kill enough people and you may become a sorcerer. Kill a great many more and you may become a god."

"At least you don't have delusions of grandeur or anything."

"No delusions, Ms. Riley. I am an ant, a worm…a parasite surviving on the shit in a worm's asshole."

"Now you're making sense."

"But it need not always be so," Valafar continued. "It is the pursuit, the process, the *becoming* that really matters. If a single, nasty little world must be reduced to ashes in this most noble endeavor—surely that is a small price to pay for transcendence?"

"Aaaaaand now you're boring me again."

"When I am alone at the end of days I shall run amongst those ashes, I shall wallow in them, and I shall be a more beautiful, a more wonderful, a more *perfect* thing than could ever crawl forth from the blood, filth and cum that lubricates this—"

I raised the forty-five and shot the preacher in the forehead. I saw the flame in his eye wink out just before the bullet pierced flesh and bone. The man sank to his knees and toppled over on his side. I took a look at the corpse with my witch sight and the black cancer growing inside it was gone. I walked up to the man, knelt and pulled his spirit from his body, binding it to the driver's seat of the Cadillac. I reached down and gently closed his eyes.

When I stood up, Terrence was at my side. He stared down at the body for a moment, and then covered it with a thin, frayed blanket from the motel. "You feeling me now, Domino? Ain't none of us going to be the same after this."

I nodded and reached around Terrence's wide back with

my gun hand, pulling him to me and resting my head against his shoulder. "I feel you, Terrence," I said. "But who knows? Maybe some change will do us good."

The drive down to Inglewood from Oberon's place had taken two hours, even with the traffic spell. The freeways were choked and the surface streets weren't much better. I could have saved a lot of time by just getting on the phone and telling Terrence his days as a boss were over, but I hadn't been willing to do it that way. I felt pretty good about that, and if I hadn't gone to see him he might be dead. But now I had to get back up to the warehouse district south of downtown, and if anything the traffic was even worse. The civilians didn't yet understand a zombie apocalypse was underway, but they knew some bad shit was going down and it seemed a few million were seizing the opportunity for some paid time off.

I stayed on Manchester at the entrance ramp to the Harbor Freeway when my traffic spell didn't open enough space in the gridlock for me to ride a bicycle through. I drove east on Manchester to Alameda and turned north. I was swimming upstream against all the traffic headed south out of the city when some asshole with a fully loaded pickup turned in front of me from Gage and promptly shuddered to a dead stop, lying on his horn. Ahead of me was a sea of cars packed door handle to door handle across all four lanes. The BMW and Bentley dealership on the corner was being looted—more like vandalized, since even if you could steal a car you wouldn't be able to drive it anywhere. Several cars in the outside lot were burning, others had been smashed, and rioters had broken out the plate glass and were getting started inside. I pulled out my cell and called Chavez.

"Where are you?" he said when the line connected.

"I'm a little over three miles from the club, but I'm not moving. I'm going to have to hike it. What's it look like there?"

"We're standing room only, D, and the civilians are freaked the fuck out. But hell, it's already a fucking riot outside so I'm not sure how much worse it can get."

"Get a handle on it, Chavez. Any other problems?"

"The usual. We've had some zombies try to get in. Some are just hungry, others don't know they're dead and they're just as scared as the living. We put them down."

"Okay, I'm on the move. No idea how long it will take me to get there." The distance wasn't far, but there was a pretty good chance the zombie apocalypse would slow me down. I slipped the cell phone in my pocket, drew my forty-five from its shoulder holster and got out of the car.

The asshole in the pickup truck got out, too. He pulled a golf club out of the back and stalked up to the driver's window of the Camry in front of him. He reared back and swung the club like a baseball bat, starring the safety glass. The zombie who was driving the Toyota pushed the glass the rest of the way out of the frame and reached for the asshole, trying to drag him inside the car. She was a middle-aged Latina and her skin was gray and blotched. She grasped for her attacker and snapped yellow teeth at him.

The asshole dropped the golf club and ran. A small, high-pitched voice screamed from the open cab of the pickup. "Daddy! Don't leave!"

I stopped in the middle of the street and looked north at the ragged line of cars that choked all four lanes, and then some. I heard gunshots, though I couldn't see the shooters and didn't know who their targets were. Then I ran over to the pickup and ducked my head inside. Two little boys, the oldest no more than six or seven, sat huddled together on the bench seat. They were crying and shaking from head to toe. "Your daddy went to get help," I said. "He asked me to take you someplace safe. Will you come with me?"

The youngest boy just shook his head. The oldest said, "We're not supposed to talk to strangers."

I could juice the kids and feel bad about it later. It would be the smart thing to do. "I know, little man, and that's usually real good advice, but it's not safe here. Maybe if we weren't strangers, then you could talk to me. I'm Domino, like the game." I smiled and held out my hand. The oldest boy looked at it for a moment and then shook it. "I'm Ethan and this is Dylan," he said.

"It's very nice to meet you, Ethan and Dylan. Will you let me take you to a safe place?"

"How will we find Daddy?" Ethan asked.

I could find the guy easily enough. I wasn't sure the kids weren't better off without him. I understood getting a little freaked out by the zombie apocalypse, but you don't run off and leave your kids. "I'll find him," I said. "Once you're safe, I'll find him and bring him to you. I promise. Okay?"

Ethan nodded and they slid across the seat to me. I helped them out of the truck and took Ethan's hand. "Now you hold on to Dylan's hand," I said. "And no matter what happens, stay right beside me. Do you understand?"

"Yes, Domino," Ethan said, taking his brother's hand.

I looked north up the street and then back at Ethan and Dylan. I pulled juice from the streets and dropped protective wards on the boys. "It's not far," I told them. "But it's going to be really bad." I spun up a charm and let the magic flow over them. "Keep your eyes down at your feet. Don't look at anything else unless I tell you. And if you see anything, don't remember it." I didn't want to use magic to compel them, but I figured this was no different from the protective wards.

"Yes, Domino," they said in unison.

"Good. There are a lot of bad people around here, and I don't want you to be scared if I have to fight, okay?" The boys nodded, but they didn't seem convinced. I squeezed Ethan's hand and we set off into the slaughterhouse.

It didn't take long to put my suspicions to the test. We'd just started down the sidewalk when a gang of looters came out of a lot filled with commercial trucks. A punk who looked like he was in his late teens dropped one of the cardboard boxes he was carrying and CDs spilled out. He saw us and grinned.

"Check it out," he said to his friends. "Someone brought us a MILF!" The friends all laughed. There were five of them. The leader bent down and pulled a knife out of his boot. "Come here, bitch," he said, walking toward me. "You give it up real sweet, we won't hurt the kids."

I extended my hand to him, palm out. "Vi Victa Vis," I said, and punched him through a chain-link fence into the grille of a large panel truck. His homeboys dropped their loot and ran. Ethan and Dylan started bawling but their eyes stayed on their sneakers.

It took us more than three hours to walk through the endless warehouse district that stretched south from the edge of downtown. By the time we got to the intersection at Washington, I'd lost track of how many spells I'd cast. We saw a few rioters and a lot of zombies. A large pack attacked the gridlocked cars at the railroad tracks near Twenty-Fourth, and I learned my wallflower spell didn't have any effect on Zed. I couldn't say whether it was smell or some arcane sixth sense, but the zombies locked onto us immediately. There were too many for the ghost-binding spell and they came at us too quickly, so I had to use fireballs. The screams of dying zombies and the smell of burning meat terrified Ethan and Dylan and further slowed our progress. I told myself the charm I'd used meant they wouldn't keep it with them long. We kept walking.

I dropped another dozen zombies between Washington and the Santa Monica Freeway ramp. Most of them were stragglers, and I had time to use the ghost-binding spell before they could get close. A few jumped out from behind cars and attacked, and I had to use force magic to create some space. A couple of them were armed. One middle-aged woman in sweatpants and a long, bloodstained Dodgers T-shirt came at us with a butcher knife in one hand and a hammer in the other. She leaped down from the roof of a blue minivan, and I barely had time to trigger my repulsion talisman before she landed right on top of me. The force magic knocked her across the street, and she was impaled on the climbing hooks of a utility pole. The woman wriggled on the hooks like a fish on the end of a line until I stepped up and tore her spirit from her body. I used my telekinesis spell to pull her body down.

Ethan and Dylan stayed at my side through all of this, their eyes glued to their sneakers.

I heard the zombie horde before I saw them. At first I thought it was another riot in progress down by the freeway. It sounded like a riot, like a mob—a cacophony of shouts and screams that blended together to create a dull roar that raised the hair on the back of my neck. Then I saw them pouring down the off-ramp from the freeway into the street. It reminded me of the footage I'd seen from Victoria Park. A lot of the zombies fell as they scrambled and staggered down the ramp, and the others just kept coming, climbing over the fallen and grinding them underfoot. I could see more zombies marauding among the cars up on the freeway. Some of the living had crawled over the barrier and hung from the overpass. Others jumped or fell to the street below.

I looked around for a defensible spot but didn't see any attractive candidates. With no other options, I picked up Ethan and Dylan and carried them to a tractor-trailer rig that had been abandoned in the gridlocked traffic. With one of the boys under each arm, I spun my jump spell just as the first zombies reached us. Ethan was tucked under my right arm and I didn't have a good grip on him because I was still holding the forty-five. I lost him when we landed on the roof of the trailer and he slid and tumbled toward the edge.

"All movements go too far!" I shouted as he fell over the side. The telekinesis spell caught him and pulled him back just before he reached the eager, outstretched arms of the zombies below.

There was plenty of food for the zombies stuck in the traffic jam, both down on the street and up on the freeway, but we attracted enough attention that our truck was quickly surrounded. The more enterprising zombies began rocking the trailer. Others threw rocks or junk they picked up off the street at us, hoping to knock us off our perch. I had Ethan and Dylan lie down flat on the roof of the trailer, and I spun my defensive shields to protect us. Zombies began climbing onto the cab of the truck to get at us and I knocked them down with force magic. I didn't have time to use my witch sight, and I couldn't be sure all of them were zombies. I told myself there was no way a living human could survive long enough to climb up on the truck.

These zombies might have been brighter than the average movie zombies but they were every bit as relentless. I thought after a while they might notice they weren't getting anywhere with me and decide to look for easier prey. But once the idea we'd be their next meal got into their heads, it stayed there. The sea of zombies around the truck kept getting bigger and bigger as more of them noticed us. They were a carpet of decomposing flesh completely covering the street and empty cars and they stretched as far as I could see.

There was no break in the shouting, screaming and wailing of the hungry dead. It grew louder and louder as more of them swarmed around the truck. It was impossible to think. Could I fight my way through so many zombies with the children in tow? I couldn't even be sure how many of them there were. I could start throwing fireballs and other destructive spells, but could I keep it up long enough to reach safety? I could call Chavez for reinforcements but I'd be putting anyone he sent in terrible danger. I might have been willing to do it anyway, but even if they could reach me it would pull them away from defense of the sanctuaries.

If it had just been me, I was pretty sure I could have walked to Pasadena without a zombie getting its rotten hands on me. I could make it, but I wasn't sure Ethan and Dylan would. I needed help.

"Adan," I called, reaching out with the juice.

"Domino, where are you?" he said, the words echoing in my mind. "Are you in trouble?"

"You could say that. I'm on Alameda down by the 10. I've got a couple civilians with me—little ones—and we're surrounded. I could use a hand, but I don't see how anyone can get to me."

"Open a gate," Adan said.

"What?"

"Open a gate to the Between and call me, just like you did with Honey."

"Oh," I said. "Oh, yeah."

I did as he instructed. A shimmering hole opened in the thick, heavy air and Adan stepped through onto the roof of the truck. He was still wearing the black fatigues and his sword was in his hand. He looked down at the writhing mass of zombies surrounding the truck.

"I told you the brain-scented perfume was a bad idea," he said.

I laughed. "Do brains even have a scent?"

Adan's grin turned into a hard line. "To them, maybe. Who are your friends?"

"Ethan and Dylan. They've been with me all the way from Huntington Park."

"Tough kids. Okay, let's get out of here."

"What's the plan?"

"This," he said. He spread his arms out to his sides, one hand palm-out toward the zombies and his sword held aloft in the other. *"Ar shiúl,"* he shouted, and a ground-level shockwave exploded from our position and expanded like a ripple on the surface of a pond. The zombies swarming the truck were either flattened where they stood or hurled through the air at such speed it was like a gray blur rolling away from us.

I looked around at the destruction. "Holy shit. Is that the sidhe language?"

"Gaelic," Adan said. "I failed to master the sidhe power words."

"The Gaelic ones seem pretty good."

Adan grinned and nodded. "Let's go." He reached down and scooped up Ethan in one arm. *"Léimim,"* he said, and he leaped to the cab and then down to the street. His power words had a real advantage in terms of speed and convenience. My quotations still had more personality, though. I grabbed Dylan and took a running jump from the trailer, then spun my levitation spell and landed easily beside Adan on a small patch of asphalt that wasn't occupied by fallen zombies.

Adan's spell had broken the zombies, but it hadn't destroyed them. As we picked our way through the bodies, they reached for us, grasping at our ankles and clothes. Others crawled or dragged themselves toward us. We cut our way through them with combat and spirit magic and finally reached the freeway overpass. A man was standing on the roof of a car on the far side. He wore a long, leather pimp coat with no shirt underneath and baggy trousers. Heavy gold chains hung from his neck and decorated his bare chest. A Nike flat cap was tugged low on his head and large, gold-rimmed sunglasses hid his eyes. One side of his face was burned black and hairless, and his ear was a fused lump of charred flesh.

It was Simeon Wale.

He held his arms out to his sides and a line of zombies pushed forward, moving between and over the immobilized and abandoned vehicles. He brought his arms down and the zombies stopped, crouching on car hoods or standing stiffly, their limbs trembling with anticipation.

I looked at Wale with my witch sight. "He's a fucking zombie," I whispered to Adan. "And he's still juiced up. How is that possible?"

Adan shook his head. "He's still got his mind and soul. That's all he needs."

"I knew you be coming to the Men's Room," Wale said, his voice echoing hollowly under the freeway. "Found you with my seeing words, but couldn't get here till just now."

"What do you want, Wale?"

"Thought I might eat you, if that's okay."

"Lot of people have tried that, lately," I said. "No one's gotten more than a bite of me yet. I'm sorry you died, Wale, but what's your fucking problem? We can still use you—you can join Anton's crew."

"See, that's just it, I got some workplace resentment. I guess you can see I got my own crew. Don't want to join Heavy Chevy's fucking crew. Don't want you telling me what to do and when. I should have been lieutenant when you got a bump. Only reason I ain't is you scared of me." He grinned, showing me a grill full of gold, diamond-encrusted teeth. "I guess you probably right to be scared of me, though."

"I don't have time to kill you right now, Wale. Maybe this can wait until my schedule clears up a little."

"I guess you got to make time 'cause I'm a hungry motherfucker."

"You honestly think you can take both Adan and me?"

"Not especially, to tell the truth. That's why I was real glad to see you got those shorties with you. It was just you and fairy-boy, I probably be in some trouble. But I figure he gonna have to protect them kids, leave you and me to do our thing."

I glanced at Adan. He raised his eyebrows and gave a little shake of his head. If Wale still had his magic, the only way we could protect Ethan and Dylan was to get them off the battlefield, quickly. I nodded and mouthed the word *Go*.

I heard Adan's voice inside my head. "It's only a few blocks to the club. Stall for time, and I'll be back." Then he sheathed his sword and took Dylan from me. *"Léimim!"* he shouted, and I felt the juice welling up from the street into him. The jump spell carried Adan and the children to the freeway overhead.

I turned and looked back at Wale. He raised his arms again and then brought them down sharply. A terrible cry rolled along the line of zombies and they surged forward. I spun my levitation spell and rose into the air, and the walking dead reached for me, howling in frustration.

Most of them did, anyway. A few of the zombies were Wale's gangsters and they opened fire. I spun my defensive shield and the hail of bullets filled the air around me with electric-blue starbursts. This was, at best, a temporary counter to the strapped zombies. For one thing, they could probably keep reloading longer than I could keep the shield up. For another, the juice I was putting into the shield was juice I wasn't using to put the hurt on Wale.

I was on Rashan's turf, now, and I could reach plenty of juice. I pulled magic out of the tags that scrolled across the blue corrugated fence to my right and the freeway overpass above. "What medicines do not heal, the lance will," I said. "What the lance does not heal, fire will." A line of red-orange flame flared to life across the street from curb to curb. I poured juice into it and it grew as if I fed it with gasoline, rising behind me like a curtain that spanned the street. Windows shattered from the heat and the first fuel tank ignited. The resulting fireball was impressive, but I was somewhat disappointed the car wasn't hurled into the air by the explosion. Hollywood did it better.

The writhing curtain of liquid fire grew to a height of at least fifty feet, and then I released it. Like a tidal wave rolling straight out of hell, it raced forward, flowing harmlessly around my body, and crashed down on the zombies in Wale's crew. The fire tumbled and splashed like lava coursing through the street and it consumed all it touched, flesh and steel alike. I could hear the zombies' screams despite the staccato fuel-tank explosions, and I reminded myself that while they were frightened they were beyond the reach of mortal pain.

The dying edges of the fire wave reached far enough to engulf the car Wale was standing on, but he leaped into the air above the flames and hung there. He started hitting me with spontaneous attack spells and all other thoughts fled as I focused on defense. I'd always known Wale had juice. Other than Rashan, he might have been the strongest sorcerer in the outfit. He was fooling himself if he really thought I'd ever been afraid of him, but I'd never trusted him, either. The evil inside him was as easy to see as the magic.

The fact was, I wasn't sure I could take him. Despite what I knew it would do to me, I would have considered using glamour on him, except I could see he was protected. I could use my fairy magic to defeat those wards, but I was pretty sure the juice would incapacitate me before I could pull them down. There wouldn't be any shortcuts or clever angles in this fight. If I wanted to beat Wale, I had to do it straight up. I began alternating between defensive magic and killing magic, spinning the spontaneous spells as quickly as my mind could give birth to them.

As we pulled more and more juice out of the street, the magic began to encroach more forcibly on the physical world. The arcane energies we were harnessing clashed in the space between us, creating a nimbus of shifting colors that danced and played along the edges of human vision. A sound that began as the soft murmur of the ocean in a sea-shell soon built to the deafening shriek of a jet engine. The nimbus between us went white, blinding in its radiance, and tendrils of ghost-light radiated from the newborn star, crawling over the pavement like spectral serpents.

Cracks appeared in the street and overpass as the concrete and asphalt was torn from within by unseen stresses. The streetlights to either side of us blew out all at once, showering the street with electrical sparks and broken glass. A manhole cover was ripped from its moorings with the sound of a tolling bell and launched into the air on a column of golden light.

The juice burned through me and it felt like the shuddering convulsions of an orgasm as I hurled it into the arcane conflagration. Then I saw Wale falter. He wobbled and dipped a little in the air as his levitation spell weakened and nearly failed. I smiled and pressed the attack, abandoning all but the bare minimum of defense. The brilliant star that turned and pulsed between us began to move, slowly at first and then picking up speed. It moved toward Simeon Wale.

He might have been dead, but Wale wasn't stupid. Without lowering his magical defenses against my onslaught, he dropped his levitation spell and triggered a jump talisman as soon as his feet hit the pavement. He flipped up and back onto the edge of the freeway overpass, teetering precariously for a moment. "A great flame follows a little spark!" I shouted, and my fireball streaked out and exploded into the side of the bridge. Wale leaped away just ahead of the spell and raced out of sight across the overpass. He moved pretty well for a zombie.

I pushed my levitation spell higher and slowly rose to the overpass. I dropped down on the roof of a U-Haul trailer and looked around. Wale was nowhere to be seen. "It is natural to give a clear view of the world after accepting that it must be clear," I said, and threw my eye-in-the-sky spell into the air. I sent it racing up about a hundred feet and panned around. Wale was heading west on the freeway, running and leaping along the line of gridlocked cars. He was heading away from the club, but no way was I letting him go.

"The kids are safe," Adan called inside my head. "Open a gate."

I almost laughed out loud. "Meep-meep," I said, and spun my Road Runner spell. I leaped from the trailer over a couple cars onto the hood of an SUV, and then I was off, racing after Simeon Wale across the stalled traffic that stretched before me like stepping stones in a pond.

Adan called again. "Domino, bring me in." This time I did laugh aloud. "Can't," I answered. "Chasing."

"Chasing? Domino, he could be leading you into a trap."

I didn't think Wale had thought that far ahead, but it wouldn't have changed my mind, anyway. I was high as a hippie at a Grateful Dead show, and I just wanted to run, and jump and rain lethal magic down on Simeon Wale's head until he was burned to a cinder.

We reached the Central Avenue exit by the time I ran him down. I jumped from a FedEx truck to the top of the exit sign and saw him streaking down the ramp below me. "Vi Victa Vis," I said, and the force spell knocked him off the ramp and down onto the Sixteenth Street feeder. He pulled himself off the pavement and turned to face me long enough to fire back with an attack spell of his own. I caught it with countermagic and snuffed it out before it even had a chance to form, and then I hit him with another force spell that knocked him across the feeder into a metal fence that topped the low brick wall fronting the street. A section of the fence went down and Wale tumbled through into a small private parking lot.

He tried to drag himself back to his feet, but I guessed enough of Wale's corpse was broken that even magic couldn't move it anymore. He struggled for a few seconds, and then collapsed facedown on the pavement. I jumped over the twisted fence and landed beside him. I nudged him with the toe of my boot and rolled him onto his back. He stared up at me with dead, gray eyes.

"Suicide by gangster," he said, and his laughter was dry and ragged.

"You might have mentioned that's all you needed from me. It would have wasted a lot less of my time."

"Wanted to know if I was better than you."

I shrugged. "You're not," I said. "You never were." I spun my ghost-binding spell and finished the job.

thirteen

The ivy covering the beige, synthetic stucco walls of the Men's Room looked as natural as double-Ds on a hundred-pound stripper. Fortunately, the vines didn't crawl up to the second story, and the glowing, red-and-silver tag that spelled out the word SANCTUARY was easily visible against the prefabricated drabness. We had muscle in the parking lot and on the roof of the club—it squatted in the shadow of the freeway and that was an obvious angle of attack if any zombies up there got the idea to do a little one-stop grocery shopping.

Inside, the Men's Room was packed to the lap-dance couches with civilians. I hadn't seen so many people in the club since a celebrity porn star wiggled through on a special appearance tour. I'd been worried about the mental state of our wards based on what Chavez had said. The juice we were pumping into the club would have been enough to give them a case of the crazies, even without a zombie apocalypse to adjust to. So I was surprised when I walked in the front door and found a fairly respectable party going on.

Chavez had both bars humming like an assembly line.

I glanced up at the ticker running over the main bar and quickly saw why—it was advertising free drinks all night. The sound system was cranked up to Armageddon and the stages were crowded ass-to-elbow with naked dancers. Judging by the standards of physical fitness and dancing prowess on display, none of them were professionals.

Adan pushed through the crowd and took my elbow. "You were supposed to gate me back in," he said, leaning in and shouting in my ear.

"Didn't really have the time," I said. "Where are the boys?"

Adan blushed. "I took them back to the dressing room. Some of the girls are looking after them."

I drew my head back and looked at him. "Are you shy, Adan? They're just dancers. They're working their way through college."

"I'm not shy," he said. "It's just...not a lot of experience with human women. It's different, somehow."

"Just remember, the club is a lot like the Seelie Court. You got to be able to dance, lie and fight. Well, most of the girls can't fight for shit."

Adan grinned. "Let's go see Chavez." We walked to the back of the club and up the stairs to the office. Chavez had Rashan's parchment map of Greater Los Angeles spread out on the desk, the corners weighted down with cell phones. Two dancers stood beside him holding cells in both hands, ready to speed dial or slap a phone against his ear if he got an important call.

"There's got to be a better way, Chavez," I said. "You could get one of those headsets. This is embarrassing—it's like a guy buys a car and then hitches it to his plow horse. No offense, ladies."

"*Chola,*" he said, glancing up at me, "we got a major

concentration of Zeds moving south out of downtown." There were red dots scattered all over the three-dimensional profile of the city superimposed on the parchment. The clump of dots at Santa Fe and Fourth Street was so large and densely packed it looked like Chavez had gotten a nosebleed.

I nodded at the map. "The bean-sidhe are feeding you the locations?"

"Yeah, we got 'em hooked right into the map. We're getting updates in real time."

"Okay, then just send some big hitters over there to clean it up. Where's Amy Chen's crew?"

"She's over in Leimert Park, D. Fucking gentrification, we don't have the juice boxes there we used to. The civilians are holed up in their churches, and Zed's hitting them like fucking Oki Dog after last call."

"Where are Jack and Honey?"

"With Ismail Akeem in Koreatown. The real problem is we got a Stag platoon down there."

"Why is that a problem? Where are they?"

Chavez reached down and pulled the three-dimensional image toward him, zooming in on the intersection. There was a tiny clump of blue dots surrounded by all the red ones. Chavez pointed to an old brick building with green freight doors. "They're pinned down in the produce warehouse. They were trying to pull some civilians out of the lofts across the street when Zed overran them. They lost a couple guys, but they were able to pull back in time. Lowell's leading them and he doesn't want to call in reinforcements."

Looking at all the red dots surrounding his position, I couldn't really blame him. "They can't shoot their way out?"

"There's less than thirty of them, *chola,* and at least five hundred Zeds outside."

Guess not. "What about the sidhe?"

Chavez snorted. "Oberon is mostly staying in Hollywood and the turf you gave up in South Central. Says his people can't hack it out in the cold. Anyway, it's good because he's taking care of business on his streets."

I nodded. The fairy king had told me what I could expect. "Where's Mr. Clean?"

"That scary motherfucker is everywhere, but he ain't exactly checking in."

"Okay, Adan and I can go pull the government out of the fire. How's everything else look?"

Chavez opened his mouth to speak and then spread his arms over the map. "Hell if I know, *chola.* Maybe better than it was a few hours ago but still not too fucking good? It's like you said—it's a numbers game and I always copied off you in math class."

"Fuck that, Chavez, we both copied off your girlfriend."

"Oh, yeah." His eyes drifted away and a little smile tugged at the corner of his mouth. "What was her name, *chola?*"

"*Their* name was Maria."

"That's right. *Las Tres Marias.* They were good at math."

"So you're telling me you don't know if we're winning."

"I'm telling you I don't even know *when* I'll know. When there's no more red dots on the map, I guess. It goes like this for a while and you think you're getting ahead of it, and then a Zed pack gets inside an apartment building or a hotel or something, and if we don't get there fast enough the map starts lighting up again."

"We're doing everything we can, Domino," Adan said. "It'll have to be enough."

"Or it won't," I said.

"It will. Are you ready to go?"

"Give me a few minutes. Mr. Clean makes me nervous and I won't have a chance to check on him if I don't do it now."

Adan nodded. "I'll go look in on the kids."

A little tinge of jealousy snuck up on me from behind and squeezed my cheeks. I turned away, walking over to the leather couch and collapsing on the soft cushions. "You need some singles?" I said, digging in the front pocket of my jeans. Adan stared at me blankly. "For the dancers...you put a dollar in their...never mind, country boy."

"I'm not going for a dance, Domino," Adan said.

Chavez looked back and forth between us, grinning. "It's a strip club, *chola*. It doesn't cost anything to look."

"Fuck you, Chavez. Go, Adan." I waved him away and closed my eyes. Sarcasm and snark can be deadly weapons, but when they misfire they can really make you look like a clown—the goofy variety, not the scary ones. I didn't even care if Adan wanted to take another peek at the dressing room. I might have worried about him if he didn't. Why did I have to say something? Why couldn't I have said something that was actually funny? Why did fucking Chavez have to hear it?

I took a deep breath and beat the moment of schoolgirl awkwardness back into the closet. Then I conjured an image of Mr. Clean in my mind, tapped the abundant juice pulsing through the club and spun my peekaboo spell. "To see what is in front of one's nose needs a constant struggle," I said.

At first I thought my spell had failed. The image that sprang up behind my closed eyelids was a gray, color-streaked frenzy of motion-blurred chaos. Then the image froze, instantly, and I found myself looking down at an expansive pile of headless zombies. A massive scimitar of silvered steel extended into my view and dripped crimson from the razor-sharp edge.

"Get out of my head," said Mr. Clean. "You know I hate that."

"Yeah," I said, smiling. "Anyway, technically, you don't really have a head. You're a spirit."

"I do have a head, as I am at present manifest in the physical world, and indeed you demonstrate that my head possesses within it far more productive material than does yours."

"That was a hell of a sentence, Mr. Clean. You might need to diagram that motherfucker for me."

The jinn's sigh murmured in my mind. "What do you want, Dominica? As you can see, I'm busy. I was about to set upon a strip mall where the dead are, as we speak, causing great distress to the locals."

"Well, I'll let you set upon it in a second. Seriously, what's with all the verbosity? Are you feeling okay?"

"The carnage is invigorating," said Mr. Clean. "I am lifted on wings of slaughter and soar on the hot, red currents of sublime and exquisite war."

"If you're having such a good time, maybe we can renegotiate the price."

"Not a chance."

"Didn't think so. Where are you?"

Mr. Clean laughed. "Where is the hatred in a man's heart? Where is the plague that steals silent and unseen through the village streets while the children lie dying in their beds? Where is the—"

"What's the fucking address, Mr. Clean?"

"I'm in Northridge."

"War is hell," I said. I had the jinn working the Valley

because he could move faster than my gangsters and the juice was probably thin enough out there to give the sidhe respiratory problems. Mr. Clean could cover more ground than anyone else I had on my side of the zombie apocalypse. "What are you doing with the heads?" We hadn't really gotten into the details, and I'd been worried about it since we closed the deal. I did *not* want to go home to a condo full of zombie heads.

"As you did not specify a location for proper disposal, I am leaving them where they fall." I saw the scimitar point down to the pavement where one of the zombie heads lay on its right cheek. It stared up at me—at Mr. Clean—out of the corner of one filmy, gray eye. It snarled and gnashed its teeth.

"I hope the Xolos are quick about cleaning up the mess. That's going to be hard to pass off as LSD in the water supply."

"Even if you had directed me to dispose of the heads properly, the bodies remain animated, as well." The jinn reached down with the scimitar and poked at one of the de-capitated bodies. Its arms lashed out and the thing grabbed onto the sword, dragging its hands along the blade. Mr. Clean wrenched the scimitar free and the hands grasped blindly for a moment before withdrawing.

"Yeah, don't do that," I said. "I just want you to bring me one head—leave the rest of them alone."

"Which head would you like?"

"The last one."

Adan and I zigzagged our way over to Mateo and headed north up the narrow street lined with body shops, ware-houses and distribution centers. Taggers had put down most of what passed for paint jobs on the concrete and brick that crowded us on either side. If anything, the street was even more choked with abandoned vehicles than Alameda and the freeway had been. There were a lot fewer cars, but a lot less space to cram them in. We moved quickly, running and leaping along the metal highway, occasionally pausing to liberate a dead motorist that hadn't yet turned and gone hunting. Most of them were so badly mauled I wasn't sure they'd be mobile even when they went Zed. We didn't spot a single zombie up and about.

At Seventh Street, the sprawling warehouse district began to give way to stores, bars, restaurants and the occasional loft or apartment building. We saw shattered windows and splintered doorways, and the businesses were empty and silent.

When we crossed Sixth Street, we heard the noise. It didn't sound a whole lot different from the obscene choir I'd heard when the zombie horde attacked us on Alameda, except this time it was punctuated by staccato bursts of gunfire. Adan and I stopped on the hood of a greenish-gold Chevy beater and looked at each other.

"How do you want to do this?" Adan asked.

"I figured we'd walk up and you'd throw down that blast spell. Worked pretty good last time. It ought to buy us enough time for Lowell and his guys to get out."

"Listen to the gunfire."

I did. "Automatics...some small-caliber stuff." Then it registered. "Aw, shit, some of the zombies are carrying."

"Yeah, you have to think the automatic fire is coming from the soldiers. The rest of it, though—that's got to be zombies."

"Who are you and what did you do with the country boy?"

Adan laughed. "I'm a quick study. This could get complicated if the zombies have guns. Even if they didn't, you had it about right—we'd basically have to walk right into the middle of them for me to use that spell. Maybe we should try to think of a smarter plan."

I nodded. "Let's move in a little closer and scout it out." When we crossed Palmetto, we could see the loft building that had been the soldiers' objective up ahead. The produce warehouse was still out of sight. The noise had grown to a dull, persistent roar and the sharp bursts of gunfire followed one after the other. I'd been around gunfire plenty of times, even automatic weapons fire, but it hadn't sounded anything like this. I might have called myself a soldier, but I'd never been in a war zone.

I flipped my head up at a large, white stucco warehouse and we levitated to the roof. We moved carefully and quietly to the edge and looked out at the vast horde of zombies that surrounded the produce warehouse across the street. There were a hell of a lot more than five hundred of them. Either the bean-sidhe were wrong, or Chavez's map was wrong, or the dead had gotten some reinforcements of their own.

"The Zed Sea," said Adan.

I glanced at him. "That's not bad," I said. "You're usually as funny as a bunion, but you show flashes of real talent. The Dead Sea would have been pretty solid, but you bumped it up a notch when you went with Zed Sea."

"Better Zed than Dead," he said.

I raised an eyebrow. "Oh, yeah, you're good."

"What's red and white and—"

"No, see, you got to know when to stop. Be patient, you're learning."

Adan grinned and then his face hardened as he looked

down at the horde surrounding the produce warehouse. "What do you think?"

The back wall of the building was a featureless expanse of red brick, but still there was a solid ring of the dead around it, at least twenty deep. The zombies in front were clawing at the brick, as if they could tunnel through the wall. The west wall had two large, barred windows. The glass was broken out and soldiers were firing through the bars. They'd thinned out the front ranks on that side, but they were less effective than I might have expected. I guessed it was hard to get a clean head-shot with a limited field of fire and a zombie horde surging around them, close enough to reach out and touch.

"They can't get to us up here," I said. "Let's just take them out. Use fire if you've got it—it'll spread. Keep it away from the windows."

Adan nodded and stretched out his hands toward the zombies, fingers spread. *"Bladhm,"* he said, and a fiery current jetted forth and spilled across the undead mob.

"Do you want the flamethrower spell?" I said, glancing sideways at him. Then I spun up a fireball and hurled it down at the massed zombies.

The initial damage was impressive, but the reaction wasn't what I'd been expecting. The zombies ran for cover. I'd seen enough zombies running around trying to eat people, it was hard to remember they weren't mindless monsters. Fortunately, while they had the right idea, tactically speaking, their execution was no better than any other human mob. They all tried to run in different directions and whole waves of them went down under the panicked feet of their comrades. Burning zombies unselfishly shared with their fellows that had escaped the attack, and fire spread through the desiccated bodies like rumors on a Hollywood set.

"Across the street!" a lone voice shouted. "On the roof of the white building! Get them!" Armed zombies scattered throughout the crowd opened fire and bullets chipped stucco off our building's facade, forcing us back from the edge.

"Smart zombies with guns," I said. "No fair." We heard breaking glass from below as zombies smashed their way into our warehouse.

Adan looked around the roof. "They're not that smart," he said. "There's no internal stairway up here. The access ladders are the only way they're going to get at us."

"How long will it take them to figure that out?"

"Probably not very long. If we want to stay here, we'll have to defend the ladders. There are six of them."

"I'm not sure what good it does to stay here, anyway. The zombies shifted around to the front and sides of the building where we can't hit them."

"We need a plan," Adan said.

"Yeah."

"Any ideas?"

"I was really hoping your shockwave thing would work. I don't have any spells designed to clear out several hundred zombies."

"We could go down and fight them on the street."

"There's too many, Adan. I don't know how good your defenses are, but they'll eventually take me down. If I don't get shot, first."

"Maybe we need help."

"We *are* the help, Adan."

"Okay, let's think it through. We don't have to drop all the zombies. We just have to get Lowell and his troops out of there."

"How are we supposed to do that? We can't even get to

the door. It would be like trying to fight our way through a mosh pit to the front of the stage. Except this mosh pit will try to eat us."

"Yeah, and the soldiers might shoot us accidentally."

"We need a distraction," I said.

"That could work. What did you have in mind? Zed's not interested in much besides eating."

"Yeah, I'll be the distraction. I'll go down there and let them get a good whiff of me, then I'll take off and they'll chase me. You get the soldiers out of there."

"I should be the distraction," Adan said. "I have the blast spell if the zombies get too close, and Lowell doesn't really know me."

I didn't like it, but he had a point. I nodded. "Okay," I said, "you're the bait. Be safe, Adan."

He grinned and put his arm around me, pulling me to him. He leaned in and kissed me softly on the mouth. "Every guy wants to be the hero," he said, and then released me. I wanted to say something—anything—but my vocal cords were momentarily paralyzed. Adan drew his sword and spun his jump spell, launching from the rooftop, across the street and onto the roof of the produce warehouse.

I smelled apples and cinnamon, and tasted it on my tongue. "What the fuck just happened?" I whispered. I looked down at myself with the fairy sight, but if there was any glamour on me it was the hormonal kind. My heart was pounding in my chest and my body felt light, like my levitate spell wanted to pick me up and lift me into the air.

Adan looked back, grinned and raised his sword, then raced for the front of the building where the zombie horde waited below, howling for blood and flesh. He jumped again when he reached the edge and disappeared out of sight. The noise intensified to an ear-grinding screech when he hit the street in the middle of the massed zombies.

I took deep, steady breaths and waited for my pulse to slow. Then I dug out my cell phone and called Lowell.

"What's going on out there, Riley? Something's got Zed all worked up."

"That'd be Adan," I said. He had more than zombies worked up. "He's leading them away from the building."

"I've got a man down in here. We need to get him out fast."

"Working on it, Lowell. Once the zombies clear out, I'll come down there and drop any stragglers. Just make sure your guys are ready to move. I don't want to leave Adan on the hook any longer than we have to."

"I've got Black Hawks circling. Once the threat is neutralized, the helos can land in the truck lot across Santa Fe. Do you and Adan need extraction?"

"No, we can handle it. We still need to thin out the Zed population a little around here once your guys are out."

"Okay, standing by."

"Yeah, good, and don't shoot me when I get down there. I need my shields for the strapped zombies."

I put the cell away and heard a scrabbling sound behind me. A zombie was climbing onto the roof from an access ladder, a black male in a red muscle shirt. He reached down and helped a girl with bright green streaks in her blond hair climb up after him. That was gentlemanly. The two of them bared their teeth and stared at me with their dead eyes. They approached slowly, warily, crouched down with their hands extended like wrestlers. Another zombie crawled up on the far side of the roof.

I didn't want to use my levitation spell because I was pretty sure I'd draw fire if I went any higher than the level of the rooftop. "Man is born free," I said, "but everywhere he is in chains." Force magic whipped around the male zombie and immobilized him. I fixed the threads of magic in my mind and spun my ghost-binding spell, pulling the girl's spirit from her body. When the corpse collapsed, I dropped the chaining spell on the man and did the same to him.

Seeing the fate of the first two, the third zombie howled and charged me as four more zombies climbed onto the roof from different ladders. "Vi Victa Vis," I said, and my force spell sent the charging zombie sprawling. I spun the ghost-binding spell just as the four newcomers charged.

"This is ridiculous," I muttered. It was like a small-scale reenactment of the whole zombie apocalypse—crunch all you want, we'll make more. I backpedaled toward the western edge of the warehouse, pulling in juice as I went. "To every action there is an equal and opposite reaction," I said, spinning a wall of repulsive force around me. The charging zombies hit the wall and were hurled away like bowling pins. One of them went screaming over the edge of the building, arms flailing.

More zombies climbed onto the roof. One of them carried a revolver and another was toting a shotgun. I reached down for more juice and my eyes started to burn. Each one of the hairs on my arms and the back of my neck stood up and started dancing. My heartbeat thudded in my chest, and blood and juice pumped through me like a rain-swollen river. I threw my hands out, pushing at the plane of force and sweeping it across the rooftop like a giant invisible broom. Zombies were hurled over the side and dropped to the street and sidewalk below.

Unless I wanted to make a full-time job out of knocking zombies off the roof, I needed to move. I ran to the edge of the building and spun my jump spell, retracing Adan's path to the roof of the produce warehouse. I ran to the front of the building and looked down. The loading area was clear, but there were only freight doors along that side. I scrambled over to the east side and finally found an access door. I dropped down in front of it and knocked.

"Riley?" Lowell called from inside.

"No, pizza guy. Open the fucking door, Lowell." The door opened and Lowell backed away, letting me in. He touched the earpiece of his headset and started barking orders. Almost immediately, I heard the sound of helicopters in the distance.

A couple dozen soldiers in black fatigues were huddled around the office and scattered through the warehouse area. Two of them were tending to a soldier lying on a make-shift pallet of tarpaulins. It looked like his left arm had been nearly torn off, and blood soaked the canvas beneath him.

"Extraction in five minutes," Lowell called. "Fall back to my position, on the quick." As if to emphasize his words, an assault rifle chattered from the far side of the warehouse where a team of soldiers covered the ground-floor windows.

My cell phone rang. "Zed's moving west across the Fourth Street bridge," Chavez said. "It's big. There might be a thousand of them."

"We've got choppers in five minutes, Chavez. Are they already on the bridge?" It had to be a quarter mile across the river and the railroad tracks. It would be close.

"They're on the bridge and coming fast, *chola*. Maybe they saw the helicopters."

Or the magic show. "Damn it," I said. "Okay, I got this. Thanks for the heads-up, Chavez." I stuck the cell back in my pocket and turned to Lowell. "We've got company,

Lowell. I'm going to hold them off—get your guys on those fucking choppers."

Lowell frowned. "You going to be okay? I can go with you."

"They're on the bridge, Lowell. I'll be fine." Even with sorcery, terrain could make a difference. The zombies would be exposed on the bridge instead of wrapped around the Stag team's hidey-hole. I went out and ran across the loading area, pausing to drop a couple solitary zombies that were more or less on my way. I spun my jump spell and leaped up to the elevated street that spanned the tracks and concrete river to the east.

I walked out onto the bridge to meet the zombie horde charging toward me. I stopped in the middle of the street between two of the old-fashioned lampposts spaced at regular intervals across the length of the bridge. I started pulling juice from the street and from the outfit tags that decorated the bridge abutments. The zombies pounded across the bridge like a barbarian horde mad for blood—which was more or less what they were, despite their lack of swords and battleaxes and except for the part about being dead. When the first ranks were three hundred feet away, I spun my fire wave spell and the orange tsunami began to build behind me.

I kept flowing juice and the wave grew to twenty, then fifty, then a hundred feet high, stretching from one side of the bridge to the other. I fed more juice to the fire and it grew hotter and hotter, shattering the glass in the streetlamps and causing the metal fixtures to glow red. I wanted it hot enough to vaporize. I knew the zombies couldn't feel pain, but I wasn't sure they couldn't still experience something like terror. There would be no horribly burned bodies staggering around on the bridge when I was done with them. There would be nothing left but grease, and ash and smoke.

When the zombie horde was a hundred feet away, I released the tidal wave and it crashed over me, thundering across the bridge and submerging the zombies in a torrent of liquid fire. The leading edges of the fire reached all the way to the overpass that crossed Mission Road. Every inch of the bridge was scoured clean. I dropped to one knee and gasped for breath as the last of the juice flushed out of me. After a few moments, the oily, black smoke began to clear. That's when I saw the demon.

Its form was an obscene parody of a woman. It was at least seven feet tall and more emaciated than any human could become and still live. Pallid flesh sagged loosely and bones protruded at hard angles like blades. Thin, greasy strands of dark hair hung down to the skeletal waist, and its breasts were tiny, withered pouches that wrinkled its sunken chest. In contrast to the rest of its consumptive frame, the demon's belly was hideously bloated, swollen to an impossible size. Black veins stood out like cracks in the fish-pale skin stretched tight over the bulging womb.

The demon's belly convulsed and contorted. It squatted with its feet braced wide apart, and dark fluids splashed onto the pavement. It grinned at me, baring broken, jagged teeth the color of charcoal. The terrible, gaping orifice between the demon's legs stretched wide, and black, clawed hands appeared, raking the stick-thin legs as something pulled itself forth into the world.

I turned away and emptied my stomach on the street. I'd seen enough to know what had wriggled out of the demon. It was a crawler. I flowed some juice to calm my shaking hands and steeled myself to look. When I did, I saw the crawler racing along the concrete barrier above the bridge abutment. And I saw a second crawler pulling itself from the demon's womb.

I fought down the nausea and tried to think. I wanted to run. I wanted to get as far away from that bridge as I could and try to forget what I'd seen. What I was seeing. You can't run from a demon. Even with my Road Runner spell, I doubted I could outrun a crawler. Or two. Nope, check that, three crawlers—another on the way. I couldn't see them from my angle atop the bridge, but I could hear the sound of the helicopters' rotors from the direction of the produce warehouse. They were on the ground—taking on Lowell's soldiers, probably. But still on the ground. I couldn't run. I had to fight.

My blood was already on fire, but I tapped more juice and spun a countermagic spell at the first crawler. The magic splashed over the demon and it froze in midstride, skidding forward along the abutment a few feet before tumbling over the side to the parched concrete of the river below.

The demon mother threw back her head and screamed. She flung out a spindly arm at me, clenching the bony fingers into a fist, and pain exploded in my chest. I fell to both knees and doubled over, clutching at my breast. "God is a scientist," I choked out, "not a magician." The magic-killing juice flushed through me and the pain subsided. It didn't feel any worse than a charley horse in my heart muscle.

I blinked rapidly to clear my vision and struggled to my feet. I reached for the juice and spun another countermagic spell at the second crawler streaking toward me along the sidewalk. The demon mother chopped down through the air with the blade of her hand and I felt my spell come unbound and disintegrate before it reached its target. Without breaking stride, the crawler coiled and leaped at me from fifty feet away. I just had time to trigger my repulsion talisman before it hit me. The magic oozed around the demon, slowing it but not stopping it. Hot claws sank deep into my flesh, and the black, featureless face filled my vision as the demon's snapping jaws went for my throat.

I grasped that smooth, blank mask with both hands, and my mind tore desperately at the street, deluging my body and spirit with magic. I cried out as I slammed the juice into a force spell. "Vi Victa Vis!" I shouted, and the hammer smashed into the demon's head and snapped its head back at a ninety-degree angle. The crawler released me and dropped to the pavement, its head lolling and twitching on its whip-cord neck. I turned the countermagic on it and kept pouring juice into the spell until the demon's body began to come apart and run liquid.

I looked up in time to see the final crawler bearing down on me. The demon mother approached with slow, spasmodic steps, hands up and ready to knock down any counter-magic I threw at the crawler. I decided to oblige her. I spun the countermagic spell and hurled it at the crawler. When I saw the demon mother's hand slice down, tearing apart the countermagic, I hit the crawler with my chaining spell. Bands of force encircled the demon. I poured juice into the spell until red and gold light began to flow just under the surface of my skin. My brain felt like it was convulsing as I forced it to contain and channel the magic. I tightened the vise around the demon and it screamed, struggling to slip through the arcane force compressing it. I tightened the chains some more and the mother screamed. I tapped more juice, feeding the spell. The chains tightened, and I screamed.

The demon mother lashed out and I triggered the anti-magic talisman on my left ring finger. A force spell smashed through the shield and struck me in the chest, and I heard ribs snap. I was punched backward thirty feet, and then I hit the asphalt and slid another ten. I'd lost the chaining spell and expected the crawler to be on me in seconds. Clenching my jaw against the pain, I struggled to sit up. The spell had done its work—the crawler had dissolved into a spreading pool of tar on the street. The demon mother kept coming, her stiltlike legs jerking and shaking with every uneven step.

I braced my hands on the street and tried to get my feet under me. The demon smashed a fist down, and force magic hammered me back to the pavement. I stared up into the sky and saw a black helicopter passing slowly overhead. I had the sudden irrational hope that Lowell would jump out of the chopper and save my ass. He didn't.

The demon began rubbing herself as she hobbled toward me. She made small, loathsome sounds of pleasure and black drool oozed from her open mouth and dripped down her chin. More fluids wet the insides of her shriveled thighs. I turned my head to the side and puked again.

The convulsions in my stomach didn't get any better—they got worse. Something twitched and twisted inside me. I managed to rise up on my elbows, and I saw my abdomen convulse, the muscles rippling and contorting. Then I saw my belly begin to rise, swelling like bread dough in the oven. The demon mother giggled and began rubbing herself harder. I felt something move inside me.

I screamed and reached for the juice, but something else was taking it. Something else was feeding on it, and the magic was ripped away from me as surely as if I'd been squeezed. The demon stood over me, now, and fluids gushed from her and spattered my legs and stomach. My belly surged and heaved, and the pain was every bit as maddening as the last time I'd used the shapeshifting magic, when I'd felt as though an alien cancer was growing inside me. In the Between, I'd known the agony would pass. This time I knew the worst was yet to come.

An image flared to life in my mind of the house where I grew up, the little bungalow my mother still lived in. This was a different time, though, long ago. I'm sitting on the floor in the living room, forgotten dolls scattered around me, watching my mother. She's sitting in the recliner—an ugly, clumsy, green thing that will vanish from the house in a few years—and she's sewing yet another patch on my favorite pair of jeans. She's young and beautiful, and the sunlight streaming through the window sets her long, dark, unbound tresses aglow. My mother is an angel, a Madonna, and the father I've never known must be an angel, too. God needed him, though, for something terribly important, and that's why he had to leave. And I'm so happy, because I know I must be special, too, and that's why I'm always alone, and no matter how ugly the world is outside these walls, our house is a little corner of heaven.

And I know I can go to this place, and I can stay here, forever. I'm standing on the wide porch, looking in through the window at my mother bathed in sunlight, and I know she'll always be young and beautiful in this place, and she'll never grow old, or suffer, or die, and neither will I. The little girl is waiting for me, that happy, hopeful child I lost just like the old recliner, and I can find her again. I can *be* her again. All I have to do is open the door. There's only darkness behind me. There are terrible things, but I won't see them as long as I don't turn around. I can go into that house and close the door behind me, and I can shut them out so they can never touch me. They can never hurt me.

I only have to open the door.

I was crying when I pulled the trigger on the forty-five

in my hand. The weapon bucked and the demon mother's swollen belly exploded in a shower of thick, black fluid and wet, ragged tissue. I squeezed the trigger again and again, and the demon shrieked and reeled back, grasping at the ruined mess her abdomen had become.

"It's called a gun, you skanky bitch," I said. The thing that had been growing inside me was gone, leaving behind a sharp, hot pain that lanced through my abdomen and groin. I sat up and blinked to clear the tears from my eyes. I steadied the forty-five, squeezing off another round that struck the demon between her shriveled breasts. "You want back in my world, you better learn how to take a fucking bullet."

Still screaming, the demon turned and tried to stagger away. I stood up, leveled the forty-five and shot her in the back. She went down, planting her face in the pavement with a sharp crack. She pulled herself to her hands and knees and began to crawl. I put a round in the back of her skull, and black spray patterned the asphalt. I walked around her until I stood in her path, and then I slammed the heel of my boot into her face. The demon mother toppled over on her side, spasms racking her cadaverous body. I filled my mind with juice and poured countermagic over her.

In twenty-three years of killing, I'd never wanted to torture anyone. More times than I could count, I'd been called on to take a life, but not once did I have any desire to cause pain. I did what I did, but if it was up to me, I did it quick. I wanted this demon to suffer, and I wanted to inflict it upon her. I didn't have any magic black enough to match what she had done to me. I spun up a ball of flame in my hand, but I was careful not to put too much juice into it. I wanted it to burn, but I didn't want it to destroy.

"Domino," Adan said. He walked toward me from the

west end of the bridge, his sword in his hand. "Finish it...
do it right."

Rage burned through me and I lashed out. The fireball erupted from my hand and streaked toward Adan. He
flicked the sword and spoke a word, and the blade flashed
white as he batted my spell aside.

"Master your fear and you'll master the beast," he said,
and he kept walking.

My lips pulled back from my teeth and I started shaking.
I felt magic flowing into me from the street, and the tags
that crawled across the bridge and the box cars that sat rust-
ing on the tracks below. I took it into me and I fed it with
hate, and a fiery tide began to swell behind me. I wanted
the demon to burn. I wanted Adan to burn. I wanted the
world to burn.

I wanted to burn.

My hair ignited but it wasn't consumed, and flames began
to dance on my outstretched hands, spreading up my arms
and crawling across my chest and back. The inferno behind
me rose higher and fiery tongues licked out, like star-fire
erupting from the face of the sun.

A brilliant emerald meteor fell from the sky and suddenly Honey was hovering before me, the dragonfly wings
a rainbow blur at her back. Her cheeks were wet, but she
was smiling.

"Jack asked me to marry him, Domino," she said.

The roiling wave of fire collapsed in on itself and snuffed
out. I crumbled to the street, falling first to my knees and
then dropping onto my side. I stared unblinking into the
face of the demon mother, and I saw it dissolve into black
tar as Adan's sword flashed down.

And then I went looking for that sun-kissed bungalow with the wide porch and the ugly green chair, the mother who would never die and the happy little girl.

fourteen

I'm sitting at the kitchen table with my legs tucked under me. My arms are crossed in front of me on the Formica table and my chin is resting on my hands. I'm watching *Scooby-Doo* on the little black-and-white TV set. The Scooby gang is in some tropical paradise. They find a flying saucer, but skeletons with a single large eye try to scare them away. The skeleton people frighten me and I bury my face in my arms when they come on the screen. The eyes are all wrong. They should be normal eyes, but gray and cloudy, like the surface of an old marble.

Mama is with me in the kitchen. She's making huevos, and corn tortillas are heating in the oven. The smell fills the room and my mouth waters. A commercial comes on and a genie with a bald head and bushy eyebrows is getting rid of dirt and grime and grease in just a minute. The genie is smiling and friendly, but I don't like him. He's very old, and he knows secrets, and he's *always* trying to sell something. The bright, shining eyes and wide grin hide something dangerous and never to be trusted.

A shadow passes in front of the window. I get up from the table and climb up in the armchair by the window to look out. I part the blinds with my small fingers—just a little—and I see a man with dark hair and large eyes standing on the front porch. He's dressed all in black, and he has an old wooden gun slung over his shoulder and a silver sword at his side. He's terribly handsome and I'm not afraid of him. He stands on the porch, looking at the front door, but he doesn't knock.

"He's waiting for you to open the door, Dominica," says Mama. She's standing beside me, looking down at me with a small smile on her face. Maybe breakfast is ready? The eggs will get cold. I *hate* cold eggs.

"Should I let him in, Mama?" I ask.

"You will have to decide that for yourself, child."

"If I open the door, I don't think he will come in. I think he will try to take me away."

"He doesn't belong here."

"But I don't want to go with him. I don't like it out there."

"You don't belong here, either," my mother says. "Not anymore."

I start to cry, the tears welling in my eyes without warning. I shake my head. "I *do* belong here, Mama. I like it here, with you. There are bad people out there, bad things. We're safe here, though. They can't come in."

I'm in my room, sitting on my small bed and playing with my favorite doll. She has a name, but I can't remember what it is. It seems strange that I've forgotten her name and it makes me sad. I decide to call her Honey, though I can't remember why. I'm shining the light on her, the light no one else can see. I don't know what it is, but I call it Glitter. I'm putting Glitter on Honey and making her walk around the room, as if she were alive. I'm certain if I can just put enough Glitter on Honey, I can make her a real girl, like

Pinocchio, and she can be my friend. It makes me sad that I don't have any friends. No one except Honey.

Honey stops and falls awkwardly on her rump, and I giggle. She turns her head and looks at me, and her doll eyes are somehow the bright, perfect blue of the summer sky. "You have to come back, Domino," she says. "We're all waiting for you. We need you."

I shake my head. "My name is Dominica," I say. "Domino is a stupid name."

"Come back, Domino," says Honey. "Please come back." Tears stream down her face, but I know it's just the Glitter. Honey isn't a real girl and she can't cry.

I'm in the kitchen looking out through the window in the back door at the tiny yard. Butterflies flit in the sunlight and Glitter falls from their wings and dances in the air. I want to go out and try to catch them, but I know it isn't safe. Something horrible is waiting out there. I can't remember what it is, but it doesn't matter as long as I stay in the house.

I see a fat man with white hair standing beside the small orange tree. His eyes are on fire and when he smiles at me, a black, forked tongue darts out, flicking at the air. He beckons for me to come to him. I turn away and run deeper into the house, looking for Mama.

She's in her room, lying in bed with the blankets drawn up to her chin. Her Bible rests on the table beside her and a crucifix hangs on the wall above her head. Something is wrong. Her hair is thin and gray, and her skin is terribly wrinkled, as if God had reached down and wadded her up like a piece of paper He would throw away. I cry out and run to the bed, leaping atop it and throwing my arms around her. She's so *thin,* like part of her has already gone and only a little remains. I bury my face in the blankets and sob.

"You're wrong, child," my mother says. "The darkness can find you here, too."

The room grows cold and I lift my head. It's dark outside now, and shadows move against the window glass. There are shapes in the shadows—black figures with no faces that scuttle like crabs, writhing tentacles and hairy spider legs, a giant that burns from the inside, a wasted corpse of a woman with a swollen belly.

"No!" I cry. "They can't come in!" I look at Mama and her eyes are gray and glassy. Her thin body is cold and still.

"You cannot run from it, Dominica," Mama says. "You must face it, child. If you do not, it will swallow the world."

"Mama," I cry, "I'm so afraid."

"I know, *cariño*. But you needn't face it alone. Your friends are waiting for you. I am waiting for you."

"But you'll *die,* Mama! You won't let me help you!"

"Nonsense, Dominica. My time on this earth will end someday, Lord willing. But I will leave part of myself behind, in you, and your children, and in theirs. That is the way it should be. You have seen what happens when the circle is broken."

"I don't know what to do."

"Go to them, child. Together you will find a way."

I'm at the front door, and I reach out and grasp the knob. It feels very large in my small hand. I turn it and open the door. The sunlight streams in and wreathes the man standing there in golden light. He smiles and extends his hand. I take it and walk out on the porch. I turn and look back.

My mother is sitting in the ugly green chair, sewing the patch on my favorite jeans. The little girl sits on the floor, making her rag doll turn somersaults in the air. Mama looks up and her face is filled with love. She smiles.

The image blurs as tears fill my eyes. I try to return the smile. "Goodbye, Mama."

Her smile widens and she shakes her head. "Not yet, *cariño*. Not yet."

I opened my eyes to a large bedroom with white walls, colorful abstract paintings and sleek, modern furniture. Adan sat beside the bed in a minimalist chair with a wooden seat and back and chromed metal legs. His face was buried in his hands. I thought he might be sleeping.

"Either I'm not dead, or Heaven hired an expensive interior decorator," I said. My voice rasped, like sandpaper on cement.

Adan looked up and smiled. He moved onto the edge of the bed beside me. "You're in my father's house," he said. "It was the safest place I could think of."

I nodded. "How long?"

"Two days. Your wounds were serious, but Honey patched you up." He shook his head. "After that, it was…"

"Yeah, I bought a one-way ticket to Crazytown."

"Not one way," he said. "You're back. You going to be okay?"

I shrugged. "Nothing years of expensive therapy can't make slightly less horrific."

"By the time I got there, it was over. I didn't see what happened."

"Something wicked came my way," I said, and shrugged. "They're demons. I guess they can do worse than try to kill you. What's the zombie situation?"

Adan nodded. "Mr. Clean is here…somewhere. He says he has something for you. It's in a box, and it's dripping—I can guess what it is. He says he either has to deliver it or you have to finish dying, thereby terminating his service to you."

"I'm touched. So it's over?"

"The zombie apocalypse is over. Mobley, Valafar and the demons are still an issue."

I laughed and shook my head. "I missed it."

"You missed the cleanup, you didn't miss the hard part. You did your part, and then some. Everyone is talking about the Battle of the Fourth Street Bridge. No one really knows what happened, just that there were about a thousand zombies and multiple demons involved. And you."

"Yeah," I said quietly, "kill enough people and you may become a god."

"What? You didn't kill anyone, Domino. You destroyed a bunch of zombies and several demons. You saved a couple dozen soldiers, including Lowell, and who knows how many others. The sanctuary network and the unified response to the zombie threat saved the city."

"Never mind, it was just something somebody said to me once." I struggled to sit up on the huge, overstuffed pillows. "So what's next?"

"We have to take down Mobley. He's the gate. Without him, Valafar can't bring more demons into this world."

"So let's go get him. Where is he?"

"He's holed up in the Salvation Army building on Compton Boulevard."

"Nice choice."

"Yeah, but we haven't been able to get at him. Valafar knows we have to clip Mobley. The place is crawling with demons. Oberon is rolling through Inglewood and Watts, Hawthorne and Lynwood. We thought that might convince Mobley to come out and fight, but I guess Valafar isn't concerned about the territory anymore."

"If Mobley can't get any juice, he won't be able to open the gate. No more demons."

"He's still got enough. He's got all of Compton down to the north side of Long Beach. And this thing with the zombies…I think it was a sea-change, Domino. We stopped it, but I don't think it will ever go back to the way it was."

"The walls are falling."

Adan nodded. "There's a lot of holes in them, anyway. Just because no new ones are opening up doesn't mean we've patched the ones that were already there."

"So Valafar doesn't care about anything except keeping Mobley alive and bringing in more demons."

"That's the way it looks. We don't know exactly how many demons Valafar has brought over. Enough to stop our efforts to get at Mobley. You know better than anyone, it doesn't take that many."

"Mobley's a tool," I said. "We can't even be sure he's ir-replaceable. This round won't be over until we send Valafar back to Hell."

"That's a heavy lift, Domino. If we get to Mobley, we'll get to Valafar. But there's going to be a small army of demons standing in our way."

"That's what I'm counting on," I said. "Are Honey and Jack here?"

Adan nodded.

"Good. Ask them to come in. I've got a plan."

"Are you quite certain a frontal assault was the best idea you could come up with?" Oberon asked.

"I like to keep it simple," I said. We'd invaded Compton in a classic pincer formation, the Seelie Court moving southeast out of Hawthorne and the outfits moving south from Lynwood. The demons had met us at Wilson Park. I stood with Oberon, Terrence, Adan and Honey on the roof of a VFW post and looked across Palmer at the darkness gathering in the park. It wasn't much of a battlefield—maybe three city blocks long and one block wide. Demons slouched from the trees at the south end, and more crawled from burning cracks in the world to join the impending conflict.

"They just finished the skatepark a couple years ago," Terrence said. "Hope it doesn't get tore up. Seems like we could have done this at a rail yard or something."

"Demons can be inconsiderate that way," I said. Once we'd seen where the demons would commit, we'd dropped enough wards around the park to keep the civilians at bay. They wouldn't know why, exactly, but they'd find someplace better to be while the desperate battle was waged against the forces of Hell.

I'd brought my heavy hitters with me. They stood together with Oberon's sidhe warriors, strung out along the street and watching the demons mass in the park. I wasn't sure how many battles it took to be a veteran, but I figured some of them qualified. Ismail Akeem and Amy Chen were down there, and they'd fought beside me in the showdown with Papa Danwe at the old factory in Hawthorne. We'd been trying to stop Oberon from returning to our world, and we'd failed. If we'd succeeded, we'd probably all be having brains for dinner. And even if we'd managed to stop the zombie apocalypse without the sidhe's help, we'd be standing there facing the demons alone.

"It's funny how shit works out," I said.

Oberon glanced over at me and smiled. "It's almost enough to make you believe in fate, isn't it?"

"It's not that funny."

"What are we waiting for?" Honey said. "Let's kill them." Her sword was in her hand, and red and orange pixie dust fell from her wings. She was wearing bright blue war paint, though I guessed it was only glamour. Oberon's sidhe warriors were similarly decorated.

"Settle down, William Wallace," I said. "Let them come."

"I'm worried about Jack," Honey said.

"I know. That's why we have to let them come."

The south end of the park had become a twisted nightmare of darkness and fire, obscene flesh and corrupted biology. There were more of the demon mothers there, and while I didn't look at them, I saw the crawlers they spawned moving forward to the front of the pack. Fire giants, like the one we'd fought at the Carnival Club, formed up behind them.

"Time for the artillery," Oberon said.

I looked over at him. "What kind of artillery?"

"Me," he said, and grinned. He walked forward to the edge of the building, raised his arms and began singing in that strange, haunting language he shared with Honey and Jack. A wind blew in from the coast, tugging at our exposed position and kicking up dust from the infield of the small baseball field. Clouds rolled in overhead, so fast it looked like vapor from a smoke machine crawling across the sky. The clouds undulated and turned in on themselves, and lightning began to flash in their bellies.

Across the field, the demons raised a terrible cry, a discordant symphony of screams, shrieks, roars and stomach-turning moans that crawled along my spine to the base of my brain and flushed my body with cold, stark terror. It was the sound of all the worst things humans had ever imagined waiting for them in dark places since they first dared to climb down from the trees.

Oberon tilted his head up to the sky as the rain began to fall, and the wind whipped his long, auburn hair around his face and shoulders. He began to glow, to shine, as if moonlight had been trapped beneath his skin and was straining to be free. The look on his face was rapturous, orgasmic, and his chant built and swelled with magic until the beautiful, secret words drowned out the demonic cacophony from the far side of the field.

A wave of crawlers raced forward, swarming across the grass and concrete toward us, and the glowering sky attacked. Jagged, crackling lines of blue-white lightning flashed down from the roiling clouds and caressed the scuttling crawlers almost gently, outlining them in fairy fire and reducing them instantly to smoking puddles of black tar. Only a handful made it through, and the sidhe warriors stepped forward to meet them, blades flashing and deadly glamours tearing into the crawlers like wild beasts.

"You're supposed to hit those guys with countermagic, first," I said to Oberon. "You got to soften them up so they don't shrug off your spells."

The fairy king laughed. "You ain't seen nothing yet," he said. Oberon threw back his head and sang, and the sky growled like a belligerent animal in answer to him. A slender funnel cloud formed in the twisting gray blanket overhead and reached for the demon horde assembled below. The tornado split in two and then another uncoiled from the angry sky. Emerald light flashed within the three vortices, and when they touched the south end of Wilson Park, the twisters spat forth an airborne brigade of piskie warriors. The piskies swarmed over the demons and the red-orange pixie dust was so thick it looked like burning snowfall.

"My people," Honey said. "We kick ass."

"Join them, if you will," Oberon said, inclining his head and raising his sword in salute. "Your House is pardoned and it is your right to stand with them. To war, Princess, and red glory!"

The blue war paint on Honey's face and body pulsed alight and green fire danced along the edge of her sword. "Until death and darkness and the world's sorrow, my King," she said, and then she was off, blazing across the field like an emerald comet falling into the sun.

"Yeah, Honey, don't let me hold you back," I muttered.

Despite the piskies' ass-kicking prowess, the fire giants pressed forward, tromping across the field and churning the turf into mud. They were armed with an array of the Dark Ages' most advanced weaponry: massive black iron swords with serrated edges, spiked balls on the ends of heavy chains that looked like they could demolish a house, mauls the size of small trees. The twisters roared through their ranks, scattering earth, foliage and playground equipment, but the fire giants leaned forward into the storm and marched on.

"What else you got, Oberon?" I said. "We had trouble with one of these guys in the club, and there's six of them here."

"Seven," Terrence said. "There's another one behind that big guy."

"They're all big guys, Terrence," I said.

"The *really* big motherfucker with the big fucking ax."

The figure striding across the field at the center of the giants' ranks towered over his fellows. He wore an ornate iron helm engraved with leaves and vines, and topped with a crown of fire that twined and branched like the antlers of a great stag. Flames burst from his eyes and from a mouth that was nearly hidden in a full beard that wreathed his craggy face like a wild tangle of spun silver.

"Oh, him," I said. "Is this guy someone we should know about, Oberon?"

The king shrugged. "Some lesser hero of the Fomoire. They have no shortage of them."

"Lesser hero, huh? Dime a dozen. That's great."

The Fomoiri hero roared a challenge and fire engulfed the front ranks of sidhe warriors. Defensive glamour flashed and glowed and most of the sidhe were spared. Some of them burned. A rumbling, baritone chant went up among the giants and rattled the windows of the VFW building below us. The giants began to run, and the earth trembled. I felt the tremors in the soles of my feet, thrumming bone-deep through my ankles and my legs.

Below, Ismail Akeem danced on Palmer Street, his thin body convulsing as he disgorged the spirits he had eaten. Amy Chen released phantasmal beasts and monsters that drifted silently through the rank of charging giants, vanishing completely within the massive bodies when they darted in to strike at their relentless, unwavering quarry. When the fire giants were only a few strides away, the sidhe rushed forward and attacked, lashing out with spell and blade to savage the demons' deformed and burning flesh.

For a moment, it appeared the sorcerers and sidhe warriors would stop the charge and cut the Fomoire down where they stood. Then the giants' blows began to land, and sidhe blood and crushed bodies fell on the grass like detritus scattered by the tornadoes.

"Time to pay the rent," Terrence said. He dropped a levitation spell and floated down to the street, and he was already spinning attack spells when his feet touched the pavement. Adan flashed a fierce grin at me and then leaped down after him.

I'd have preferred to battle the Firstborn as I had in the Carnival Club—from the Between, and with Ned in my hands. I'd decided against it because I didn't want to leave my helpless body lying around anywhere close to the battlefield. I was pretty sure I couldn't hide so well that no demons would find me, and it would only take one to ruin my day.

On the other hand, I didn't really want to see a repeat performance of the slaughter at the club, multiplied by seven and not even counting the rest of the demons on the field. I knew what they could do and I knew how effective our weapons and magic would be against them. The demons were relentless, unstoppable, and I did not believe we could stand against them.

That's why I came prepared to cheat. Mr. Clean's TV sat on the rooftop behind me. I wasn't planning to let the jinn have a piece of this fight, but I did need all the juice he could give me. I also carried the walking stick I'd taken from Papa Danwe when I killed him, for the same reason. I was physically recovered from what the demon had done to me on the bridge and I didn't need the stick to walk. I just needed the juice.

"Your first day of prison, they say you should find the biggest, baddest motherfucker on the cell block and take a shot at him," I said. "Maybe you do a little damage, maybe not, but you prove you're not a punk and the rest of the convicts will leave you alone after that."

"And that really works?" Oberon asked.

"No, it just means you get your ass kicked on the first day. The secret is, it's really for you—you prove to yourself you're not a punk. After that, you can take your beatings and whatever else comes and you can hold your head up."

Oberon nodded. "I believe it is the same at court."

"Yeah, but there's less dancing in prison." I raised my arms, with the walking stick in one hand and the other outstretched to the sky. I tapped juice from the street until my body burned with it and then I reached out with my mind and opened my familiar's veins, taking all he could give, as well.

I stepped forward to the edge of the building and pointed the walking stick at the Fomoiri hero. "Friends have all things in common," I said, and a torrent of magic rushed out of me and coursed over and through him. It was a simple friendship charm, one of the first spells you learn as a kid to make your way through life a little easier than it is for other people. It was a simple spell, but it was backed with a lot of juice. A combat spell with that much magic behind it might have seriously wounded or even killed the Fomoiri. One down, and then we'd just have six more fire giants and the rest of the demonic army to deal with.

The Fomoiri hero lifted his ax, a wicked implement more than ten feet long, and then he froze. He stood up straight, almost at attention, and stared at me as the sidhe warriors rained blows and lethal glamour upon him.

I pointed at another of the fire giants who spun a spiked ball and chain around his head before whipping it down upon the glowing, multicolored shield Amy Chen raised to defend herself. There was a blinding flash as the ball impacted the shield. Amy fell to her knees and the shield began to burn, orange flame devouring the colorful light until it dimmed and then extinguished.

"Kill," I said. If I'd known the demon's name, I might

have been able to issue more elaborate orders. On the other hand, that might have just gotten me in trouble.

The Fomoiri hero turned and brought his ax down on the knobby skull of Amy's adversary. The blade cleaved through the giant's head and bit deeply into its torso. Fire and darkness billowed out of the terrible wound, and the demon collapsed into a pool of smoking tar that began to disintegrate and blow away on the driving wind.

"Kill," I said, pointing to another demon. The Fomoiri spun the ax in his hands and buried the blade in the back of a giant that had grabbed Terrence in one massive, gnarled fist and was lifting him toward its fiery maw. The demon collapsed and disintegrated, and Terrence tumbled free, rolling to his feet and immediately spinning attack spells that tore into a giant that was hammering at Adan's defenses with a huge, two-handed hammer.

"How long can you keep this up?" Oberon asked. "Perhaps I can go for coffee."

As if summoned by his words, a trio of crawlers scuttled over the edge of the building and leaped at us. They slammed into our protective circle and began clawing and tearing at it, struggling to squirm through the magic that held them at bay.

"Nice job," I said, gritting my teeth against the burn of the juice racing through me. "Maybe you can keep these guys off me so I don't get defriended by the fucking Balrog, here."

Oberon grinned and leaped forward, out of the circle, his silver sword spinning and thrusting at the attacking crawler demons. His sword didn't have much more of an immediate effect on them than my bullets had. Their inky, black flesh quivered and oozed around the blade, but golden light danced in the furrows and puckered holes the blade left in its wake. The faceless demons screamed and scrambled away, only to regroup and scuttle toward the fairy king from three directions. Oberon blurred and his sword was a glowing, silver tracer in the air. Black tar spattered the rooftop as the crawlers fell beneath the blade.

Oberon's laughter carried on the wind. "They'll have to send better than these pathetic creatures if they wish to bring low the Lord of the Shining Host," he shouted.

I winced.

The thing that crawled onto the roof was like a giant centipede, which wouldn't have been so bad except that it was formed from the bodies of human children, one torso extending from the shoulders of the one before in a long, repulsive, fleshy chain. The chubby little arms served as the demon's legs, and they scrabbled furiously against the asphalt as the creature undulated across the rooftop. The demon's cherubic head was topped with golden curls, but the face was torn open and something insectile protruded from the torn, bloody mask.

"Discretion is the better part of keeping your fucking mouth shut, King."

The front section of the demon rose up, baby arms waving, and the bug head made a wet chittering sound. The entire length of the creature's body convulsed and black fluid sprayed from the insectoid mouth. The fluid vaporized when it struck my protective circle, giving off an oily black smoke, but Oberon was covered in it from head to toe.

The king screamed and fell to his knees. His sword clattered to the rooftop as he clawed at the black fluid that sizzled on the exposed skin of his face. It ate away at the flesh and I could see bone glistening underneath.

"Oh, fuck me," I said. "Hold the charm on the giant as long as you can, Mr. Clean." I hefted the walking stick in my hand and stepped out of the circle. I dropped a spell on the king to kill the hostile magic, and then I turned to the demon. I extended the juju stick and poured juice into it.

"Vi Victa Vis!" I shouted, and the demon swayed and nearly toppled onto its side as the force magic impacted the aesthetic travesty it called its head. It screamed, its voice that of a child in the throes of a tantrum, and it spat black fluid at me. I triggered my magical shield, and there was a flash of sapphire light as the acidic spittle vaporized against it.

This proved to be my one and only sucker punch, because the next few spells I threw its way rolled off it like rainwater from the Lincoln's hood after a good waxing. Flesh tore as insectile jaws extended farther from the human mask and snapped at me.

"Okay," I said, "we'll do an old-school beat-down." I triggered my jump spell and leaped over the demon, twisting in the air and smashing the walking stick's silver pommel down on the golden curls. The juice I channeled through it flashed with the impact, and it tore through the thin veil of skin and bone to burn the demon flesh beneath.

I landed in a crouch on the other side of the monster. It reeled from the blow and then steadied itself. Its head whipped around and I heard that wet, chittering sound again. I hit my jump spell and leaped away as the black, acidic fluid sprayed across the rooftop.

"All movements go too far," I said, but I didn't cast the telekinesis spell at the demon. I tore the large air-conditioning unit loose from the roof and hurled it at the creature. It tried to evade the improvised projectile, but its midsection was smashed and pinned against the asphalt by the heavy machinery. I poured juice into the telekinesis spell, pressing down on the air conditioner with all the strength I could muster. I heard tiny bones snapping and the dry, brittle sound of chitin giving way.

I raced to the back of the building to where a second story extended above the lower roofline. I spun my jump spell and leaped up, and immediately spotted another air-conditioning unit identical to the first. "All movements go too far!" I shouted, and wrenched the machinery from its moorings. I lifted it high and sent it tumbling through the air until it was poised over the demon, and then I hammered it down on the thing's head. There was a tremendous crash and black fluid squirted from beneath the crumpled metal.

The demon's loathsome body wriggled and twitched, and I was all out of air conditioners. I jumped down to the lower roof and ran to the edge of the building. I spun the telekinesis spell again and picked up a VW Beetle parallel parked in front of the post. I lifted it into the air, flipped it around so the car roof was facing down, and then slammed it onto the demon's writhing body. Then I lifted the car and did it again and again, until the VW was little more than a crumpled ball of metal and the demon had been reduced to black paste on the rooftop.

I ran over to Oberon and knelt beside him. Acid burns marred his beautiful, porcelain skin and one eye was a puckered ruin of angry, red flesh. "Oh, Jesus," I whispered. "King, I can't heal this. I can give you some juice to numb the pain."

"Help me up," he rasped. "I am not dead, and thus I am not beaten." He extended his hand and I took it, pulling him to his feet. He touched his face gingerly. "How does it look?"

"How does it feel?"

"Like someone dunked my head in Hell's toilet, and flushed."

"Looks about like it feels, then. Don't worry, you're still prettier than any man needs to be." It was a lie—even the fairy king couldn't make acid burns look good.

"Let's finish this, Domino," Oberon said.

I nodded. We turned and walked together to the edge of the building and looked out across the field. The better part of the battle was already finished. Mr. Clean had held the charm on my giant friend long enough for him to be attacked and slain by lesser demons, but he'd taken a lot of them with him. The bodies of fallen sidhe were scattered across our end of the battlefield, but the survivors had pressed forward with Adan, Terrence, Ismail Akeem and Amy Chen, and they'd joined forces with the piskies to slaughter the remaining demons.

Oberon and I jumped down and crossed the street, and then walked together side by side toward the fading battle. "It's hard to imagine," I said as I surveyed the carnage.

"Let me guess," said Oberon. "This was just, what—perhaps fifty of the Fomoire? You're trying to imagine what the next battle will look like, and the one after that."

"Yeah, I guess so," I said. "And I'm trying to imagine how we'll stop them."

"We will find new allies to fight beside us, Domino, and new weapons to wield against our enemies. In the end, we will fight and we will win, or we shall perish from this earth and all the worlds beyond. It has always been thus. Do not try to fight a battle before your enemy has taken the field."

We joined our friends and fought with them until long after the sun had fallen into the sea. When it was over, twenty-five sidhe were dead and more piskies than I could count. All of my people were wounded, but miraculously, all of them were alive. Ismail Akeem had lost his left arm in the battle, but he'd replaced it with the ghostly apparition of a healthy arm. He said the new arm would be good for wrestling with spirits before he ate them.

Adan's right leg had been shattered when a giant fell on him. Honey had used her healing glamour on him and he was able to walk. He insisted on staying with me, so I loaned him Papa Danwe's walking stick.

"What's next, Domino?" said Oberon.

"Round up your sidhe and sweep the area," I said. "Make sure there are no more demons skulking about, and if there are, take care of them. Amy, Akeem—go with Oberon and lend whatever assistance you can."

"What of the rest of you?" the king asked.

I looked over to where Jack hovered beside Honey. He nodded once. "We're going for Francis Mobley," I said. Adan, Terrence, the piskies and I left the park and walked south to Compton Boulevard. There was one more demon to face before we could rest.

fifteen

We found Mobley in the Salvation Army building's soup kitchen. It was pretty sorry as inner sanctums went, and overall just a less than dramatic spot to make your last stand. We'd run into some of the Jamaican's gangsters in front of the building and a few more guarding the doors of the soup kitchen. None of them had put up much of a fight.

Francis Mobley's dreads flowed from beneath a red, green, gold and black Rasta hat down his back and past his hips. A full, bushy beard concealed most of his face, and he wore a white silk suit with no shirt. He stood in the center of a pentacle that had been drawn on the tile floor with chalk, and black candles burned at the five points of the star. His body was rigid and shaking, as if he were in the grips of a seizure, and his eyes were rolled back in his head. His lips moved as he silently mouthed the words of an incantation.

As we approached, his eyes began to burn. White froth formed on his lips and soaked into his beard. One eye popped and was followed closely by the other, and flames licked out of the sockets. Mobley's body relaxed. One hand reached up and wiped the white foam from his lips.

Valafar grinned at us. "I wasn't sure he would do it," he

said. "I've been whispering in his ear, always whispering, warning him that he would not survive this meeting unless he opened himself to me. Oh, the others, sure, he agreed to let them use this wretched body long enough to crawl forth into this world, but me? I think some part of him always knew if I ever got inside and sank my teeth into his soul, I wouldn't leave until there was nothing left of it to sustain me."

"We knew you'd come," I said. "No way you'd give up your gate without a fight."

"Is that what this is, then? A fight? You would test yourselves in battle against a Lord of Hell?" He turned up his hands and flames erupted from the palms.

"I heard you were more of a low-ranking general," I said. "But no, since you asked, we don't think it's going to be much of a fight."

"No doubt you're right about that," the demon said, looking around, "unless you've brought your little army with you. In that case, we might have a bit of sport."

"The truth is, we're a lot alike," I said. "Your people and mine, I mean."

Valafar laughed. "You are no more than a pathetic parody of my race. You were given all the tools, sure, but that little seed of weakness was planted deep in your souls. Empathy, I think you call it, or conscience. Humanity," he said, spitting the word like a curse. The forked tongue darted out and licked his lips. "Whatever you call it, I can tell you this much—it tastes delightful."

"Yeah, just like us," I continued. "Someone I know referred to us as a small measure of spirit imprisoned in flesh. That was made really clear when the Xolos were taken and human souls were unable to escape their corpses. People like us, we need help dying. We can't escape the prison on our own."

"Fascinating," Valafar said. "Would you care to die now?"

"You know the most horrible thing about the zombies? You'd think it would have been the cannibalism, but it wasn't. The worst thing was they were just people. A lot of them didn't even know they were dead."

"Yes, well, humans are imbeciles."

"It's not that easy to tell, though, is it? The flesh is still animated and the soul endures. It's an easy mistake to make."

"For a human, I suppose."

"Or the Firstborn," I said. "We really are so much alike. That's why I was so sure you'd crawl up inside Francis Mobley without ever realizing he was already dead."

The fire in the demon's eyes dimmed and the flames dancing on his upturned hands winked out. He looked down at Mobley's body. "What..." he stammered. "How?"

Jack raised his hand and smiled.

I laughed. "The big fight at Wilson Park? That was just to get your attention and draw your demons away from Mobley. Just long enough for one of the King's Knives to slip in here and do his work. It was quick and painless—Mobley didn't even notice. I figured you'd be trapped, just like a human soul. I noticed you bailed pretty quick when I shot that preacher you possessed."

"Clever, but so what?" Valafar spat. "Even trapped within this rotting meat, I will destroy you."

"You probably could," I said, "but we're not going to have a fight." I brought my fingers to my lips and whistled, and my Xolo padded into the room. He sat on his haunches beside me and looked up, his tongue lolling from the side of his mouth. In the mortal world, he had a family and a good home. He wore a collar and a dog tag. His name was Noe.

Valafar laughed. "That pathetic cur is no threat to me."

I reached down and scratched Noe's ears, and then I looked up at the demon. "He's not here for you, Valafar," I said. "He's here for Mobley." The Xolo barked once and leaped to his feet, and then he faded from view as he crossed over to the Between.

"No," the demon said. His eyes flared and he backed away toward the far side of the circle. "It's not...you can't..."

"You said yourself, you're just a parasite. I'm guessing you won't last very long in there without a human soul to chew on."

The demon threw back his head and howled, and then the burning orbs flickered out. Mobley's human eyes stared sightlessly at us for a moment before he toppled over and fell facedown on the tile.

Honey flew to Jack and tackle-hugged him in midair. She tangled her fingers in his hair and kissed him long and hard. "My hero," she whispered when she finally came up for air.

"Save it for the honeymoon," I said. "We haven't even had the wedding yet."

On Honey's insistence and with Stag's grudging authorization, we held the ceremony at the Ashram. I argued we could find a good spot in L.A., and failing that we could always go to Vegas, but Honey wouldn't hear of it. She said the Ashram was a sacred place; I wasn't sure if that was because Hecate was there, whatever she was, or because Honey had a thing for New Age eastern mysticism. I guessed it was probably Hecate.

The location proved to be a logistical nightmare. The

convergence of two major ley lines meant there was more than enough juice for the Seelie Court, but there were enough dry spots in San Bernardino County they couldn't just take the freeway. We had to build gates for them in the compound, and they had to make the trip through the Between.

Just about everyone I knew was at the wedding. The outfit represented, with Terrence, Chavez, Adan, Ismail Akeem and Amy Chen all attending. Shanar Rashan even returned from sabbatical in time to make the event, though I wasn't sure how he'd heard about it. Oberon, Titania and representatives of the sidhe nobility attended. The king's face was healed but he was wearing an eye patch. If anything, it made him look more charming and roguish than ever. Lowell and Granato were there. They were too busy worrying about what a fairy wedding celebration might do to government property to really have a good time. My mother attended, radiant in her simple yellow dress and white hat. Other than me, she was Honey's closest friend in the mortal world and she wouldn't have missed the wedding even if the zombie apocalypse had still been in full swing. Detective Meadows even showed up for the affair. She'd seen enough of the dark side of the underworld, and she deserved to see the wondrous and beautiful side for a change.

The wedding was strange in some ways and familiar in others. We all gathered in a large circle with the bride and groom at the center. Titania presided over the ceremony; she spoke in the language of the sidhe, so I didn't know what words were said. I understood it, just the same. When it was over, Titania bound the piskies' clasped hands together with a white and gold ribbon, and Jack and Honey kissed for the first time as husband and wife. Honey was so happy and Jack looked so proud, it made my heart swell, and I had to flow a little juice to keep the tears out of my eyes. That's me—a hard case to the bitter end.

After the ceremony, there was food and drink and dancing. I danced with Adan for what seemed like hours, and we clung to each other without speaking. Later, I took a glass of champagne and walked alone through the grounds. I found Honey sitting on the branch of a tree with her back pressed against the trunk. She was crying.

I dropped the glass and rushed over to her. "Honey, what's wrong? Did you and Jack have a fight?"

The piskie laughed and wiped at her eyes. She shook her head and smiled. "No, everything is wonderful. I'm just sad because Jack will leave tomorrow."

"What do you mean he'll leave? You just got married."

"We'll make love tonight, Domino, and we'll make a baby. And Jack will leave when the sun rises."

"He's going to knock you up and then split?" It really *was* like the barrio.

"Well, yeah," Honey said, frowning at me. "After he gives me a baby, what else is he supposed to do?"

"He's supposed to stick around and be a husband and father!"

"That's what human women want. I'm a piskie," she said, as if I might have forgotten.

"You don't want your husband to stay with you?"

"I do, more than anything, but that's why he has to go."

"You're not making any sense, Honey."

"What I feel right now, today, that's what I want to hold on to. And I couldn't very well do that with Jack around all the time."

"Why not? You just have to keep love alive, keep the home fires burning, all that shit."

Honey laughed and shook her head. "Men are better in

the wild, Domino. You can tame them if you work at it hard enough, but it takes away everything that made them interesting in the first place. Then you're stuck with a best friend and roommate who won't clean house and hates to go shopping. What's the point?"

"He could help you raise your child."

"What the hell does a man know about raising a child? And why would a mother want to let him try? My family will help me raise the baby, Domino. If it's a boy, Jack will return for him when he's old enough. The boy will go a-wandering with his father and learn to become a man. If the child is a girl, Jack will visit and spoil her with gifts and affection, but he won't stay long enough to do any permanent damage. That's the way it's supposed to be."

"So you only get one night with your husband, and then he leaves."

Honey smiled a wicked smile. "Yeah, for now, but Jack and I both know what the morrow brings. And oh, gods, Domino, what a night it will be! It'll be enough to keep my home fires burning until the next time Jack comes home."

Adan rode back to the city with me after the wedding festivities wound down. I drove straight to my condo and parked the Lincoln. He followed me up without asking why I wasn't taking him home. When we got inside the house, I threw my jacket on the couch, grabbed his hand and pulled him into my bedroom.

"Mrs. Dawson is in there," he said.

"She can watch or she can leave."

"But Domino, tomorrow…"

"Shut up, Adan," I said. "I don't care about tomorrow." I turned him around, pushed him down on the bed and pounced before his protests could escalate. Maybe it was a week of fighting zombies and demons, or maybe it was the fairy wedding. Maybe I'd been working up to it for a while. Whatever it was, I didn't care. I wanted it. I needed it. Sometimes it really is as simple as that.

L.A. had survived the zombie apocalypse, but Adan and I made love like it was the end of the world.

Later that night, I awoke to find my bed empty. I got dressed and drove out to Venice Beach, and I found Anton on the boardwalk. He sat on the grass under a palm tree, wearing sunglasses with a cap pulled down low on his face. He leaned against the tree and stared across the sand at the moonlit surf rolling in. I sat down beside him and we watched the sea for a while.

"When I came to this country, this was first place for me," he said finally. His voice was so dry and harsh it was hard to understand the words. "I got the taxi at LAX and I told him to bring me here. He dropped me off and I paid him and then I stood in this spot with my suitcase and looked at ocean. It was old, pink suitcase from Soviet times. Babushka gave it to me when I left. I could afford to buy the new one, but I took it so I would remember her. I bet I looked funny standing here with pink suitcase."

"There are stranger sights in Venice than a Russian gangster with a pink suitcase."

Anton tried to laugh and it sounded like a smoker's hacking cough. "I remember I'm thinking, this is the place where any man can be a chief. Any man can be a boss."

"I'm sorry, Anton. I guess it never worked out that way."

He looked at me and smiled, the leathery lips stretching away from yellow teeth. "You make joke with me, Domino," he said. "It was everything I dream about that day. I had good life here. Babushka would be proud of me."

"I'm sure she is," I said, my throat tightening on the words. "Maybe it's time to go see her, now."

"Da," he said, nodding. "Now it is time." He struggled to his feet and turned to face me. He took off the sunglasses and dropped them in the grass, and he looked at me with those dead, gray eyes. "Will it hurt, Domino?"

"No, Anton," I said, and my voice broke. "It won't hurt at all."

Noe stepped up beside me and sniffed at the leg of Anton's track suit. The dog turned its head up to look at me, and whined.

"Goodbye, my friend," I said, and I nodded to the Xolo. Then I turned and walked away. I'd have some guys claim his body from the morgue. I owed Anton a nice funeral, with pretty flowers and a good coffin with small pillows inside.

The next morning, I awoke to a deep rumble from the street that rattled the windows. I went to the French doors and drew the sheer curtains aside. Adan was parking a canary yellow Harley-Davidson Panhead at the curb on the other side of the street. The saddlebags bulged and there was a large pack tethered behind the seat. Jack stood on the oversize chrome headlight casing looking up in my direction. His eyes found mine and he touched his hand to his heart. I flipped him off and dropped the curtain over the window. I went back and sat down on the sofa and waited.

Adan buzzed from the front door of the building and I ignored it. A few minutes later, he rang my doorbell, and then knocked a few times when I ignored that, too. He killed my wards, juiced the lock and came in. He was wearing a scuffed, black leather jacket with a lot of zippers and buckles, faded jeans and black engineer boots. He took off his aviators and stood in the hallway, watching me.

"You're leaving," I said, "with Jack."

"I tried to tell you last night, but you didn't let me. I wanted to explain."

I shrugged. "What's to explain? You're running away."

He came in and sat down in the armchair across from me. "I'm running from all this," he said, gesturing around the room with his sunglasses. I knew he didn't mean the room. He leaned forward with his elbows on his knees and stared at me. "I'm not running from you."

"I'm here, aren't I? I'm part of all this. So you're running from me."

"Come with me, Domino," he said, and I heard the earnestness in his voice. "We'll hit the road, sleeping in motels and taking our juice where we can. We can be like Bonnie and Clyde."

"And Jack," I said. "Bonnie and Clyde and Jack."

Adan smiled. "Yeah, and Jack. At least for a while."

"Well, fuck you, Adan. There's a war here. You know I can't leave."

"Why not, Domino? L.A.'s getting the front edge of the storm, but it'll be everywhere before long. And there aren't any sorcerers out there to protect people. No outfits. What happens when demons start showing up in Podunk, Iowa? What happens to those people?"

"They're not my problem."

"We can *make* them our problem," Adan said. "Just as easily as my father made Los Angeles our problem. It's *our* choice. No one owns us. We choose our responsibilities, Domino. I know you think you're the only one who can run this thing, but the outfits will get along without you.

My father is back. He can make Terrence captain. The city will survive. Out there, they've got nothing. No one."

"So that's your plan? You're going to walk the earth? Do you see yourself more as Kane or Jules?"

Adan looked at me with that infuriating blank expression on his face.

"*Kung Fu? Pulp Fiction?*" He didn't know much about pop culture if he didn't know Kane or Jules.

He shook his head. "I don't have to walk, Domino. I've got my bike."

I clenched my jaw and bit down on the anger rising into my face. "Why, Adan? Why can't you stay? What's so fucking bad about what we've got here?"

He shook his head. "It's not bad," he said. "It's just not mine. I don't belong here, Domino. Maybe it would have been different if I'd grown up here. I don't know. But I didn't. Oberon took me and it turns out he can't just give me back. I don't know if I can explain this. I don't fit, Domino, or the world doesn't fit me. It's like walking around with my shoes on the wrong foot. And I have to fix it, I have to find my place in this world, or it's going to drive me mad." He stopped and shook his head. "Please, try to understand."

"I understand. You're in Japan, and you're fucking clueless. If there's nothing keeping you here, then go."

"I tried to make a list last night," he said. "Two columns. On one side, reasons to go. On the other side, reasons to stay. It wasn't a very good list, because I could only think of one reason to stay."

"That reason obviously wasn't enough to outweigh your bike, and the open road, and Jack, and some fucking motel in Podunk, Iowa."

"It almost *is* enough. Even though everything else is all wrong, it's almost enough. But I know if I stay here, I'll lose you, too. Every day in this city, I feel like I'm fading. I'm that little kid again in the woods and I'm *completely* alone. I'm a ghost."

"You're not alone," I said. "I'm here. I can't see the future, Adan, and grown-ups don't get guarantees, but we're good together. There might be something for us if we try. Like Oberon and Titania. You said it yourself, they've got it. And they still manage to rule a kingdom together."

"You don't understand them. Both of them would watch the world burn—starting with the Seelie Court—if they were forced to choose. But you? The outfit, the war...the people you think you have to protect will always come first."

"What makes you so sure?"

Adan nodded and his eyes locked on mine. I saw something there, but I couldn't tell if it was hope or desperation. "Because if I'm wrong, you'll come with me. You'll walk away, Domino. You'll choose us, or a chance for us, whatever it might be."

I was quiet for a long time. His little trap made me want to tear his heart out and shove it down his throat. But I was still in the trap, fair and square. He wouldn't stay unless I could put him—put *us*—in front of the outfit. If I wasn't ready to do that, I was no different from the sidhe who sat on their horses and watched him fight alone. And if I *was* willing to do that, I'd be willing to go with him. It was really as simple as that.

"You're not wrong, Adan," I said. "I won't watch the world burn for you."

"I know. You're not Oberon or Titania. You're better than them."

"I'm sorry."

He nodded. "It would have been great, though, wouldn't it? Just you and me and the road."

"Yeah, it would have been great," I said. "Even with Jack as a third wheel."

Adan gave a little laugh. "We could have ditched him."

He stood and started toward me, but I shook my head. "Just go," I said.

Adan went to the door and paused, turning back to look at me. "Maybe in another life," he said. Then he walked out and closed the door behind him. I knew it was the last time I would ever see him.

My eyes snapped open and I heard the fading chant of three voices in my head.

> solitude mourns the empty spaces
> calling torn roses taste of plague winds
> blade and chalice the color of mirrors
> star seal dances the hyperbolic equilibrium

The Panhead rumbled to a halt on the street outside and I went to sit on the couch. I knew what I'd seen was real. It was the future, and it was about to happen. Hecate had shown it to me. I wasn't sure what all the fucking poetry meant, but Hecate obviously didn't want it to happen. I didn't, either.

I waited until Adan let himself in. The jacket, the jeans, the boots, the sunglasses—everything was exactly the same. Déjà vu crashed over me and I felt light-headed. I stood up and looked at him, steadying myself with one hand on the back of the couch. He pulled off the aviators and returned my stare.

"You're fired," I said.

His jaw dropped open and he just looked at me for a moment. "What?" he said finally.

"As wartime captain, I've determined that your relationship with the sidhe makes you vulnerable. Your presence makes the outfit vulnerable. So you're out, as of right now."

Adan shook his head and looked down at his boots before raising his eyes to mine once again. "What about my father?"

"I'll tell him how it is. If it's related to the war effort, my word is law. He might bitch and moan about it, but I think that's a personality trait that runs in the family."

Adan shook his head again and laughed. Then his smile faded and he fixed those huge, dark eyes on me. "Thank you, Domino," he said.

"You're out of the outfit, but you're not off the hook," I said. "It's occurred to me that I need eyes and ears beyond the city limits. I need some intelligence—I need to know what's going on out there. You and Jack get the job. Maybe you'll run across other outfits in other towns from time to time. You'll make contact with them on our behalf. And when I find myself up to my chin in zombies, demons or whatever the hell's coming next, you'll bust ass back here and lend a hand."

"I will always come, Domino. Just as Jack will always return to Honey when she is in need."

"Good. Then get the hell out of here, I've got work to do."

I turned away, but Adan stepped up behind me and pulled me into his arms. He turned me around to face him and lifted my face to his, and then he kissed me like a warrior-poet on the eve of battle.

I went out onto the balcony to watch him leave. When I

opened the French doors, the scent of apples and cinnamon was picked up on the breeze and carried from my home. Adan swung onto the Panhead and Jack dropped down onto the gas cap. I smiled at the piskie and touched my heart. He grinned and blew me a kiss.

Adan pulled out the kick-starter and rested his foot on it. Then he turned and looked up at me. "Anton invited me to the Mocambo club," he said. "I can travel fast through the Between. Maybe we could get a drink sometime?"

"What are you talking about?" I said. "Anton's dead."

"Yeah, but he came to me this morning just before dawn. He said there are a lot of ghosts looking for someone to lead them. He said to tell you it's the kind of place where any man can be a boss."

"And he took over the club?"

"That's what he said. And you should see him, Domino. I guess his ghost never discovered junk food. He's lean and mean. He's going to run this town on the other side. I should warn you, though, he put Abe Warren on the payroll."

"I'll be damned."

"So what about that drink?"

"I'd like that," I said. "You've got my number."

Adan nodded, grinned and started the bike. He gunned the throttle to wake up the old engine and then waved at me. He held my gaze for a long time. Finally, he slipped the aviators over his eyes, put the bike in gear and rode away without looking back.

Maybe Honey was right and men were better in the wild. Maybe we all needed to wander, to find our own place, and maybe our paths through life would diverge for a time. But those separate paths could bend back toward each other, too. X marks the spot.

There's a kind of magic in that.

★ ★ ★ ★ ★

acknowledgments

Summer in Minneapolis is a magical time—it's warm, sweet, green and far too short. This year, I spent nearly all of it in my office, sitting at my desk in front of an open window, writing *Skeleton Crew*. This was great for me—the book was tremendously fun to write and I'm so fortunate to have had the opportunity. Writing isn't a spectator sport, though, and it wasn't so great for my wife. And so, Mashenka, thank you for giving me this summer, with constant support and without a word of complaint. This is your book, too.

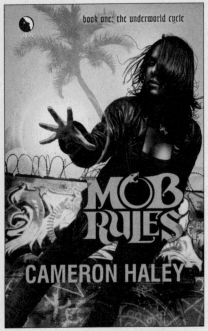

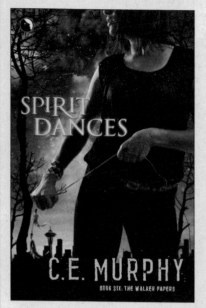

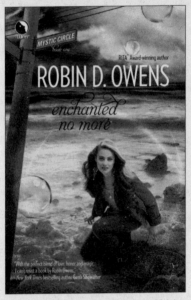